ADVANCE PRAISE

Motro is a magical author. Her stunning stories add a masterful contribution of love and understanding to humanistic Holocaust literature. – **Shraga Milstein, Holocaust survivor; Mayor of Kfar Shmaryahu, Israel 1983-1998**

* * *

Helen Schary Motro's *The Right to Happiness* is a compelling series of short stories, each unique in their own right, readable in isolation, but each building one on the other to offer the most pointed insights into the post-Holocaust experience of survivors and the second generation. Having grown up surrounded by children of survivors and of those who found refuge in the New York on the eve of World War II, I had a deep familiarity with her characters and the world that she depicted and thus an intensified appreciation for what she has achieved. One can read these stories as an elaborate depiction of Post Traumatic Stress Syndrome in all its variety and intensity. Reading it after October 7th and during a visit to Israel, I wonder how soon in our world, Jews will be able to experience a post-traumatic world, but when they do, they could hardly do better than using Motro as their guide. – **Michael**

Berenbaum, Former Director Holocaust Research Institute, U.S. Holocaust Memorial Museum; Distinguished Professor of Jewish Studies, Director Sigi Ziering Institute, American Jewish University

* * *

Intimate and gripping tales that tell small human stories yet reveal greater truths. You feel the love and care of the writer for her characters. – Martin Fletcher, former NBC News Bureau Chief, Israel

THE RIGHT TO HAPPINESS

AFTER ALL THEY WENT THROUGH

STORIES

HELEN SCHARY MOTRO

ISBN 9789493322684 (ebook)

ISBN 9789493322660 (paperback)

ISBN 9789493322677 (hardcover)

Publisher: Amsterdam Publishers, The Netherlands

info@amsterdampublishers.com

The Right to Happiness is part of the series New Jewish Fiction

Copyright © Helen Schary Motro 2024

Cover image: Central Park by Ola Schary, oil on canvas

All Rights Reserved. No part of this publication may be reproduced or transmitted in any form or by any means, electronic or mechanical, including photocopy, recording or any other information storage and retrieval system, without prior permission in writing from the publisher.

CONTENTS

The Smoker	1
Three Hundred Zlotys	12
The Parade	15
King of Yiddish	28
Homecoming on Riverside	43
Korczak's Boys	60
Iron Eagle on West 11th Street	83
German Lessons	106
Love of the Land	116
My Musical Education	143
The Right to Happiness	155
Glossary	209
Acknowledgments	211
About the Author	213
Amsterdam Publishers Holocaust Library	215

For Michael, always

To remember is a kind of hope.
– Yehuda Amichai

...[E]ach of us eventually comes home to the thing that we have always been, to the thing that we really are.
– Alexander McCall Smith, *Bertie Plays the Blues* (A Scotland Street Novel)

Except where noted, this book is a work of fiction. Names, incidents, dialogue, and all characters and events with the exception of some well-known historical figures and events are products of the author's imagination or are used fictitiously and are not to be construed as real. Any similarity to real individuals, living or dead, is coincidental and unintended.

THE SMOKER

Anna kept her cigarette-butt collection in a tin Band-Aid box. She stashed it at the bottom of the old wooden toy chest that still stood in her room, raising the lid with the cut-out hearts, sticking the box deep under a jumble of her oldest forgotten dolls – dolls with tangled hair, some without limbs, some naked, some with eyes that had fallen back into their heads.

The butts were Anna's practice materials. Most she collected from sifting through the ashtray on the coffee table after her parents' guests went home. The trick was to sneak in first thing in the morning while her parents were still sleeping and before Gertrude arrived to straighten up. The best cigarettes were hardly smoked and had traces of lipstick coating the filters – coral or fire-engine red. Anna took them all – Pall Mall, Benson & Hedges, Parliament, and Kent. She cherished one brand especially – Southern Tapers. Not because of its flashy name but because she imagined European cigarettes must have resembled them – long, thin, elegant.

Both of Anna's parents smoked as they told her about her grandmother from Krakow. She wondered if her other grandparents had smoked. She never met any of them. None had made it through the war.

"Your grandmother Annushka – you are named after her, Anna – was invited to the performance of the Italian opera troupe on their gala tour," her mother said.

"Did you go, too?" Anna interrupted the first of the many times she heard the story.

Her mother dismissed Anna's question with a wave. "God of mine! What a question! I wasn't even born then. It was in the Twenties that the Italians sang there. I was born later."

"When were you born, what year?"

"In the Thirties," her mother answered vaguely.

Later, Anna learned it was exactly 1930. That made her mother nine when the war broke out and 15 when it ended. Did that make her a child survivor?

"So how do you know about what Grandmother did in the opera?" Anna asked.

"It made her the talk of Krakow," her mother resumed with enthusiasm. "They were still talking about it when I was a child. In the parterre where they held the reception, they say my mother Annushka drank champagne and puffed on a Turkish cigarette in her ivory holder. It was a big – how do you say it? – a big *scandale*. The whole Jewish society of Krakow, modern as it prided itself to be, was buzzing. Your grandmother Annushka was extreme, very daring. She came home and laughed. She didn't care what anybody thought."

I am like Annushka, thought Anna. I don't care, either.

Tiny white elephants carved in bas relief ran round and round the holder, connected trunk to tail. Now the elephants lay for good, neglected in her mother's jewelry drawer, wrapped in tissue paper. They never saw daylight except when Anna unrolled the tissue to peek at them. The ivory was yellowing and brittle, but when she picked it up and held it to the lamp, squinting, the light through it glowed rosy and translucent.

Sniffing the inside, Anna detected a faint scent that she imagined to be foreign tobacco. Even the holder's origins held melodramatic romance. It had been given to her grandmother by a disappointed suitor, an engineer – a *cavalier*, Anna's father called him – before he learned of her engagement to Grandfather after the Great War.

"The engineer could not get over the loss of Annushka," Anna's mother declared. "So he became a communist and left for Russia. Nobody in Krakow ever heard from him again."

"Why not? Why not?" cried Anna. "Didn't he have any family? His parents? Or sisters?"

"It's a good time to practice piano," her mother said, turning away. It was the end of the story for the day. That's the way it was – people surfaced, they played their parts, and then they dropped out of sight, off the end of the earth.

The holder was the only piece of life from "Before" that her mother managed to salvage. Everything else – her dresses, photographs, books, apartment, friends, parents – vanished. Her mother had instinctively snatched up the cigarette holder as she fled, escaping from the apartment building and running for her life.

She told Anna proudly that she kept it hidden in her bodice for the rest of the war – through "everything that I went through." Anna often wondered what secret place a bodice was, and what was that "everything" her mother had to go through. She was tempted to ask, but she never did. In the rare moments when her mother spoke of things that happened in the time "Before," Anna knew better than to interrupt. Questions distracted her, disturbed the flow, and brought the narrative to an abrupt end.

Her grandmother's cigarette holder was here in their apartment, precious and real. Exotic as a foreign guest and equally out of place. The cigarette holder was proof that "Before" existed.

Anna planned to be a smoker, too. She wanted to be good at it – to inhale smoothly, blow perfect rings, light up easily on windy days. She knew it was important to practice early. "Whatever you learn to do when you are young will stay with you forever," her father was fond of repeating.

Cigarettes were one of the most important parts of life. Desperate smokers in the war bargained away their last ration coupon for a quarter of a cigarette. Anna read that in a book. It said smokers suffered more from lack of nicotine than from lack of bread. Hunger for a cigarette never passed – she knew that. Cigarettes were *that* important.

Of course, now the war was over. Time after time, her parents told her how lucky she was not to have known its terrors. "You were not there, thank God, you can never understand what we went through," they'd say.

"What? What happened to you?"

"Better not to know."

She lived surrounded by cigarette abundance, by cartons and packages in every store. People carelessly left them lying around, forgot them on cafeteria tables, asked strangers casually if they could spare a weed, smoked only one puff and then tossed the rest away when the intermission bell rang, ground out perfectly good ones into the gutter. Often, she had the impulse to pick up butts from bus stop curbs, but she resisted. This was America, this was "after the War." Things could not disappear, and neither could people.

Anna came home from school to find Zosha from Peru sitting in the living room eating the flaky pastry her mother brought home from the Hungarian bakery in Yorkville. Of course, Zosha wasn't really from Peru. She just lived there now. Zosha visited them every year when she traveled from Lima to the United States to sell leather skins to American wholesalers.

Zosha had lived upstairs from her mother in Krakow; they had been in and out of each other's homes all their lives. They were together on and off until the very day of liberation. "A miracle we were on the same transport," her mother said. Her mother brightened up for weeks before Zosha's visit, and when she came, her mother chattered and wore makeup, even during the daytime. The first time Zosha came, Anna was trotted out for an awkward introduction; now a nice hello was all that was required.

Zosha looked straight at Anna and went right on talking, whatever the subject was, even when Anna showed up unbidden and with a proprietary flounce plopped herself down on the couch diagonal to the one where her mother and Zosha sat, teacups on saucers balanced on their knees. But while Zosha kept talking, when Anna entered, her mother's expression froze and the chatter dried up.

Zosha's skirt was pulled tightly over two plump thighs, and the nylon of her stockings shone in the yellow circle cast by the fluted lampshade. The waves in her hair shone, too; the electric light brought out an unusual red, a shade between orange and chestnut that Anna had never seen. That's what made Zosha look unmistakably foreign: the color of her hair that nobody in America had, and other things, too, just different enough to mark her as a foreigner – the fitted, woolen suits in shades of lilac or mauve with thick patent leather belts and shiny oversized buttons, and the matching patent leather pumps on spiked heels. Zosha did not so much as walk, she teetered. Her lips were smeared a moist, thick cupid crimson.

Anna peeked at Zosha's stole on a hanger in the hall closet. It was black and white, like an animal running in the snow. When Anna touched it, it felt as soft as the rabbit she had once been allowed to hold at school. After Zosha had taken the taxi back to her hotel, her mother told her father over supper, "Imagine, real chinchilla she was wearing!" That made two Spanish words in Anna's vocabulary: Zosha and chinchilla.

As soon as Anna sat down in the living room when Zosha was there, her mother's tone changed, dried up to the familiar. If Anna didn't get up to leave, her mother would invent errands for her so she could be alone with Zosha. Anna could imagine her mother as the serious child she told Anna she used to be, but it was hard to imagine Zosha as any more sober than she was now in Anna's living room. Anna was sure that Zosha never wore tragic looks or talked about "Before" or what might only have been "if."

Stubbornly, Anna sat, but the talk remained wooden. Zosha picked up chocolate cherries and dusted almonds with her plump, ringed fingers, licking her lips after each. Her mother lit a cigarette. Anna watched the match fizz up and then her mother's breath blowing it out.

Today was no different than the other times. Her mother would never say anything interesting while she was there. Anna went back into her room and sat down beside her empty desk. The four o'clock February light was dull gray. It was time to turn on the overhead lamp. But Anna hunched over with elbows on the desk and chin in hands, immobile, dreaming. Her homework assignment, already done, lay neat and folded away in her book bag.

The apartment was silent, as usual, but it was a different quiet because of the guest, a quiet that held the promise of being broken. In her house, doors were never closed – there were no sounds to keep out. Things were orderly, static, and silent.

It was a good time for Anna to practice. A perfect time. With Zosha here, the truth was a half-step closer. "Before the War" didn't seem so much of a never-never land.

Anna chose her longest cigarette – less than one-quarter gone, and with an intricate coral imprint on the filter. She rarely used this one. She took the cigarette out of its tin box and imagined how it would look inserted in the ivory elephant holder. She had once or twice dared to insert cigarettes from her collection into the mouth of the precious relic, but only when her parents were out.

She held the cigarette between two fingers, pursed her lips gently over the lipstick traces, and sucked air in as hard as she could through the dense yellowed filter. Standing in front of her mirror, Anna cocked her head and examined herself, took turns holding the cigarette with the right hand and the left, then closed her eyes and inhaled again. She kept the breath with its tobacco hint inside her as long as her air held out.

When she opened her eyes, she was not alone. Zosha was looking back at her from the reflection. Anna's arm fell like a lead weight. She knew Zosha had seen the cigarette. Worse, the Band-Aid box stood out in the open, its treasures visible. Even so, she absurdly closed her fingers around the cigarette to hide it and held it inside her fist.

Without saying anything, Zosha came in and closed the door behind her. She gestured to Anna's wooden desk chair. "I may sit?" she asked.

Anna's face burned. She shrugged, hoping her expression didn't betray her shock. Zosha started to talk: "You've heard stories about your glamorous grandmama, Anna. But your mother never tells you about the dark side."

Anna's ears perked up. Would Zosha tell her things? Would she finally hear something, anything, to fill in the gaps?

"As the war wore on, your grandmama became desperate," Zosha said. "As soon as food coupons were distributed, she traded her share for cigarettes. She was able to get only three, maybe four, to last her for a week. Annushka rationed cigarettes like other people rationed bread, allowing herself a puff, maybe two, each time she lit one. Matches, too, were not unlimited. God, believe it – even matches we counted."

"How can anyone count matches?"

"We did, believe me, we did many impossible things. But I want to tell you about your grandmama. Where was I? Ah, yes, Annushka made one cigarette last for a few days, but they would always run out before she could find a new supply. Then Annushka began to pace back and forth like an animal."

Her eyes on Zosha, Anna sat down cross-legged on top of her old floral floor rug, smoothing and resmoothing the fringes with her empty hand. The other hand kneaded the cigarette she was concealing. Her back leaned uncomfortably against the bed. Anna shifted position. Zosha looked up and stopped talking. Anna was afraid the spell was broken.

But Zosha resumed. "She went out to prowl the streets. I myself saw her hunched over outside once. I didn't recognize her at first: a skinny, old woman with thin gray strands bent double over the gutter. Then she turned her head and I saw it was Annushka. Her raw fingers scratched at the pavement. Maybe by some miracle, a few grains of tobacco had been overlooked. Her nails were ragged, broken, the skin on her fingers was raw, and their tips shone of blood. Those same glamorous fingers I had seen so many times during my childhood gleaming with lacquer. I stopped beside your grandmama, and I started to heave her up to stand, but she looked up at me with hateful craving. She spat the words out, 'Let me go! Let me be!' Her face was pinched, eyes scanning the ground. Your grandmama was right to push me off. There were butts to be found if a person foraged hard enough.

"Before the final deportations, we all lived crammed together in that cold apartment. Cousins moved in. Our family had to join as well.

"Your grandmama dwindled, became sick, too weak to get up, lying on the bed covered with everybody's coats. She was cold, so cold, shivering without any blankets. She lay coughing. She coughed her lungs out. Nobody slept.

"It was me who was able to sneak some medicine for her because my Uncle Zigmush was a doctor in the one remaining clinic. Before the war, he was only a student, but when there were no doctors left, they treated him with reverence as if he were a professor. Everybody was ready to do favors for him; he had access to whatever pitiful supplies of drugs were to be had. So I brought medicine from Zigmush, and your whole family was so grateful. Your grandfather lit up when saw me. *Me*, who had been in awe of tall mustached Grandfather Boris, who had made me so tongue-tied. 'Little Zosha,' he cried. They all looked at me as some kind of, some kind of *savior*…" Zosha trailed off.

"But your grandmama's coughing didn't stop. Nothing changed. We all watched her waste away. Every time I entered the apartment, her bed seemed emptier. If anything, the coughing became louder. We couldn't bear to listen to its hacking. On the floor next to the bed were old shirts torn into strips soaked in bloody phlegm. After she died, Uncle Zigmush told me that the famous medicine had been nothing but vitamin B pills. It was the only thing left on the shelves.

"So dear Anna, forget this nonsense." She gestured to Anna's fist hiding the cigarette. "Go out and play. Meet your friends. Sing, run! Let your grandmother be the last addict. Don't be like her. Maybe she would not have survived anyway – who knows? – but her end was cruel. And your mother had to watch, day in and day out. Wringing her hands, crying until her eyes became dry, and nothing, nothing to give her mother to ease her suffering. Throw out those filthy cigarettes, I beg you!"

Zosha got up and smoothed down the horizontal creases in her skirt. Her expression altered; she became the Zosha whom Anna knew. Zosha looked around the room and said, "Next time I'll bring you a rug made out of llama wool. Here it will look lovely, marvelous! Llamas make the best wool, you know, and I know just where to get the best quality! I'll bring you a llama wool sweater too, I promise."

Anna didn't look at Zosha and didn't meet her smile. Zosha threw in, almost as an afterthought, "Don't look so sad, don't worry, my little Anna, our little conversation – your cigarette..." She swept her hands around the room, and said, "These things I won't breathe to my dear friend. Your mother has been through enough."

Zosha held out her fleshy arms, but Anna shrunk back. Nevertheless, Zosha planted quick moist kisses on both cheeks with her cupid lips. The heavy perfume on Zosha's neck mixed with the sweet smell of pastries.

"I'm so glad we really talked!" Zosha exclaimed. "I can see from your face you understand. Just like your mother and I talking together when we were young. But these days, Anna, it's so hard to see her always with her serious expression. I try to cheer her up. And you know, she cheers me too." Zosha exited, blowing a kiss at the door.

Anna uncurled her fingers. The cigarette was mangled, the paper ripped, and the filter flattened. Shreds of stringy tobacco stuck to her sweaty palm. Anna was not sad. She was furious. To have been caught red-handed! She glowered and vowed never to be so negligent again.

She was so angry that she spoke out loud: "From now on I will make sure – 100 percent sure – that no one is home. I will close the door. I will lock it."

It occurred to her that no matter what she said, Zosha might still tell her mother about her cigarette collection. How could Anna trust that strange, foreign woman? Zosha's loyalty would be to her mother; their ties went back to a more important world.

Tomorrow, Anna would have to find a new container. For the time being she stashed the Band-Aid box on the bookshelf behind last year's history book, *Explorers of the New World*.

Anna put both elbows on her windowsill and pressed her nose against the pane. She looked out at the windows across the alley, trying to catch glimpses of other people's lives. When she was grown up, she would go to the opera, too. At the intermission, she would place her program on the velvet seat. She would glide out in her ball gown to the lounge. Her shoulders would be bare. Her escort would hand her a fluted glass brimming with champagne. In the other hand, she would hold her grandmother's ivory holder lightly between thumb and index finger, while her pinkie would point up toward the ceiling. The elephants would run around in circles, trunk to tail. Anna would close her eyelids, tip her head back slightly, and inhale, inhale the marvelous smoke as deeply as she could.

She was in America, after all. Things could not disappear here. Neither could people.

THREE HUNDRED ZLOTYS

Based on true events

My name is Helena Zakrzewska. It is May 1945. From one day to the next, the Russian soldiers arrive. People fall upon them with flowers. The forever war that wiped out the past is suddenly over. The soldiers commandeer the house of the peasant woman where I am staying, but they strum the balalaika and sing melodies all through the night and leave us be.

My old name comes back – Ola. It feels as if it doesn't fit me anymore. I have almost merged into Helena, the person who hides behind a facade, the tall woman with dark hair and dark eyes who raises suspicion.

I return to the rubble of Warsaw. I hear that charities are in the city to help survivors. That's why I come back. No other reason. I know everything is bombed and burned, everybody from my life sent away.

I have no money. No money at all left. I ask, "Where is HIAS? Where is USA Relief?" But the agencies haven't arrived yet. The peace is too new in May 1945. There is no HIAS, there is no

Jewish Relief Agency, nothing, and everybody is so poor in Warsaw.

I look around and all at once I see Jews walking in the streets. Unmistakably Jews. I thought there were no Jews left. I thought I was the only one. And yet here they are – meek, slouched, thin, sallow, timid. But clearly Jews.

I, too, walk along the streets. I walk freely in the city even though it is in ruins, and it is wonderful to breathe the spring and not tuck my head into my chin and not have to be Helena Zakrzewska anymore. I feel her sliding off my shoulders and down my back.

But I ask myself, why I am still hungry if there is no war?

Suddenly, I hear nearby a voice: "Ola! Ola! Darling Ola!" A lilt that I know from my childhood, a slight lisp where the front teeth do not quite meet. But I cannot place that voice so quickly. It is like a dream. There is nobody left from my past, that one thing is sure.

And then I see her standing in front of me, but she is no longer a girl. She is no longer the girl who sat a row behind me in Latin lessons. She is no longer the girl I slept next to in a cot in summer camp in the Polish woods. She is still the same beautiful, petite, smiling, laughing Rega. Although so thin, her hair is shiny still. Even after this terrible war.

We fall into each other's arms. It is like the movies. She is the first person from my past who reappears. She is alive, Rega is. Alive like me.

And right there on the street, Rega reaches into her pocket, deep, deep. I am so happy. My heart pounds. I am sure she has bread to give me. But not. She starts to pull out bills. She uncrumples them and pushes them into my hands. So much money: 300 zlotys. Enough for food for a week.

And we embrace and we go our own ways, separately, because that's the way it is at that time, because despite the peace we are still nervous to stand next to other Jews in public.

Years later, when we are both living in New York and walking together and we bump into acquaintances of mine, I always turn to them, while we are waiting for the light to change on 57th Street. And before we cross the street, I put my arm around her and say, "This is Rega who gave me 300 zlotys when I didn't have anything at all."

THE PARADE

Television was my refuge. Every afternoon I plopped down on our leatherette ottoman, avoiding the scratchy tears in the vinyl, watching our black-and-white set, and eating handfuls of Frosted Flakes dry out of the package. The programs pictured perfect American families, and I willed myself into the action. I became the child playing Chinese checkers in the den on the slipcovered couch, running outside to buy a popsicle from the ice cream truck, dressing up on Halloween. None of which existed in my real life.

My father didn't need conversation when he mopped the hallways and stacked the chairs in the Slotkin Yeshiva School for Girls. And there wasn't much for my mama to say as she stood behind the stainless-steel counter, wearing a white apron and nylon hair cap, dishing out hot lunches. My parents hardly spoke English. They didn't have to.

Their jobs enabled me to attend Slotkin Yeshiva tuition-free. Because my parents were not religious, I was sort of a double outsider: also on scholarship and also not a child of the regular observant families. But as much as I protested that I wanted to go to public school, they wouldn't hear of it. They were leery of public schools.

"Don't want you to be ganged up on by strangers," Papa said. "In Slotkin, you'll be safe. He had no idea that I already was a stranger – to the girls in my class.

"Good girls stay close by," was my parents' mantra.

My given name is Malka Shulamis, and that's what my papa would call me, using both names, which made me feel important and special. But my mama always called me Zisele - "my sweet."

Mama made some money another way too. In the evenings and weekends, she was a milliner. Religious women from the neighborhood were her clients. They crowded our little apartment on Sundays trying on hats to buy for their Sabbath synagogue visits. I ran around the hat stands, weaving in and out between the customers' feet.

My mama was not old, I knew, but she looked so different from the perky TV mothers in their pastel cardigans and sleek straight skirts. In school my mama's shiny hair was hidden by her nylon cap; that and the shapeless apron made her unnoticeable.

The hats Mama made were full of life and color, with velvet around the brims. Sometimes even tiny birds peeked out. But there was no color left in Mama. She was a dull brown, like a little wren hopping among the rain puddles on the sidewalk.

"I don't throw nothing away," Mama told me. "I learned that in the camps. Everything was precious. A spoon was a treasure. And a tin bowl – that could save your life."

"Why? Why?" I asked. "What if you didn't have some old tin bowl?"

But Mama never continued. That's the way it was with her. She would blurt out a sentence about "the War" but then catch herself and clam up no matter how hard I begged her to go on.

"No, Zisele, not for you to hear those things. May you never know such times."

When I tried to ask Papa, he shook his head and changed the subject. And later I would hear him speak angrily to Mama for mentioning "the Past." Because "the Past" was a subject so taboo nobody was allowed to broach it.

"It's not for Malka Shulamis to hear such stories," he rebuked her. "Malka Shulamis is an American girl. She belongs to the New World. Such things as we knew will never happen here."

As I listened, I became angry. If that's true, why don't they treat me like an American girl? Why can't I behave like everyone else?

I conformed, more or less, to my parents, to the school, and to the outside world – dutifully wearing my ugly, navy pinafore and heavy, white leggings. Studying prescribed subjects I didn't care about: Torah Stories for Girls, the Meaning of Modesty.

At home, it was only a mixture of Polish and Yiddish, the languages of their former life. That they spoke quickly, spitting out the words and using endless intonations. Their English was flat and halting, as was their approach to the big world around them, which they penetrated only when forced. When asked a question in English, my parents often nodded their heads up and down, up and down, mouthing, "Yes, yes." But I knew better.

Mama and Papa sat at the kitchen table on Saturday nights. The lamp shone down on Papa's hands as he counted out the bills, putting aside the money we would need for the upcoming week.

We lived in a neighborhood of families like us, other refugees from Europe whom my parents sometimes visited on Saturday afternoons. Then there were people from other poor or immigrant groups from whom I was warned to stay away, although I knew the real Americans lumped us all together.

All I wanted was out there in the other world – the shadow world I saw on TV that twinkled with irresistible appeal.

I should have counted myself lucky to be able to watch television at all, which I did constantly until my parents got home late afternoons wrung out from their long workday. The few times I ran into school in the morning bursting to talk about my shows, the other girls opened their eyes wide and told me either that their homes didn't have a set or that watching TV was forbidden. Television was switched on only for snowstorms, hurricanes, or – God forbid – "an emergency."

I looked forward to the holidays when our threesome family was home together. Not because we did things or talked, but because I knew Papa and Mama were nearby.

My best holiday of the year was Thanksgiving because it was my favorite TV day. Even Slotkin Yeshiva was closed. Although they did not care about American holidays, my exhausted parents were happy they didn't have to arise at six to open the school gates by seven. They lolled in their polyester robes as late as they wanted. Time stretched out luxuriously, and they went down for a walk on Flatbush Avenue.

I, on the other hand, spent the morning immersed in the most glorious spectacle ever to be devised: the Macy's Thanksgiving Day parade, a three-hour-long cavalcade. I didn't move from the ottoman, sat as close to the TV as I could get, my nose almost touching its 17-inch screen.

Marching bands, movie stars waving to the crowd, jugglers, skipping clowns doing cartwheels. Floats like carriages for kings and queens: the pirate ship from Peter Pan, Cinderella's coach, the Little Engine that Could, Peter Rabbit on an oversized rolling lettuce. Giant balloons sailed two or three stories above the crowd's heads: Felix the Cat, Pete the Magic Dragon, Mighty Mouse. Most glorious was the colossal white torso of Snoopy the dog floating like the incarnation of a beautiful dream.

People lined the avenues ten deep and children pushed to the front so they could see, squeezing between the legs of anybody who would yield an inch. They sat on the curbs, faces fixed in expressions of wonder.

I was in Brooklyn, New York, technically in the same city as the parade. I felt I could almost reach out and touch it, but it might have been on another planet.

From the time I was in the third grade I begged my mother, "Next week is the parade. Can we go? Can we go?"

But she always demurred, saying, "That's not for us, Zisele, leaving Brooklyn, traveling so far for such nonsense."

"But why not us? Why not?" I cajoled. "We never do anything. There's no school, you have no work, nothing to do. You can see Macy's with your own eyes – the world's largest store."

I suspected it was the journey that frightened her – that we would have to take the subway from our home in Brooklyn and travel on the train into Manhattan.

Because Mama was afraid of trains. I knew that without being told why.

Actually, Mama was afraid of lots of things, especially loud noises. When the buzzer rang from downstairs, Mama's body tensed. If I was in the room, she looked around as if searching for a place to hide me. She jumped up when she heard a police siren. At the wail of an ambulance, she started, her eyes pools of instant fear, hands flying up to her cheeks. After a moment, she would relax, embarrassed. "It's just those... those..." Mama apologized. "Sorry, Zisele, don't let me frighten you."

When I reached the sixth grade I began to beg early to go to the parade, from the beginning of November, but without much hope.

Suddenly, out of the blue, my mother agreed.

Why did she do it, I wonder now? Was it because I had begun to gain weight from all that TV watching? Started to look distracted? To daydream even more than before? Maybe somebody told her a mother-daughter outing would draw us closer. But I suspect another explanation: Perhaps Mama felt that I was old enough and

American enough to be her guide in that strange labyrinth of the subway, that I was her shield. Maybe she really wanted to visit Macy's.

Back then, I didn't waste time wondering what motivated my mama. I pounced on her decision with ecstasy.

"Papa, too? Papa, too?" I jumped up and down.

"Papa needs to rest, to rest his back," Mama answered. "It will be the two of us, Zisele, a girls' holiday."

But Papa was opposed. "It's a holiday," he warned. "The trains will be empty. A woman and a little girl alone... who knows what might happen?"

But I begged and begged. Papa looked at me, yearning written all over. He relented.

On Thanksgiving morning, I put on my winter coat for the first time – secondhand, but new to me. The buttons at the waist were tight, but I didn't tell Mama. She had fished out this gem from the school rummage sale. It was green and red plaid wool and had a matching hat topped with a fluffy green pompom. Had Mama made hats for children, she would have created something this perfect. I twirled around the room, glamorous.

"Mama, I love it!"

My mama wore two sweaters under her brown duffel coat. It would be cold to stand all that time outdoors on the street, she said.

We were off, headed for Manhattan. The very word sounded magic. My mother would see how easy it was to enter the world of the others. It would be a new beginning,

Mama talked to Bluma, the school secretary, who advised her to head to 34th Street, where the grand finale of the parade route ended next to the Macy's store.

"Bluma told me exactly how," Mama said. "'The B train at Atlantic Avenue will take you straight there,' Bluma told."

"Did Bluma write it down?" I asked. "I can read the directions."

"Bluma said no need for directions – it's just the B train straight there. But I asked again and again, and so she wrote down the names of the last few stops before the one where we must to get off."

We left early, in plenty of time to see it all, from start to glorious finish.

"Be careful! Be careful!" Papa stuck his head out of our second-floor window as we left. "Malka Shulamis, hold Mama's hand!" I felt him following us with his eyes.

I knew the final float would carry Santa Claus, the incarnation of happiness and comfort, who would bellow, "Ho ho ho! Only three weeks until Christmas!"

I skipped down the street, my low rhythmic voice repeating, "Ho ho ho! Ho ho ho!"

We headed down Flatbush Avenue to the Atlantic Avenue station. The walk was far, but my feet felt like they were flying. I tugged at my mama's hand.

When Mama purchased the subway tokens, I hopped from foot to foot as she took out her change purse, unzipped it, and counted out the coins. The floor reverberated and rumbled underfoot. I was nervous we would miss our train while my mother fumbled with her dimes and quarters.

She handed the attendant enough for her and a half fare for me.

"My girl, she is not yet 12," Mama said. "Just 11 years old."

"Oh?" The attendant looked skeptically at me, bulky and round-cheeked. "Are you sure?" He scowled. "She looks pretty big to me. Pretty large for 11."

Mama started to stammer.

She bit her lip and whispered to me, "Zisele, you talk. Tell him when falls your name day."

I felt myself turn red; my cheeks burned.

But the attendant turned away and waved us on through.

In the corridor there were so many notices, so many initials for different subways, so many arrows. Finally I found the sign for the B train.

"Here it is!" I said.

I led the way. We followed the arrows, went up and down and around until we found the platform. Above our heads a big sign said "B".

I craned my head to try to see if anything was coming from the dark tunnel down at the end. My mother snatched my arm and yanked me close, holding me firm by her side as she kept her back plastered against the grimy white tile wall.

We waited – ten, 15, 20 minutes.

Finally, a tiny rumble turned into a roaring. Mama's grip tightened. We rushed into the train's doors as soon as they parted. The car was almost empty, with only four or five others in the car.

Mama unfolded a sheet of paper from her handbag and pushed it under my nose. "Look well!" she instructed me. "Tell me when we pass the stations Bluma wrote down."

I read out loud: "Grand Street, Lafayette, West Fourth, 34th Street-Herald Square."

"After the West Fourth, get up quick," Mama instructed. "Get ready to get out. The next stop will be ours: Herald Square."

We sat side by side on a bench for two, me next to the window, but all I could see was my reflection in the black glass. I looked at myself in my green hat with the pompom. I tilted it to one side and then the other like a beret, finding the best angle. It was a wonderful, special hat, fitting for this special day.

I daydreamed about what lay ahead. The majorettes in white uniforms with gold buttons twirling batons. A rotund Humpty Dumpty perched on a moving wall. If I waved hard enough at Snow White with her blond hair, maybe she would jump down and give me a hug. Maybe Mama would buy chestnuts to take home to Papa. Maybe she would get me candied peanuts.

Stations went by – Prospect Park, Church Avenue, Beverley Road. At each one, hardly any passengers got on the train. Wasn't anyone else from Brooklyn going to the parade? Then stations named for letters started: Avenue H, Avenue J, Avenue M, Avenue U.

When would we get to the stations Bluma wrote down?

The train became emptier and emptier. Finally, it stopped and the doors just stayed open. Tiles on the wall spelled out black letters: "Brighton Beach."

I looked sideways at Mama. She was bracing her body, expecting the train to lurch into motion.

Nothing happened. The car stopped vibrating. All was still. I got up and leaned out the door, looking up and down the vacant platform. After a while, a man in uniform entered from the staircase.

"Go, go, ask," Mama said.

"Mister! Mister!" I cried. "When does the train get to 34th Street?"

He stared wordlessly, disbelief on his face. Then he snorted. Then his expression softened, facing two bewildered stranded travelers, a girl dressed up in a cheap coat and her shabby mother.

"Ladies," he said, "This is Brighton Beach, the last stop on the B line. Right now, you're at the very end of Brooklyn. If you want to go to 34th Street, that's in Manhattan. The opposite way. You have to cross over the platform, turn around, and take the train in the other direction."

He saw our stunned expressions, and he softened.

"Go up the stairs, here," he said kindly. "Cross over to the other side and take any train – the B or the Q – whatever comes. They all head where you're going, into Manhattan."

Silently, like dumb cattle, Mama and I did what he said.

The platform was deserted. We sat down on the bench. Time went by, precious minutes. We should have been at the parade long ago. We might have missed the beginning. But I consoled myself. Things always started slow and got more elaborate as the parade progressed.

No trains came.

I began to fidget. The station was heated with hot air blowing down from filthy black vents. I felt hot in my heavy coat. I took off my pompom hat and stuffed it into my pocket. Mama's face was glistening. She unbuttoned her coat.

I kept asking Mama to show me the time. I peered into her lap at her hands and looked at the heavy stainless-steel watch with its ugly green hands weighing down her delicate wrist. An incredibly long 27 minutes – 27 minutes! – went by.

Finally, we heard rumbling under our feet. Mama stiffened, and she clutched my arm.

When the empty train pulled up, we got in, but the doors stayed open instead of pulling out of the station. Something must be wrong.

A conductor appeared.

"When are we leaving?" I asked, my voice almost cracking.

"Missy, just have a little patience, will ya? Today is Thanksgiving, in case you forgot. The whole subway system is on a skeleton schedule. Everyone knows that."

Mama didn't seem to be listening.

"Sit tight," he continued. "You'll get where you're going sooner or later."

Mama and I didn't talk the rest of the trip. She sat still, hands crossed over her bag. Rigid as the subway rumbled on its tracks underneath the city. I kicked my legs on the dirty floor, crossed and uncrossed my feet.

The subway snaked its way through the big spread-out borough of Brooklyn, stopping in reverse order at the lettered avenues we had passed before: then at Beverley Road, at Church Avenue, at Prospect Park, past Atlantic Avenue.

I looked at Mama's watch. It was two hours, 15 minutes since we had gotten on the first train. It felt like a whole day had passed.

Still, we had left so early. Soon we would arrive. More passengers got on at every stop until the train was almost full. Most held bakery boxes tied with twine or gift cartons of whiskey with bright red gift bows. On their way to festive Thanksgiving celebrations.

Our train screeched to a stop at 34th Street Herald Square a little after noon.

I ran out, wanted to dash up the stairs. But Mama was slower and stubbornly held my fingers tight.

I preened my ear for strains of trombones, for drums, for the noise of the crowd. We were too far underground to hear anything.

I burst out into the raw air of the street.

The parade, the parade! I hoped we could still get at least a partial view. I was still young enough, I hoped, so that grownups would let me push through to the curb.

But 34th Street was deserted. Litter lined the empty sidewalk – I trod on a single mitten, on ice cream wrappers, glitter, and crumpled streamers. Wind gusts scattered the debris.

Mama muttered under her breath. I strained to hear. "Like after an *Aktion*," she whispered. "Empty like after an *Aktion*…"

Starting to panic, I tugged Mama's hand forward up toward Seventh Avenue, searching.

Maybe the parade didn't turn down 34th Street. Maybe we'd meet the crowds on Seventh Avenue.

But Seventh Avenue was the same story. Quiet. Eerie. We skirted past the big hulking building where enormous letters painted in red on a white background announced: "Macy's, The World's Largest Store." An iron grill covered its revolving doors. Macy's was closed.

Then I saw Snoopy. The deflated sagging frame of the giant balloon was collapsed on the pavement in the middle of the avenue. Air was hissing out of him. Workers scrambled over Snoopy's deflated bulk like ugly insects, loosening the ropes off the straps attached to his body.

How could this happen? Tears of fury streamed down my face.

I whirled towards Mama. I screamed at her, screamed in English, "We missed it. There's nothing here. We missed *everything*."

I screamed it over and over, louder and louder. "*Everything! Everything*! We missed it all!" I wrung my hands in despair. Mama tried to hug me, but I avoided her arms.

A cop came over. "Yup, girlie, you said it. Parade's wrapped up almost an hour ago." He glanced over at his partner. "Jim and me are only here because we had the bad luck to pull the holiday shift. Everybody's left for Thanksgiving dinner.

"That's where you and your mother will be headed soon, too, I'm sure, to a nice turkey dinner. So better just calm down, girlie. The parade will be here again next year."

Chill gripped me. Wind froze my head. My earlobes stung from the cold. I put my hand in my pocket for my hat, feeling for the green pompom. But my hat had fallen out somewhere. It was gone.

KING OF YIDDISH

"*Schmaltz!*" Solly cries out.

The man on the subway bench opposite him jerks his chin up from his newspaper. When he sees Solly is just an oldish guy with a fringe of gray hair sticking out from below a plaid driver's cap muttering to himself, the man shakes his head and loses interest.

It is the middle of the day and the train is almost empty. But Solly isn't sitting on any of the vacant seats; he is too wound up. He clings to the handrail, swaying with the strap. He needs to feel the jolts of the car screaming over the tracks. The express hurtles uptown from WZMA radio's decrepit offices on Hudson Street, churning toward the Bronx.

Schmaltz, Solly laments. The language whose poetry he once recited has been reduced to that most American of Yiddishisms. It's dissolved into chicken fat, glutinous and cloying.

He can't banish dark thoughts. The language of his youth, his lifeblood, clogs the vessels around his heart. It's become a bowl of drivel doled out to seniors hunched over walkers. To shivering retirees in ratty wool coats on the benches that divide upper Broadway, chapped lips stretched over yellowing teeth, the light in their eyes reduced to a flicker of recognition at melodies from their extinguished youth.

No matter, he tells himself, you will no longer announce it. Nobody will hear you.

He mutters to himself the whole trip, his unexpected way home to the Bronx at midday. Solly has never traveled at this hour before, never expected to.

The Bronx, a place no one wants to come from or go back to. The last bastion of unglamorous immigrants. The borough he's been commuting to and from for the last 31 years, the 31 years since 1947, trudging up the stairs in the gloom of the train trestle, then walking the five blocks to the apartment he and Bluma were lucky to get from the Housing Authority when they arrived as refugees the year after the war ended.

Of course, Bluma and Solly speak Yiddish between them and Solly reads the Yiddish press daily. But they became good Americans. Every election they vote – Stevenson, Kennedy, Johnson, Humphrey, Carter. Straight Democratic. And Solly is a union man through and through.

Soon after they arrived, a HIAS representative had cautioned them, "America is a great country with a big heart. But the only way you can get ahead is to speak English. Your local PS offers night classes for immigrants."

"PS?" Bluma asks.

"That stands for Public School. You can learn English for free!" he says, beaming.

Bluma was reluctant. "Ach, Solly, my age is too old to put anything new into this head of mine! Besides what do I need a royal English for? To buy tomatoes on Allerton Avenue? Believe me, they'll be glad to sell to me in Yiddish."

But Solly would not let go. "Bluma, you talk nonsense. You're not an old woman, far from it. And between you and me, Bluma, your head is the sharpest. How you always kept all the figures in your memory, and the inventories, and the list of all the customers at your father's factory. And afterward, the names of all the departed from the ghetto."

It was a mistake to mention the ghetto. Bluma's face turned stony. They had survived together, but she never talked about it.

Still, he pressed on, trying to convince her. Without admitting it, he wanted Bluma to accompany him to night school so he didn't have to plunge alone into the unfamiliar English sea.

"Just try one week," Solly cajoled.

At the graduation ceremony a year later, Bluma was awarded the Certificate of Outstanding Achievement. Their Proficiency in English diplomas have been hanging side by side in the living room ever since, in identical pencil-thin black frames, Bluma's embossed with a gold emblem. Specks of dust have crept between the glass and the diplomas.

Night school gave Bluma a new start. With her head for figures and her new proficiency in English, Bluma made a big career in their corner of the Bronx. Bluma worked her way up to head bookkeeper at Swiftee Collision Auto, the big parts and body shop off the Cross Bronx Expressway.

Solly's success in English has been more modest. He is never at home with it. He admires the language, but it remains a shining locked fortress. He only breaches it haltingly, flinching at the looks people give him, how he grinds out English words like a dolt with the accent of an ignoramus.

Maybe because he has given his whole soul to the Yiddish language, he has little left over.

Before the war Solly was a member of not less than three poets' circles. But most of all he loved to act. By 1938 he was invited to become a permanent member of the Classical Players that performed Shakespeare and the great modern dramatists translated into Yiddish. It was the most prestigious troupe of Yiddish actors in Vilna, and Solly was one of them.

He was young and virile, a strong 25 years old, his abilities at a peak. He played Chekhov, he played Ibsen. But his dream was the same as every actor's: the part of Hamlet. In the summer of 1939, it was about to happen.

"Uninsky is finishing the translation," the director told Solly. "In time for the fall season. I'm going to pass you the rough script. Take a look, but don't memorize it yet. Things might get altered."

Solly couldn't resist. He practiced the soliloquies as he strode up and down the avenues of his native Vilna. He declaimed under his breath as he accompanied Horatio Mordechai to the park. His heart swelled to watch his boy's chubby legs pedal over the lanes on his tricycle.

A date was set for the opening night of *Hamlet*, but it was never to be. "To be or not to be," Solly recited bitterly.

Their whole lives were overturned, not only *Hamlet*.

Uninsky and the director were among the first to be killed.

Solly survived, and Bluma, but when they came to America, they left behind the ghosts of their two sets of parents, Solly's three sisters, and Bluma's twin brothers. Plus the unknown grave of Horatio Mordechai, the most beautiful toddler in Vilna. Solly had lulled his cries with the children's poems of Y. L. Peretz and translations of Wordsworth. But he couldn't banish the pain of starvation and the fever of typhus.

In America, Bluma and Solly were a tight unit. Bluma accomplished the boring work of organizing, filing, planning, paying the bills. Because of her, Solly was free to remain the *artiste* – able to dream, to recite, and to serve whoever still yearned to hear the tones of their native tongue.

Solly understands English, but through the decades, he's been comprehending less and less of what's spoken around him. What an irony – that English is not enough after all. First it was Puerto Rican Spanish cackling around, the raucous shouts of boys under basketball hoops and the staccato of women in tight tank tops, beefy thighs overflowing onto the stoops, their orange hair with black roots showing through. After a while, his ears got used to it; Spanish became white noise he didn't notice.

But new sounds have barged in. Often, he can't pinpoint the languages. He surmises from the hues and features of the speakers that they might be Korean, Sri Lankan, or Taiwanese. Polish, at least, he recognizes.

These people don't know it, but these are the ones to whom Solly owes the loss of his livelihood.

Thank you very much, Solly mouths sarcastically under his breath toward the Polish woman in a faded pink polyester scarf hurrying to clean offices. He shakes his fist at the startled taxi driver from Bangladesh double parking his cab and drumming impatient fingers on the wheel. He grimaces at the skinny Korean with wispy hair on his way to stack boxes in the garment district. These are the culprits who have elbowed Solly out.

In their kitchens, in their workrooms, in their garages – wherever they have radios – they listen to Solly's station. They know exactly when to tune in to hear their native language. His crotchety Yiddish station has heard the cry of modern times and transformed itself accordingly. WZMA now emits perky polkas, soupy Russian ballads, and music filled with Asian gongs. It is racing to catch up with the immigrant languages of the hour. As new languages fill the streets of New York, Yiddish is being displaced.

WZMA, do these greenhorns even know what the letters stand for? That the station was named after a giant? Zelig Meir Alter. Hero of the Garment Workers Union. An organizer, a placard bearer, an orator. Never afraid to stand up to the police or anybody else. Zelig

Meir Alter leading thousands in Union Square to support Sacco and Vanzetti, to free the Scottsboro boys, to cheer on FDR. And, like so many giants, forgotten by history. Alter's legacy has been reduced to three initials of a second-rate radio station whose listeners have no idea who he was.

Solly admits Alter was once unfamiliar to him as well. "You never heard of Zelig Meir Alter?" they asked him fresh off the boat, incredulous that Alter's fame hadn't spread to Europe, wasn't as well known to Jews there as Dreyfus and Trotsky.

But Solly has come to bless Alter's legacy and thank him a thousand times over. For it was to Zelig Meir Alter that Solly owes his one and only job in America.

It wasn't his first choice.

Even in Europe before the war, before Solly heard of New York's Second Avenue, he knew there was a street in that city lined with famous Yiddish theaters.

"Go down to Second Avenue and show them who you are," urged Bluma as soon as they got settled in the Bronx. "All they have to do is hear you recite; they will snap you up."

So Solly took the subway down to the old Yiddish theater district and trudged hat in hand over to Second Avenue.

Seeing his expression, still unused to Jewish American cockiness, his timid way of walking, his newcomer's clothing, they shook their heads almost before Solly began to speak. He couldn't get through any doors, let alone do a reading. In the fifth theater, the coarse manager, a toothpick dangling from his lips, spelled it out: "Unemployed Yiddish refugees are a dime a dozen, Pops. Didn't you know?"

Solly walked miles up Second Avenue, rolling that new expression around his tongue – a dime a dozen. By the time he got within sight of the Queensboro Bridge, he'd recovered. "No, no, you bigshots," he told himself. "Solly Solomon is not a dime a dozen. What I saw playing in your theaters was nothing classical, just low-level melodramas. Maybe the war killed off serious Yiddish theater as well as serious Yiddish actors."

The trip to Second Avenue was a failure. No place in America for this Yiddish actor. But through his despair, Solly felt relief. Even after all he had been through, he felt superior – the debased Yiddish stage in America was not for him.

Then, like a miracle, he read an advertisement in the *Jewish Daily Forward*.

"They are asking for an announcer at a Yiddish radio station. What do you think?" he asked Bluma.

"Theater it's not, Solly, but you'll still have to use your voice."

And that radio station, the radio station named after Zelig Meir Alter, handed him a place in the sun. He landed the job one year after he arrived in 1946 and never budged.

Solly arrived promptly at 9:15 a.m., hung up his jacket on the door hook, drank a glass of tea with lemon, thought hearty thoughts, and cleared his throat. At ten, he began to project from deep in his lungs into the microphone: "A good day, Yiddish listeners, this is sonorous Solly Solomon with a big hello again at WZMA, the radio that talks your tongue."

When he broadcast, Solly again became the linguist; consonants and idioms and plays on words rolled off his tongue. His audience was wide. He reached out to fellow refugees and to the old-timers who had come to America before the war and settled on Essex Street, on Ocean Avenue, and in the Bronx.

After about ten years, around 1957, WZMA decided to rebroadcast all of Solly's daytime programs later the same evening. The words the station manager used when he told Solly they would start replaying a taped version still ring in his ears. "Wildly popular," he called Solly's show.

The sound guys told him, "Your Yiddish sounds different, pure."

Solly nodded his head modestly. But inside he was crowing, "Of course. No wonder. I'm from Vilna, the crown jewel of Yiddish. And I was a nobleman in that castle of spirituality and intellectual ferment.

"Even in ghetto I performed. I survived that burning cauldron, that nest of extinction – a miracle. I can't understand until today why me. Why me, and not my precious Horatio Mordechai?

"I brought with me here to America the only possession I had left: I brought my royal Yiddish. Who else would use the word royal to describe a bastard language? Yiddish royal?" He laughed at his own joke.

Sure, they complimented him, but what did it mean? The station replayed his shows, but they didn't raise his pay. It's like the American expression he learned early on, and which he found so many occasions to repeat: "That and a token will get you on the subway."

Yet he could say that he was happy. He, budding actor of the defunct Yiddish stage of prewar Vilna, rebirthed himself into the broadcaster of WZMA's Yiddish hours. And became "wildly popular," no less. News, commentary, comedy, melodrama, and, above all, song. Solly broadcast it all, a smorgasbord of Yiddish for all the displaced refugees and immigrants who had somehow saved their skins in Europe and been lucky enough to be accepted through the golden gates of America.

They called themselves the surviving remnant, after a biblical term. Industrious they were, and upwardly mobile, striving to act American. But their hearts pined for the disappearing cadences of their youth, for their upbringing, for their mother tongue.

And he, Jacob Solomon – Solly to all – fed it to them with all his heart for 31 years. WZMA was more than a job, it was Solly's vocation.

Thirty-one years passed like a dream. He never took a Florida vacation. He never called in sick.

Alas, Solly didn't see the handwriting on the wall.

"Such is the fate of many great men," Solly bemoaned to Bluma. He should have guessed when the horseradish and then the egg noodle companies phased out their advertisements, when the show was cut to four days and then three, edged out by the Ukrainian Hour and then the Korean Hit Parade. Solly fumed, Solly stormed out, said he would not accept the cuts. But he always did. What choice did he have? Where else could he go?

And then, salvation swooped toward him. Out of Stockholm, Sweden, of all places. Who would have predicted that their little Isaac Bashevis Singer would stand on the podium in Stockholm like an ancient hero upon Olympus? Singer, whose work in Yiddish Solly first read serialized in the Yiddish press, and who became the first Yiddish novelist translated into English to hit the big time.

"Bluma," Solly said proudly, "they're displaying Singer's *The Family Moskat* in the window of the Browser's Bookshop! Yes, our Singer they're showing off. In Manhattan!" He stood with his forehead pressed against the glass, admiring Singer's book in between a novel about a factory girl in the Midwest and *Easy Holiday Cakes to Bake at Home*, almost as proud as if he had written it himself.

When the greatest honor of 1978 Nobel Prize in Literature was bestowed upon the Yiddish author, Solly's language burst out of the closet in glory.

The same diminutive Singer whom Solly had met at the station when he came to give a reading over the radio. Singer, pink and bald like a newborn baby, but with the imagination of a genie. Singer, who had recognized Solly, even talked to Solly personally, who smiled at him when Solly handed him a copy of Singer's book to autograph. Who said to Solly, "On Sundays, mine ears are all yours, Solly."

On the day of the Nobel ceremony, the entire WZMA staff gathered in the coffee break room overlooking the moving trucks and the furniture storage companies and tuned in to the radio broadcast live from Stockholm. They listened to Singer delivering his speech in the language of exiled refugees to the exalted audience dressed in silk and tuxedos.

"Oy, I am higher than the sky," Solly beamed when he heard Singer's singsong voice accepting the Nobel Prize in Yiddish.

The whole crew was silent, rapt. Next to Solly stood Moish, the last Yiddish programmer, wiping away tears.

When Solly heard Singer's speech, he knew Yiddish was safe, and Solly Solomon was safe along with it.

This morning, a few weeks later, almost New Year's 1979, Solly is called into the business office, down the dirty hall from where the real work of the station took place. His heart sings. Is he up for a bonus for New Year's? Or maybe, finally, a raise? Yiddish, after all, now has status. Yiddish has risen to the Nobel category.

"You're looking wonderful, Solly!" says Adele, the deputy station manager who started as a girl Friday a few years after Solly was hired. That smart cookie had surely risen. "The years do you well. Sit, sit. You might have heard about the negotiations, Solly. Well, they've been concluded, and…"

"Ah, great relief! I know about the talks, we all do. I was supposed to be the union's rep – seniority," Solly says, half modestly. "But because of – well, what can I say – call it bad luck, I was passed over. And then we were so upset when management's talks with the union were postponed. A wonderful thing that's behind us now and…"

"No, Solly," she interrupts, *"other negotiations.* Higher-level negotiations. A deal's been concluded. WZMA's been sold."

"*Sold?* Who would buy?"

"Our station's new owner is Cartwright Communications, a media conglomerate, Solly, based in Boulder."

"Boulder? A rock?"

"No, Solly, Boulder, Colorado."

"Colorado!" he blurts out. "What do they know of Yiddish? Who ever heard of Molly Picon, or Martha Schlamme, or Dzigan & Schumacher in the Rocky Mountains?"

Adele's jaw drops. She looks confused.

Silently, he chides himself, "Even at a time like this you try to joke, Solly."

A soliloquy of eloquence wells up inside his head. Will a corporate heart bleed for homebound old listeners in the recesses of Washington Heights or the byways of the Grand Concourse? For bony fingers turning the dials on transistor radios until they catch our station, the aged ones stuck like unwanted extras in the spare bedrooms of their kids' houses in Roslyn Heights or Fort Lee? Who knows, are there still thousands out there? Hundreds? Maybe only dozens? But these thoughts he keeps to himself.

Don't lose your head, Solly, he cautions himself. He raises himself in the chair and sticks out his chin like before a big speech. "So when do I get to meet them, the new bosses?" he says.

"Let me explain something Solly," Adele resumes. "Something basic about economics. The bottom line of a radio station is revenue. Not literature, not nostalgia, not charity – revenue. There's just no more sponsorship left for Yiddish. None. Sorry, my friend, times change. Our listeners speak Russian, Vietnamese, and, above all, Spanish."

He feels the ax falling.

Adele continues, "From now on, WZMA will be focusing on languages more in demand…"

Solly stops listening. He celebrated too soon. Instead of a raise, it is the death knell. Even I. B. Singer and his Nobel couldn't save the neck of Solly Solomon.

What they mean is not "Sorry." It is "Vamoose, Sol, scram."

In plain English, or Yiddish, or any language, he's fired.

"Take your time to gather your things, Solly," Adele says. "After all, you're like family."

That and a token, he thinks to himself.

He opens the drawer of the metal desk he's sat at for 31 years. But Solly never needed any props. In it are just a ratty cardigan and folding umbrella. Plus five unopened boxes of Tilden's honey lozenges – Solly's secret remedy and backup in case his voice should become hoarse on the air. It never did though, not once. He leaves the lozenges behind for the next guy.

Solly exits the premises with the plaid driver's cap he's always worn in the broadcasting room and his heavy white mug with *Astoria Savings Bank* printed in red. As he goes down in the elevator, he notices the inside of the mug has absorbed tea stains and is discolored with rusty streaks. He sets the cup down on the curb next to the litter bin outside the subway stairs. It is still a good cup, with no cracks, no chips. Somebody will pick it up.

And that's why, for the first time, Solly finds himself traveling back to the Bronx before rush hour. As the train leaves Manhattan and passes the station signs for 149th Street, passes Jackson and Prospect and Intervale Avenues, he realizes his error.

After all, there is only one Isaac Bashevis Singer. Solly conflated himself. Like the heroes in Greek tragedies, Solly has given in to hubris.

Solly rides home to Bluma. He walks over to their squat brick apartment building on Holland Avenue. Bluma will see his tragedy for what it really is. She remembers when Solly played Prospero in

Yiddish, when he recited to Horatio Mordechai, when he carried his language to America precious as a violin in a silk-lined valise. She knows Yiddish is the instrument of his life. What will it be like now that it's been blacked out?

Bluma will commiserate while Solly licks his wounds.

She sits at the kitchen table, a pencil behind her ear, poring over Swiftee Collision Auto's quarterly report.

After he stammers out the news, Bluma jumps up as fast as she can manage these days. Solly is still wearing his coat, but she puts her arms around him.

"Wicked!" she cries. "Heartless, to fire a man of over 60. Solly, you've given them half a lifetime of service. No, you've given them your whole life here in America."

"Especially to hear it from Adele," Solly says sadly. "By the time she joined the station, I was already a veteran."

"That scrambling pusher. I pegged her early for a shark." Bluma leans both arms on the table and her voice rises. "She would kill off everybody if it saved her own skin.

"But," adds Bluma, sitting down abruptly and pulling out a clean sheet of paper, "let's figure out how we can manage." She taps her head. Solly knows she is calculating the figures before she writes anything down.

"Let's look at the bright side, Sol. Medicare and your union pension will see us through." She seems cheerful, even. Almost ready to plan that long-delayed vacation. That's Bluma; she knows how to shut the door on the past.

But Solly is not ready for pragmatism. Solly is not ready to become realistic.

He puts on his coat and his broadcasting cap and walks over to the Pelham Parkway. A beautiful road, really, the Pelham Parkway. More a park than a thoroughfare. But like Yiddish, sadly past its prime. No credit is given to the Pelham Parkway, having the bad luck to find itself in the Bronx. The trees have grown larger in 31 years, although try as he might, he cannot recall how tall they were when he arrived.

He sits down on a bench to catch the angle of the winter sun and remembers how he burst with pride when Singer declared in Stockholm, "Yiddish has not said its last word." Maybe not, he tells himself, but I, Jacob Solomon, have said mine.

The sun slides down behind the buildings and shadows darken the bench. He feels his words dwindle and drain out, feels himself becoming mute.

A boy of about ten in an unzipped flannel jacket whizzes by on a bicycle, doubling back and forth, circling, passing Solly again. His jacket rises behind him like a cape in the gusts of wind. He is whistling.

His Horatio Mordechai would have become such a bike rider, would have loved riding like that. Solly pushes the pain away. But his mood remains dark.

Despondently, Solly thinks about what's waiting, about an unwanted Florida vacation.

Then it hits him, the Idea. He sits bolt upright, his hands give a mighty clap, the sound sharp in the cold air. He leaps up, flings his arms wide, and tosses his cap high into the air.

"Miami!" he whoops. "Miami!"

The boy screeches to a stop in front of Solly's bench. He stares at Solly, an old man jumping and gesticulating.

Solly addresses the child in the big announcer's voice he used for his listeners. "That's where they've gone, all the ones who've left New York – to Miami. Not all the Yiddish listeners have died of old age. No – they have relocated! And I will, too. Yes, I am saying: in spite of everything! I will, too!"

Solly stabs the air. The boy grips the bicycle handles and puts one foot on a pedal, but he keeps still, listening.

"Lonely native Yiddish speakers sweating on lounge chairs," intones Solly. "Yiddish speakers indifferent to Coppertone and Cuban coffee and the hit parade. Yiddish speakers longing for one thing – to hear their mother tongue."

Solly raises his arm like a conquering emperor. His voice regains poetic resonance. "And I, I shall give them their Yiddish back! Solly Solomon does not disappoint!"

HOMECOMING ON RIVERSIDE

As soon as Henny spied her dead grandparents climbing out of the taxi, she raced across the side street and down West End Avenue toward her building. The yellow cab had just pulled up in front of her building's canopy. With her sharp child's vision she recognized them at once from two blocks away, even through the heavy snow.

The doorman rushed over to the curb. He popped open an oversized black umbrella high over the gray heads of the Grandparents, protecting them from the wet snowflakes. The doorman's gestures lost their flourish when he saw the couple's old-fashioned appearance – Grandpa's double-breasted suit, Grandma's chignon, Grandpa bent slightly at the waist, standing aside to let Grandma enter first.

Henny ran toward them, face into the wind. Her breath stabbed between her ribs as she raced down the deserted pavement. Through the corner of her eye, she read the "Don't Walk" sign at the crosswalk flashing blood red. The hard plastic handle of her book bag banged against her knees. Icy pinpricks hit her hot cheeks, melted, and ran down beneath her collar.

The Grandparents would be bewildered by the lobby's twisting corridors and multiple elevators: the front elevator, the rear elevator, the service car. She could almost hear them struggling to ask: Did they have the right address? Did their son Ignash Kanowitz live there? They wouldn't know to use the new name – that their Ignash had become Eugene and that Kanowitz was reborn as Kane. If she didn't get there right now to steer them, the doorman would turn them away, out into the snow. This time he wouldn't shield them with the umbrella.

Henny wondered if they had a place to stay in New York, if they knew anybody. They would have come all this way for nothing, all the way across the years. They wouldn't know how close they had come to seeing their son again, and his wife whom they remembered so young – and to meeting her, Henny, their only grandchild. She *had* to make it.

This time she would catch them, for sure. Eighty-third Street, 82nd Street, she ran, panting. She was almost there.

"I'll take you upstairs!" she'd shout. "I know who you want!" For once, there would be no empty chairs in their living room.

She hoped the Grandparents would understand her. She hoped they could speak English. At least a little. There would be time later for them to learn more, Henny would be there to help. Henny raced past the building next door, pushing her way between a couple walking from the doorway toward the open door of a taxi idling in front of the canopy. She felt their disapproving stares at her rudeness as she brushed past. She saw Grandma go into her building and then Grandpa's thin frame disappear after her into the open doorway.

The doorman in his crimson wool uniform tipped the visor of his cap toward Henny and smiled his gold-toothed smile as she dashed in, breathless, intent to catch up.

But it was the same story again. The elevator door snapped shut just as she arrived to slip in and join them. She hit the buzzer over and over. But it was too late. The elevator whirred, chains creaked, as the car ascended. Next time, next time I'll succeed, she vowed.

"What youse in such a rush for, little missy? That hungry for your dinner are youse?" the doorman asked in the hearty voice he turned on for the tenants and their children.

Henny shook her head in bewilderment and shuffled from foot to foot. She was still breathing hard from the run, and her knee was hurting where her book bag had hit it.

The lobby was empty except for the doorman giving her a puzzled look. He turned around and stood impassively facing the glass entrance doors, looking out into the boulevard, his thick arms hanging down and back turned toward her.

Henny's shoulders sagged. She had lost them again. And she knew why. She hadn't played by their rules. She hadn't resisted the urge to chase after them.

Henny learned to recognize the grandparents from the blurry photographs stashed in the back of the bottom drawer of her parents' dresser. The photographs she had come across wrapped in wrinkled white tissue paper held together with crisscrossed rubber bands. She had studied them for so long that she would know them anywhere.

And it wasn't only Grandpa and Grandma, it was also the other set, her mother's parents, the ones she called Poppa and Nana. Coming upon Henny one day sitting on the carpet in front of the dresser with the photographs spread out around her, her mother swooped them up. "These are fragile, they're all we have! Not to touch!"

Grandpa, Grandma, Poppa, Nana – she had given them those names. In Henny's house, the Grandparents were never mentioned.

On the middle shelf of their living room bookcase stood the leather-bound album, maroon with a gold border, framing the words "Family Photos," with parchment paper between the stiff laminated pages. Putting triangular black holders on each corner and measuring with a ruler, her mother meticulously pasted in all of Henny's photographs as soon as the films were developed: Henny's first time toddling around the coffee table, blowing out candles at her second birthday party, straddling a pony at the children's zoo, singing at a Thanksgiving assembly.

Two years ago, when she was nine, Henny asked her mother, "Why don't you put your parents' pictures in the album, too? And how about Daddy's parents? Why are they all in the drawer? Don't you ever feel like seeing them?"

Henny's mother looked at her sharply and then away. "I haven't gotten around to it," she murmured, running her fingers through brittle, dyed hair. Then softly, through pinched lips, she repeated the familiar mantra: "Now is not time for talking about it."

Henny would be smarter now than to ask a dumb question like that. She would know better than to expect an answer. In her house, silent questions hovered in the air, answers were hardly ever articulated. Question marks were the invisible cobwebs of their lives, accumulating in all the scrubbed corners of the apartment.

The photographs lay on, undisturbed and lonely in their paper shrouds. The bureau was their coffin.

On Sundays, fathers in her class took their kids up to Yankee Stadium to watch the game. Henny's family also took a drive. But they continued past the stadium to the Bronx to visit old Cousin Bella. Bella had come over "before the war." Before he died, Bella's husband traveled by subway to work in the garment district.

Henny wished they could ride by subway, too, instead of in the monotonous overheated car, but her parents declined.

"Why you want to go in a dangerous train next to strangers when you have the nice clean back seat for yourself?" her mother said.

Henny shrugged. "It'd be fun, maybe," she stammered. "Could we try it? Or maybe I could go alone! Yes, that'd be OK – the best."

"Henny..."

"And you could meet me at the subway steps. It doesn't cost much!" Her voice speeded up in her efforts to persuade. "It will work out! I saw a subway entrance near Bella's house. I'll show you!"

Her parents laughed without answering. Even though they didn't talk to her much, or want to answer her questions, they always arranged to keep her nearby.

Cousin Bella lived in a brown brick apartment building with a musty odor in the hallway and a self-service elevator with a sticky gray floor.

Week after week, in a voice high-pitched with anxiety, Bella called, "Who is there? Is that you, Ignash?" She repeated the same words even though they telephoned her every time, last thing before they left their apartment. And besides, Henny thought, who else would Cousin Bella be expecting?

Opening the door, Cousin Bella looked at Henny's parents mournfully and sighed. Her father sighed back. "Yes, yes, Bella, that is how it is," he said. "We have you, at least."

They filed straight into the kitchen and took their places on the metal chairs with red plastic cushioning. Henny shifted to avoid getting scratched from the crack in the plastic running across her seat. Cousin Bella shuffled to the stove and picked up the kettle filled with hot water she had simmering. The three grownups sipped strong dark tea, transparent in thin glasses with glass handles. They blew on the hot liquid, leaning their heads close together across the oilcloth tablecloth and talking Polish. At the fourth place set for Henny was a thin paper napkin folded into a triangle, a glass of tepid milk, and a piece of candied cake. She nibbled off the glazed sugar. Then she raked the top of the cake with the tines of her fork, creating a pile of crumbs. She extracted all the raisins and ate them one by one. The grownups talked away.

Henny ducked through the swinging door into the living room.

The dark television lurked in front of the closed drapes. She turned it on, hoping this Sunday the set would be in a good mood. Henny's thighs stuck unpleasantly to the plastic slipcovers on the armchair opposite the television, so she moved and sat cross-legged on the cold linoleum floor close up in front of the small screen.

One arm of the V-shaped antenna was broken in half, hanging down at a disjointed angle, and wavy lines across the middle periodically disrupted the reception on the screen. Voices became unpredictably garbled. The only station that always had good reception was the channel screening the ballgame being played nearby in Yankee Stadium.

Henny never watched the ballgame. Baseball per se held no interest, even though she would have given anything to go to a game, the ones she heard chewed over in school on Monday mornings. "Did you see that homer in the top of the sixth?" "Would've loved to catch the ball that came into the stands!" Henny had no idea what they meant. But she longed to sit high up in the bleachers and shout "Steal that base!" with everyone else, eat hot dogs. and wipe mustard off her chin.

No matter how snowy the screen got – if there was any picture, however bad – Henny stuck to her shows: *Father Knows Best*, *Leave It to Beaver*, *Ozzie and Harriet*. She immersed herself in the plots of the short episodes. What's the proper attire for roller skating parties? How to get along with the boss's wife? Which way is best to earn last-minute money to buy flowers for your parents' anniversary? She envied how the characters smiled at one another and put their arms lightly around each other's waists, the mother wearing a perfectly ironed shirtwaist dress, full skirt ballooning demurely. She felt warm and full when the inevitable happy resolution was accomplished.

In the background, through the crack in the kitchen door, Henny heard her parents talking with Cousin Bella. Through the staccato of Polish, she recognized the recurring names of people she had never met. Their foreign names ended with vowels: Moishele,

Helka, Golda, Yankele. Mostly it was her mother and Bella who conversed even though Cousin Bella was really her father's cousin. They often finished off by turning to her father and asking, "Ignash, do you remember?" Her father mumbled a response or kept silent.

Sometimes, the TV refused to work at all, no matter how hard she jiggled the antenna or spun all the buttons on the front of the old set and even the hidden ones on the back. There was nowhere else to go except Cousin Bella's room with the threadbare bedspread in faded damask pink looking soiled. The Venetian blinds were always shut, and when Henny poked a finger between them, there was nothing to look at but the cracked concrete of the treeless street.

So Henny headed back into the kitchen.

When Henny entered, the conversation stopped short, and the three heads looked up.

"TV's busted," Henny pouted.

Cousin Bella reached into the drawer next to the silverware and pulled out the old set of dominoes with the missing double-four.

Thrusting them at Henny, she asked, "Here, why not to have fun playing?"

Henny stood the dominoes up in a row like soldiers, then knocked them down. She stacked them in piles until they collapsed. She listened in to stories where the only words she understood were the names of towns she knew she would never see and the names of people who were dead. When they mentioned someone, Henny anticipated the sad inflections in her parents' voices and their lowered tones, which meant their end had been met.

On the way back home, she reached over the back seat and tugged at her mother's sleeve, begging her to retell the story in English: "What happened to your brother Marek? How old was Marek when he died?"

"Ignash, it will be an accident with that driving!" her mother said. "Clean off the window!"

Henny's father turned the windshield wipers on and off, off and on, trying to clear the fog. The steam on the inside of the windshield became opaque. Her father tried wiping it with his palm. All the while, Henny's mother gave urgent advice. Finally, he fumbled in his pants, squirming in the seat until he dug a handkerchief out of his pocket and smeared little circles on the glass, holding the wheel with the other hand. Henny's mother reached over the seat and snatched the handkerchief.

"Do you want to kill us? Drive with both hands!"

They had succeeded again, as they always did. Henny's question was buried.

As they left the Bronx, Henny waited to pass under big concrete arches supporting access to the George Washington Bridge. After that, she would stare at the outline of the roller coaster across the river on the Palisades of New Jersey.

She wouldn't dream of suggesting that her family go to an amusement park. Theirs was not a family for rides. Not like her friend Maureen's parents, who took Maureen and her sisters twice a year, in spring and fall. Maureen described how she screamed and buried her head in her father's shoulder on the roller coaster. "We get to have two cotton candies each!" she said. Henny hoped Maureen would invite her to join – one extra girl wouldn't make a difference, she was sure, to the four sisters or their parents. She was sure there were no silences when Maureen's family traveled in their powder blue Chevy with the girls squeezed into the back seat. She opened her eyes wide to try to make them look very shiny and asked a lot of questions, hoping to plant the idea of an invitation in Maureen's mind. But the seasons rolled past, and Maureen did not ask.

"I hate to visit Bella!" Henny scowled in the back seat. "Why can't I just stay home?"

Glancing at her mother, her father muttered, "Next year, when you're older."

But the next week, they suddenly relented, just past her 11th birthday, repeating the injunction over and over the hour before they left about not letting in strangers: "Never, *never* unlock the door."

Yet as Henny sat at the piano bench getting ready to put in her obligatory practice, her mother said, "Are you sure, Ignash, that we should leave her? What's worrying me is that she wants to be by herself. It's not healthy to a child to be so much alone." Henny was used to hearing herself talked about in the third person as if she were far away or invisible even though she was sitting large as life in the same room.

Her father was already in the elevator, with Jimmy the operator in white gloves holding the door open for her mother. Henny's mother hesitated, her hand on the doorknob of the apartment, pleading, "Maybe you'd like to come after all, Henny? You know you always have a good time with the television there. Maybe today Bella buys a babka."

Henny shook her head, impatient for the departure. At last, they disappeared.

For the next few visits, Henny's father asked her to reconsider and join them. Then it became a given that Henny stayed behind when they went to Cousin Bella. Henny detected her parents' relief at being able to leave her. The only thing she regretted was that she wouldn't hear the freedom her absence permitted them: freedom to speak freely to each other about the topics to which they alluded in half phrases and glances when she was within range.

As soon as her parents left, Henny unbolted the front door, leaving it closed only on the chain. That would make it easier to open fast to welcome the Grandparents. She waited as long as she could, forcing herself to look at her watch for ten minutes to be sure her parents had already reached the car and driven away.

Then she flew through all the rooms, flinging open each window as wide as it would go. She went from one window to the next, leaning out from every one as far as she could, the ledge pressing down on her waist. Cupping both hands around her mouth she called out, "Grandpa! Grandma! I'm here!" or "Nana, Poppa, this is Henny! You can come over now!" Then to be sure they understood, she cried, "It's Henrietta calling from up here! I'm Henush!"

Her calls ricocheted against the walls of the building on the opposite side of the courtyard, and she heard her own voice echoing back. From the windows facing the street, Henny directed her calls downward, repeating them in between the horns of the taxis below and the screech of cars' brakes stopping short at a light.

None of the Grandparents had yet responded. But she kept on, hoping they might pass by and look up and see her leaning out high above them from the seventh floor, her hair whipped by gusts of wind.

Then disaster struck. As she leaned out of the window calling down, Henny spotted Mrs. Scheradsky from 5B across the courtyard looking right back up at her. Henny had unmasked herself – she was exposed. She imagined the glint of recognition in Mrs. Scheradsky's eyes. Heart pounding, Henny ducked inside the window and crouched low. She dashed to the front door, double locked it, and hurried to turn on the television set to the loudest volume. Henny perched on the couch twisting her hands, waiting for Mrs. Scheradsky or her husband or Jimmy to ring their bell. Worse than facing Mrs. Scheradsky, who would doubtless tell Henny's parents about her strange behavior, now the Grandparents would be frightened off and hide for sure.

After 15 minutes, Henny began to breathe quietly. She didn't dare call out of the windows again that day. From then on, she scanned the windows opposite hers in the courtyard beforehand, making sure no one was around when she summoned them: "Nana, Poppa, Grandma, Grandpa, look up here, look at me!"

After calling for the Grandparents, she proceeded to visit them. Henny headed into her parents' bedroom.

She stopped in front of the dresser. Her fingers groped into the back of the bottom drawer and removed the rubber band bindings from the loose snapshots.

Nana squinted at the bright sunshine behind the photographer, pulling the brim of her hat over her forehead to shade her eyes; Poppa's hand rested lightly on the soft fur of Nana's collar. Both looked straight at Henny. They were glad to be among family again. Sometimes, the borders of the photographs crumbled off onto the bureau as Henny held them, little beige crumbs like ashes. She carefully collected them into her cupped palm, then blew away the tiny specks.

Even though the Grandparents hadn't yet visited her at home, Henny saw them often. She found them behind her as she stood in line for the crosstown bus on a rainy morning; Poppa sheltered her with their umbrella and kept her book bag dry. Or she noticed them on the curb while waiting for a green light to sidestep the dirty slush on Amsterdam Avenue. Handing over a dime for a sooty comic book at a newsstand, she sensed someone looking over her shoulder, and turning, stood face to face with her namesake grandmother, the one who had been gassed in a camp called Chelmno. Henny had overheard about gassing trucks, how the people had been crammed into the back of sealed vans and then poison air pumped in. But Henny's grandmother didn't look like someone who was suffering. Grandma looked just like the photo Henny knew, her chignon in place, her eyes kind and peaceful. Smiling, Grandma took her by the hand, and together they began descending into the darkened subway stairwell. By the time Henny reached the bottom stair, Grandma was gone.

Arriving home, Henny found Viera sitting perched on the living room couch beside her mother. With Viera, Heddy's mother suddenly had so much to say, the words pouring out. The women laughed together, too; it was so strange to see her mother laugh. Henny loved to sit in her room and listen to them talk. Unlike her mother's other friends, who were Polish like her mother, Viera was from Hungary. So with Viera, her mother had to talk English. If Henny left her door open, she caught most of the conversation.

Viera was her mother's first friend in America before Heddy's parents located survivors from their hometowns. She had sat next to her mother at the public night-school English classes for refugees. Even though she was from another country, Henny's mother said they were both the same, both from the Other Side, and she got along better with Viera than with Americans who could Never Understand.

"Understand what?" Henny asked.

Henny was beckoned to play Viera a piece on the piano. "Viera so anxious to see how much you have improved since last time," coaxed her mother.

She walked down the narrow hallway trying to postpone entering the living room for her unwilling recital. She was rounding the hall corner when she was stopped short by Viera's words:

"Henny is healthy and so pretty, but you know, pardon me to say it, but your daughter seems to spend the time all by herself. Does she always play alone?"

"Oh, Henny *loves* her dolls," her mother replied quickly. "Still plays with them even up to now. And she has – how did her teacher put it? She has her... imaginary playmates. She is holding big conversations with them. I am watching from the window. She is talking miles a minute to the empty space beside her as she is walking. Even she leans toward them and is moving with her hands. About it I went to speak to her teacher."

"What is the teacher saying?" asked Viera, leaning forward. "A teacher surely had something thinking about this!"

Henny's face burned. She flattened herself behind the corner wall outside the living room, straining her ears.

"The teacher told me many children do it, so it's not to worry about," her mother said. "She assured me the child out of it will grow. So all children. The teacher said so. But I am watching her all the same. I do not say anything to my Henny, but I watch. I want only one thing – for my Henny to be happy."

"Yes, let her be happy," nodded Viera.

Henny ran back to her room and grabbed her winter coat, then turned on her heels and ran down the hall to the front door. She heard her mother calling out to her, but she kept on. Henny fled into the hallway.

In the overheated corridor, she buzzed for the elevator, then buzzed again. All was still. The elevator ropes and pulleys weren't starting up in the shaft. She kept her finger on the bell. The buzzer screamed in her ears, but the elevator didn't come. She knew sometimes Jimmy went down to the basement and didn't answer for several minutes. When he returned, a pleasant heavy odor of tobacco enveloped him.

But this time, Henny couldn't bear to wait. The vestibule was a cage. She put her shoulder against the heavy fire door marked Service Stairs and pushed it open. She ran down, the taps on her heels reverberating on the metal steps. The khaki walls bore down upon her; the smell of garbage from the incinerator hung in the moist air.

Henny raced seven flights to the bottom and found herself in front of the door that said Main Lobby. She turned the handle and pushed, but it did not budge. She could not get it to open. Henny began to sweat. Her coat hung heavy on her shoulders. She imagined having to climb all the way back up. What if the door at the top wouldn't open either? She gripped the sticky knob again and butted against the door, but it stayed shut.

Maybe the doors only opened from the outside? Henny unbuttoned her coat, and called, "Help!" Nothing. Then in a louder voice, "Mommy, Daddy! Help! Jimmy! Jimmy!" She sat down and gulped for air. Her back was wet from sweat, her face hot in her heavy coat. She stared at the concrete floor. She stood up and pounded on the door and called out, "Jimmy! I'm stuck in here. It's me – Henny. Henny Kane from 7A! Please help, somebody, help!" Henny's voice broke.

She leaned her whole side against the door. It loosened a crack. At last, she managed to swing it open. Henny raced through the brightly lit lobby, streaking past her reflection in the full-length mirrors. She bolted through the entrance doors, pushed them open herself, not giving the startled doorman a chance to hold them.

Henny bounded down the side street to Riverside Drive, then across the road into the park. Empty. Nobody. She hunted for them everywhere, on their favorite bench near the flagpole at the Soldiers' and Sailors' Monument. She checked the benches outside the entrance near the park's perimeter. She scanned the empty playground. But even as she searched, Henny didn't have much hope. She knew it was against the rules to look too hard.

What they wanted her to do was to walk slowly, to appear engrossed in her own concerns. They needed her to feign indifference. Then, when she least expected it, they would appear. The Grandparents insisted on it: to materialize only on their own terms.

Henny knew from experience that if she arrived early for her piano lesson and waited patiently on the bench outside the park, looking at the river in the distance, her father's father, who disappeared one icy day in Lodz, would walk up and sit beside her. Clutching her sonatinas and composition book, she listened to him recount how children in the ghetto were wrenched from their parents and deported to Chelmno. "All the children under ten years old, en masse" he said, so softly, so sadly. "In one week."

"Like the Pied Piper of Hamelin!" Henny piped up.

"Not exactly," said her grandfather, and he cupped his lighter-than-air fingers upon her head.

Henny cringed to recall her words, when she had been younger and not very smart. Grandpa told her of his own roundup in the street, about the truncheons and the trains. He accompanied her gently through the stone gates of the park and they strolled, his warm arm around her shoulders. Down they went along the winding paths to the boat basin. They leaned against the black wrought-iron rail together and watched the pungent smoke colored Hudson drift by. Her heart beat, dreading the time he would leave her. She never knew when that inevitable moment would come.

Now Henny strode purposefully downhill and downtown through Riverside Park, through the tunnel toward the boat basin.

She stared across the river at the utopian silhouette of the giant roller coaster on the Palisades. The image crossed her mind of Maureen and her family in their powder blue Chevy, laughing through rolled-down windows as they whizzed over the George Washington Bridge.

The week before, she had been lucky. She had spun around to face the serene smiles of her maternal grandparents, her Nana and Poppa, who had been shot together with all the people in their town one screaming afternoon in the clearing of a pine forest. New snow had hung heavily on the emerald boughs of pine, muffling the bullets. Henny snuggled between her Nana and Poppa on the park bench with its peeling paint, her arms linked tightly through theirs.

The Parks Department man in his olive uniform had shuffled by. Oblivious, his cheeks ruddy with cold, he concentrated on spearing crumpled candy wrappers off the path with his pointed stick.

In what accent the Grandparents spoke and what their words were she could never exactly recall, but Henny precisely pictured their sad smiles, dry as the brown leaves that swirled around her in the park. When the Grandparents came to visit her, Henny was protected. She was encircled by the threadbare woolen sleeves covering their lifeless arms. She always lay her head on Nana's shoulder. She knew Nana didn't find her too heavy.

Today Henny stood perfectly still, her back pressing against the balustrade by the river. She looked up at the line of apartment buildings majestically lining the avenue, at their windowpanes burning in the reflection of the cold sun soon to set behind the Palisades.

Then she saw them, all four, just emerging from the tunnel underpass. The two grandmothers walked first, arm in arm. Their faces wore happy, gentle smiles as they talked. Henny knew they were saying good things about her.

A few paces behind came Grandpa and Poppa. Grandpa was opening his mouth in a wide circle and gesturing with his hands. Poppa, his hands clasped behind his back, leaned forward toward Grandpa, listening. Grandpa must be telling one of the jokes he was famous for.

The two couples strolled downward toward the river on noiseless footsteps. They approached Henny, and she waited for them, with all the time in the world, her back leaning on the balustrade. She would wait, she decided, until the Grandparents were very close before running from one outstretched pair of arms to the other, until she had been embraced by each one. Until all four kissed Henny first on one cheek and then the other.

With mounting anticipation, Henny prepared to go back upstairs to interrupt her parents. No matter what they were doing, it was always partial. In the background lurked their burden, the shroud of their furtive grief.

Henny would fling open the door, the Grandparents trailing behind her: Nana and Grandma hesitant lest they interrupt, Poppa and Grandpa with hats in hand, all four wearing shy smiles.

Then, in triumph and in grandeur, Henny would present her orphaned mother and father with their own reincarnated mothers and fathers – the Grandparents. They would all stand in the hallway, without thinking to take off their coats, and hug one another in a tight ring, their arms entangling, embracing each other without borders, as the golden afternoon sun over Riverside encircled them in a halo.

KORCZAK'S BOYS

The letter lay before him on the peeling green paint of his steel desk. In a few moments, Gideon Biro would know the decision on the most unorthodox proposal of his career – and the one about which he felt most passionately. After months of correspondence and three personal trips to up Jerusalem to the office of the Ministry of Education, the answer had arrived.

Gideon's idea had met furious opposition.

At the last meeting, the minister of education asked dubiously, "What's your main impetus, Gideon, for having your group of delinquents – er, I mean former delinquents," the minister corrected himself hastily, "make a journey to a concentration camp in Germany? Do you honestly mean to give them free rein in Europe? Experts have warned the risk might be too great."

When Deputy Superintendent Regev came out strongly against his proposal, Gideon came close to losing everything.

"Subsidize a trip to Baumwald Concentration Camp? For those kids from the Ramon Reformatory?" the deputy superintendent asked incredulously. "They've never even heard of Baumwald." He jabbed the tip of his ballpoint into the air. "And even if they did, they have no identification with any Nazi camp – nothing whatsoever. Or with the whole European experience in the war, for that matter. After all, while Europe was in flames, *their* parents were selling tobacco and hashish in the bazaars of Damascus and Tripoli. As far as these people are concerned, the war was the reason so many of the Ashkenazi Jews are here in Israel hogging all the good jobs. No, giving these boys a trip to Baumwald means one thing – throwing out public funds. Money that could be better spent in a million other ways."

"Like what?" abruptly interjected the minister without looking up from the paper on which he was jotting down notes. "What would you suggest?"

"Like, for example, giving them more equipment – lathes or model engines for technical training – some kind of machine – to prepare them for the real life that awaits them," Regev said, holding up both smooth hands in exasperation. "Let's be realistic about our expectations for them, after all. Let's not forget which kind of boys we are talking about."

Seligson, the head of the appropriations committee, broke in. "For sure! Sending these hooligans out is only asking for trouble," she said. "They have no idea how to behave in normal Israeli society, let alone cutting them loose in Europe. They are even worse than the element they come from. Why else would they land up in your reformatory, Gideon?" Her lips puckered in disapproval. "Granted, you have done well with them. All of us at the Ministry appreciate the success you've had with these difficult cases. That being said, sending them abroad goes a step too far.

"After all," she added, "when we send out youth groups, they become our representatives. Representatives of the State of Israel. Who among us would like these delinquents to be our envoys? Surely, even you, Gideon, wouldn't want these boys to appear in your name. They are not Israel's finest – far from it."

Heads around the table nodded in assent.

"I can appreciate your apprehension, both of you," Gideon said, trying to keep pleading out of his voice, attempting in vain to catch the eyes of the officials around the table. "But our students at Ramon are far from the stereotypes you imagine. They are on the way up, ready to be treated like other kids. They know Israeli teens get a chance to be on youth delegations to Germany and Poland. Seeing the evidence of Nazi crimes against the Jewish people – their people – will cement my boys' determination to become mainstream.

"Nobody wants this delegation to succeed more than I do. It would destroy my boys' egos altogether if they came back in some way personally diminished by this odyssey. I wouldn't take that risk, now that they are just getting on their feet, starting to believe in their own potential. I have faith in my boys, and if you knew them, I am certain you would, too."

He turned to Seligson and Regev. "Come down to Ramon, both of you," he said. "We're not all that far away. Get to know the boys and see for yourselves."

Regev coughed and straightened the angle of the pad of paper lying before him, lining it up with the edge of the table. Seligson unclasped her handbag and began rummaging inside. Neither looked up. There was a long silence in the conference room.

"So, shall we put this up for a vote?" asked Regev, turning toward the minister. Several heads around the table glanced at their watches and then nodded. Gideon knew he was sunk.

"Wait a minute!" came a voice from the far corner. It was Leonid, Gideon's former classmate. "I don't think the Ministry ought to be railroaded into a negative decision."

At the university, Gideon and Leonid had been lumped together by their other classmates as "those two from Eastern Europe" even though Gideon had come to Israel before he was ten and Leonid had arrived from Russia in his early teens. Gideon came to consider the ostracism as one of the luckiest breaks of his life – Leonid remained his friend and champion ever since.

"Not all of you know Mr. Biro," Leonid said. "Look at his face – the scars are still fresh. You don't have to be geniuses to guess that Biro didn't get them from cutting himself shaving."

All the heads around the table stared openly at Gideon's face as if they hadn't been casting surreptitious looks at the discolored skin before. Then they quickly averted their eyes. Gideon sat still, pressing his palms against the tabletop.

"He wasn't in an auto accident, either," continued Leonid. "No, the cuts were inflicted by the knife Sammy Abujaan kept hidden in his pocket when he was brought into Ramon."

"Leonid, please," Gideon protested, "this is unnecessary."

But Leonid plowed ahead. "No, Gideon, I think your colleagues should hear this," he said. "These pencil-pushers should know what's really out there in the field."

Leonid was never afraid to call a spade a spade. And because of generous grants he solicited and won from foreign donors, Leonid had the knack of knowing nobody would dare to stop him from speaking his mind. Leonid turned to the others in the group.

"When Sammy first arrived at Ramon six months ago, he tore away from his police escort and lunged at Gideon as he entered the room," Leonid said. "The slash was not deep, but it was bloody. Luckily, the officer was on his feet. He hit Sammy with a karate chop to the back of the neck and whipped out a pair of handcuffs. The cop yanked the boy by the hair to haul him out of Gideon's office. Gideon pressed a wad of paper from his desk over the cut, trying ineffectually to stop the blood. Bright drops fell on Sammy's file spread out in front of him. Everybody knows that an attack like that would put Abujaan behind lock and key for a long time, underage or not.

"Then as they were almost out the door, Gideon raised his hand and said, 'Stop! Leave the boy here as planned.'

"Stunned, Sammy raised his eyes to look at the man he had attacked. The policeman was reluctant. He made Gideon sign a paper before leaving Sammy behind. 'Don't say I didn't warn you,' the cop muttered. 'These types never change.'

"I'm not telling you this to make a ploy for sympathy," Leonid said, looking at the faces of the Ministry staff around the room, but he directed the angle of his posture in the direction of the minister. "Two years ago, Sammy was put away for using broken glass to cut a teacher's aide. Today, two years later, Sammy has moved up to the academic track. He knows he has to keep up in order to engage in competitive sports. And last spring, Sammy won second place as a featherweight in the national youth boxing championships – those are the competitions that Gideon got approval for Ramon to join. Now he's training hard for this year's matches and also serving as boxing coach to younger boys."

There was a murmur around the room.

"Truants and delinquents who seemed finished for good have changed beyond belief," Leonid went on. "And the important thing to remember is that Sammy's story isn't unique. Momi came in as a chronic arsonist. Ori vandalized every piece of property he could lay his hands on. Maurice bullied and beat younger boys. To see them today, you wouldn't believe what you read in their files. They are so attached to Ramon, some volunteer to stay an extra year working on the grounds in exchange for room and board. And when you hear the word Ramon, you should substitute the words Gideon Biro. Gideon Biro made Ramon the miracle that it is, and his boys recognize that.

"It's true, Gideon's scar won't ever disappear," Leonid continued. "It doesn't make him the handsomest of men. But when he looks at himself in the mirror, it's like that scar is proof that he put himself on the line for his kids. And whenever Sammy Abujaan or the other boys look at Gideon's face, they know it, too."

Gideon turned directly to the minister. He felt himself begin to plead, so he tried to hide the wanting in his voice. "Granting these boys this experience will help them make the best of the poor hand in life that's been dealt them," he said. "Sending them out, just as we send so many other of our high school students, will give them proof that we believe in them, too, that they, too, are part of our nation. My students have come a long way from the days when they vandalized stores and were chronic truants – I've brought all the test results with me."

Gideon pulled out a sheaf of papers from his vinyl briefcase and held them up. "You've all seen what these boys can accomplish when we give them a chance," he said. "This trip to Baumwald, to see with their own eyes what they themselves might have had to undergo just because of their nationality, of their religion, I am certain that it will cement their identity and their commitment to our society as it does for other Israeli teenagers we send out on delegations to Germany and Poland every year.

"My boys have proved they can achieve as much on paper as those richer boys from Tel Aviv and Haifa – the boys with two parents, coming home to their own room in a nice apartment with money for discotheques and driving lessons. Give my boys a chance. They will prove themselves." Gideon ended, looking straight into the minister's eyes.

Gideon had a burdened heart on the way back until the bus pulled over on the side of the highway 45 minutes past Beersheba into the desert. He knew that Regev's arguments and Seligson's suspicions expressed the prevailing view in the Education Ministry about the Ramon Reformatory. They allotted just enough funds to keep it afloat, covering the salary of the skeleton staff, minimal maintenance, and not much else. While schools in the heart of the country were getting air conditioning and computer networks, Ramon hardly had the budget to give the boys enough balls for the soccer fields or to stock the skimpy library. Gideon walked heavily under the hot sun down the cracked asphalt road leading him to Ramon.

But his heavy thoughts were banished when he entered the classroom of his 11th grade and the boys clustered around him. These were the boys who had made such tremendous headway since they arrived in Ramon, shrugged off by exasperated relatives or accompanied by youth services policemen gripping their arm in one hand and a court order in the other. He smiled at Ori, Maurice, and Menashe, and they smiled back.

***

Gideon stared at the letter with its official seal. He picked it up, but before slitting it open, he turned the angle of his head upward toward the portrait. The large canvas representation of the Polish orphanage director hung on the wall opposite his chair, in muted tones of beige and olive, with the accent on the brooding forehead and troubled eyes. Eyes that never really met his own. The painting was the only personal touch Gideon had added to the institutional decor allocated to his headmaster's office in the public reformatory.

People who came into Gideon Biro's office often supposed the painting to be Theodor Herzl, or maybe Sigmund Freud. Of the few who inquired, most did not recognize the name when Gideon answered diffidently, "It is a portrait of Janusz Korczak," as if that settled it. But more and more often, despite Gideon's tone of finality in stating the obvious, people asked, "Who? Janusz who?"

So Gideon became used to reciting a shortened resume of Korczak's life. Few were aware, nor seemed particularly interested, when Gideon explained that Korczak was a radical among the pedagogical establishment in post-World War I Europe. "Korczak believed in encouraging young people's self-respect by giving them unconventional freedom," Gideon said. "His philosophy was maligned, branded as anarchistic."

Gideon hoped his visitors would see the parallel to his school Ramon, a parallel that to him was obvious. But people's ears really only perked up when Gideon recited the story of Korczak's martyrdom.

"In the Warsaw Ghetto, Korczak headed an orphanage.

"Korczak was so well known an educator that even the Nazis offered to spare his life," Gideon would say softly, "but Korczak chose instead to accompany his orphans on the death train from the Warsaw Ghetto to Treblinka rather than abandon them in the moment of their mortal danger. He perished with his children."

That's when most people started to nod. "Oh, yes, now I remember," they'd say. "The orphanage director. I think I saw a TV documentary about him, but I had forgotten his name."

A few recognized Korczak's name right away but had no idea how the martyr had looked. These people looked up at the portrait with new enthusiasm and often could not hold back from exclaiming, "Korczak! Really? Did you *know* him?"

Gideon shook his head, bemused. "Know him? How could I?" he replied softly through his crooked, scarred mouth. "I was born *after* the war." He smiled a smile that might have been embarrassed or sardonic. Gideon was not yet out of his 30s, but something aged in his aspect, something immensely fatigued, made it common for people to assume he had witnessed firsthand the wartime events he knew so much about.

Gideon told himself that whatever the letter contained, the verdict had been decided days or even weeks ago, and nothing he felt or did could affect it. He took a deep breath. Under the heading of the Office of the Deputy Minister of Education, Gideon saw enough to grasp the gist of the message: Yes. A yes! The text authorized sending a delegation of 15 students to Baumwald Concentration Camp in late April. Attached to the letter was a copy of a bank transfer signed by Seligson. Gideon looked up into Korczak's face on his wall and then leaned back and closed his eyes, smiling.

"They let you have it because of what you stand for, Gideon," Leonid told him two weeks later as they sat on the steps outside the conference hall. They were at the university in Jerusalem sharing coffee from Leonid's thermos. The meeting, "New Trends in Educating Challenged Youth," was the one event that Gideon made a point of attending every year. Too often he found sociological conferences less than illuminating. But it was important to keep abreast of new research. With some success, he had adapted Harry Conner's famous techniques pioneered in the Detroit inner city schools to Ramon, and now Conner and Gideon had an ongoing correspondence, exchanging ideas and observations.

Today, though, Gideon came to share his victory with Leonid.

"I didn't feel that I'd convinced either Seligson or Regev in that meeting," said Gideon. "If anything, it was you who changed their minds. But I guess in the end they were with me. At least the minister must have been."

"Listen, Gideon, be realistic," said Leonid. "The Ministry bureaucrats couldn't care less whether the Ramon boys go or not. What they'd like best is just for Ramon and everyone in it to keep as quiet as possible. But you've become a legend in the field, Gideon, devoting yourself to those young candidates for prison. You live what everyone else talks about. You are the educator who has given up a good job with overachieving kids, cooperative parents, and easy conditions in the center of the country. How many people with the opportunities you were offered after you got your doctorate would have gone off to the wilderness to apply academic theories on rejects that everybody before had struck out with?

"Those new appointees like Seligson and Regev, they write you off because they are too new, but to the old-timers in the establishment, like the minister, nobody would have the guts to refuse you, Gideon. They look at you down there in the desert three hours from a decent library or the opportunity for a cultured conversation and they are embarrassed. And they know that you have made those poor deviant boys admire you and perform far more than any of the other principals elsewhere with a thousand-fold more resources have managed. The people in Jerusalem know you've accomplished this miracle because the boys love you. The pencil-pushers look at you and they are ashamed of themselves – these bureaucrats in their cushy jobs with their car allowances and their all-expense-paid conferences twice a year. They couldn't reject your proposal to send a delegation from the Ramon School to Baumwald – just as long as they don't have to be the ones to accompany those boys."

"What about Seligson and Regev?"

"They made no objection."

"So the decision was unanimous?" asked Gideon.

"Unanimous, yes, in a manner of speaking," answered Leonid. "Some people in the Ministry figured they might have more to gain by letting the delegation from Ramon go to Germany."

"What do you mean?"

"Don't dismiss the opposition," Leonid continued. "They haven't come over to your side at all. They're just lying low. It didn't look seemly for them to vote against the disadvantaged. But Regev's group is convinced this delegation from Ramon will slip up, create some unpleasantness. As frequent as Israel's contacts with Germany have become, they are still far from normal, and any small incident has the potential to escalate into a political event. In Regev's eyes, your boys will always remain thugs – rehabilitation or no rehabilitation.

"Look, look over there," Leonid said, pointing at a group of three men exiting the main doors of the conference hall. "See that man in the middle? That's Regev's buddy, Abramov. He has been working his way up the ranks. Abramov's been assistant principal at that school in Jerusalem now for five years. All the good positions in the big cities are locked up. Thanks to you, Gideon, Ramon has become professionally respectable, and Regev would like nothing better than to stick Abramov in there in your place. He is looking to prove your magic aura is nothing but a mirage."

"Why is Abramov relevant now?"

"Normally, these memorial groups go out as a matter of course," Leonid said. "But everybody at the Ministry will be watching your delegation at Baumwald with a microscope, waiting for a slip-up. Just let those boys of yours do anything wrong and the finger will be pointed straight at you, Gideon. Remember, keep on your toes."

"I have faith in my boys."

"I have faith in *you*, Gideon. Just remember, you're not home free yet."

"Are any of us ever?" answered Gideon.

The next week, Gideon rode the bus north again. This time, he got off before they reached the capital, at a bus stop in the middle of nowhere. He walked beside the scrub brush and dusty desert plants until he reached the entrance to the big state mental hospital that straddled the deserted highway between two industrial towns. Located out of the way – like prisons – so normal people won't have to be reminded of them, thought Gideon. Like my school, Ramon.

Once inside, he sat for the proscribed hour opposite his mother, her jaws locked as ever in stubborn silence, her eyes alternatively clouded and burning. Gideon had been told her illness was the result of her unspeakable traumas as a teenager in wartime Hungary.

Gideon barely remembered his Hungarian father, a Communist Party member whom they lived with in Budapest. But he did recall the molded ceilings in his large room and the iron window handles in the shape of lions' heads. When he pushed them open, he looked directly out over the Danube.

But even then, he heard people call his mother nervous. "Dora was in Auschwitz, you know," they whispered to new neighbors. "Who knows what she endured – what she had been made to do, a young, pretty woman."

It was getting riskier in the early Fifties for Communist officials to be linked to Jews. Gideon heard that later and supposed that was why his father refused to marry Dora. He went out "to buy milk" one morning and never returned.

After the Hungarian uprising in '56, his mother thought to seize her chance and emigrated to Israel with Gideon, a land where she was sure they would be wanted.

Gideon and his mother were assigned to a tiny apartment in a new city near Ashkelon. With her six-year-old boy trailing behind, Gideon's mother lugged their metal suitcases from the bus depot. They trudged at the edge of a wide street with no sidewalks. The bright light made Gideon want to keep his eyes permanently shut, and the heat was unrelenting; the boy was soaked with sweat under his heavy European clothing. There were no traffic lights, not one tree. It took three years before the town got a cinema.

His mother's violence was at first confined to the destruction she inflicted on the shabby objects inside their room and kitchenette – banged pots, angry smears on the walls. When Gideon was 12, Dora developed a new habit that was impossible to ignore. Every night, she opened all the windows and howled with feline ferocity at the streetlamp across the street. Dora's screams escalated to where they could no longer be drowned out by the radio, which Gideon frantically turned to the highest volume trying to cover up.

One night, they got so loud that a neighbor who had newly moved in and was unfamiliar with the shrieks ran in distress the three blocks to the public telephone box to call the police. The slashes Gideon cut into the ambulance tires were no use. They stuffed Dora, limp and unresisting, into a private car and took her away.

Since that night of sirens and wild gestures, Gideon had never heard his mother utter another sound.

Afterward, Gideon started to roam the streets and commit small crimes – pointless acts of destruction. He became known to the truancy officers, and finally, the court placed him in a boarding school for problem boys. It was as if by a miracle Gideon found himself in David Golumb's division. Golumb was a native of Israel who served in the overseas British army during the war. Golumb was among the first troops to liberate the concentration camps in Germany, when few were aware of the horrors. Golumb poured out his passionate stories of death and redemption to the boys he instructed. For some reason, Golumb took Gideon under his wing – perhaps it was the look in his troubled eyes – and Gideon responded.

Gideon's achievement to become principal of Ramon was the fulfillment of the vow he had made to himself at 18. None of Ramon's truant boys suspected that Gideon recognized his own young self in them. He had picked up Hebrew so well that only a practiced ear could pick up the telltale resonances of Central Europe. Gideon did not advertise his background to anybody.

* * *

After leaving his ever-silent mother at the asylum, Gideon made his customary stop at the warehouse for overstocked clothing down the road. Rummaging through the warehouse afterward had become the thing that helped him get through the agonizing visits. He was always hopeful of finding something they could use at Ramon. He had made friends with the stock manager, who laid aside irregular bathing suits or socks dyed a color that didn't sell.

This time, Gideon couldn't believe his luck – enough warm-up suits for all the boys in the delegation. The suits were black shiny nylon, with pants and matching zippered jacket. Hard as he examined them, Gideon could find no apparent defects.

Back at school, Gideon asked Simona, who ran the laundry and did whatever mending was necessary, to sew the school's name within a Star of David emblem onto the back of each jacket. Simona nodded and stuffed all 15 jackets into two plastic trash bags, hoisted one over each shoulder, and lugged them off to her uncle's fabric store.

When she presented the finished jackets proudly to Gideon, he saw that all the Jewish star logos were bright egg-yolk yellow – exactly the shade the Nazis had used to identify Jews.

Gideon managed to hold back a dismayed outburst, but Simona didn't miss his expression. "It was the only color felt my uncle could find," she apologized.

Time moved quickly. Four times a week, Gideon taught the boys about the Nazi era. At first, Regev was right – the war was as remote as ancient history. The boys weren't ignorant just of the Nazi past. Their knowledge of global events and even Israeli history was rudimentary.

Gideon gave few lectures. Instead, he showed films. He had each boy take on the identity of a victim or perpetrator and put on skits. He assigned them to write "diaries" of their own wartime experiences. He drove a famous Holocaust writer down from the university in Beersheba to give a reading, but seeing boys fidgeting in the auditorium, Gideon understood he had gone too far.

Still, within weeks, the boys at Ramon were on a first-name basis with Eichmann and Goring. They recognized the Wannsee Conference and Kristallnacht. They knew that trains crisscrossed Europe toward Oswiecim.

There was a small scandal when it was discovered that Menashe and Kobi were sketching a notebook of Nazi symbols – eagles, insignia, iron crosses – and that Kobi was making elaborate drawings of the plane models flown by the Luftwaffe. Once, Gideon came upon Momi practicing Nazi salutes in the courtyard, but, seeing his shocked stare, Momi looked so abashed that he didn't have to reprimand him. By and large, the boys were appalled and horror-stricken by what they learned and extremely attentive. As Gideon knew, there was nothing boring about the Holocaust. He noticed they took on an attitude of shy respect toward the school's handyman, newly intrigued by the faded purple number on the old man's wrinkled forearm.

The day before their departure, Gideon called all the boys into his office. For most, it was the first time they had been back inside that room since the day they first came to Ramon gripped by a policeman. Gideon sat the boys down, pointed to the portrait of Janusz Korczak on his wall, and proceeded with the story of Korczak and his orphans. When he had finished, he let the silence hang in the air for a few moments. Then, with a smile, he opened up the big carton in the corner by his desk and handed every traveler a new black nylon warm-up suit, each with its hand-stitched yellow Jewish star.

They left at dawn on a warm spring morning. As they climbed the steps up to the airplane, the misty air was heavy with the scent of oranges. The boys' spirits were high. For all, it was their first flight and, Gideon knew, their first "vacation." Some fiddled self-consciously with the buckles until they figured out how to latch their seatbelts. They were on their best behavior, sitting three abreast and taking up five solid rows. Most donned the free earphones and studied the laminated cards with the specifications of the airplane.

Gideon sat alone up front with the itinerary on his lap and a newly published study of alternative education he hoped to have time to read. But he repeatedly jumped from his seat and walked up and down among the rows trying to look casual. His heart was full; he felt like hugging them all, one by one. Instead, he contented himself with putting a hand on the shoulders of the boys sitting at the aisles and smiling encouragingly at the others.

Sammy sat in a window seat and kept his head turned toward the clouds. As they flew deeper over Europe, he beckoned to the others with excitement and the boys leaned over to peer at the snowy panorama of the Alps.

At noon the plane landed in Munich. Gideon looked ahead of him at the column of boys descending the airplane stairs. He saw to his horror a line of yellow Jewish stars entering Germany, one after the other. Simona's patches were more than an apparition – they were eerie replicas. Gideon was stabbed with the thought that the inadvertent irony was a premonition.

As they drove through Munich, the boys sat with their faces pressed to the windows, wide-eyed at the sleek silver cars and the massive marble buildings. They had entered a world of superior quality. The bus itself was a luxury with its clean velvet upholstery and reclining seats.

Speeding out on the highway, the bus turned in the direction of a sign marked "Baumwald 20 km," as if the place was to be signaled with no more significance than any other provincial village. They entered the clean, bustling town that had the same name as the camp on its outskirts. Bright red geraniums dotted the window boxes. Butchers in white coats hoisted bloodless cow carcasses in shop windows. He almost expected to see girls with braids halfway down their backs skipping down the immaculate pavements hand in hand. Every street looked like a postcard advertisement. Gideon met the town of Baumwald and saw that it continued to exist in the bubble of a fairytale.

The bus deposited them at a youth hostel at the far end of town. For dinner they were served greasy wursts swimming in iridescent fat. Some boys blanched at the meat and reached for double portions of hard, round potatoes.

At night, Gideon awoke shivering. There was no heat in his room. He walked barefoot into the corridor over the cold stone floor. Gideon went to check on the boys in their long dormitory. They were all awake, very cold. They were southern children after all, Gideon reminded himself. There was nothing to do – no extra blankets, and they hadn't brought overcoats. Only the black warm-up suits, which they piled on their beds as best they could. In the morning, the proprietor answered Gideon's urgent complaint blandly with the information that the Ramon boys were the first group of the season. Since the hostel was used only for summer visitors, heat had not been installed.

Although it was almost May, the morning air outside was frosty. As they waited on the pavement for the bus that was to drive them to the camp, Momi was the first to notice the snow. Isolated flakes wafted down at long intervals. The boys were ecstatic, running after the white specks, trying to catch them like small children. All dressed alike in their black nylon warm-up suits, the boys had slicked down their dark hair with water; they were soon shivering. Gideon berated himself for not thinking of gloves or at least woolen caps. He should have remembered the unexpected cold of European spring.

On the way the boys were uncharacteristically silent. As they approached the camp, Gideon felt his throat tighten. When the guard at the gate put his hand up and asked, "How many in your group?" Gideon detected fear in his own thin voice when he answered, "Fourteen and myself, sir." He was handed a white paper with arrows, directions, and printed explanations in several languages, including Hebrew. Gideon put up his hand and beckoned for the boys to follow.

They entered together in a small tight group and walked down the graveled paths, keeping close together. The black of their suits contrasted with the clean white gravel, which still bore the marks of rakes. Everything was spotless, quiet, and manicured.

The path led downhill to a brown, brick building shaped like an igloo. The boys entered through the iron gates and found themselves crowded into a small space. They strained to look at the brick oven before them. "The crematorium at Baumwald is a symbolic one," Gideon read from the white paper. "Baumwald functioned as a concentration camp, not an extermination center.

Those who died from sickness and starvation were cremated. For mass extermination, the Jewish prisoners were shipped out of Baumwald eastward into Poland."

The boys showed no reaction to Gideon's words. They strained to look, standing together in a tight clump, shoulders touching, mesmerized by the square hole in the oven, which stood with its two tidy metal doors wide open. The interior was a black tunnel. The oven resembled a large bakery, thought Gideon. Bodies could be piled in to bake like loaves of bread. Sticking out of its black mouth were the handles of an iron stretcher, empty. The boys showed no sign of moving. Finally, Gideon led the Ramon boys out of the crematorium.

It was time for the memorial ceremony. The boys walked down the path toward the amphitheater in single file.

Solemnly, glancing at Gideon for the sign to enter, they remained huddled together in the entrance courtyard. Momi started to speak, but the rest glared at him so strongly that he quickly desisted.

As the boys filed into the cozy, wood-paneled amphitheater, they were directed toward the left side, where a row of 15 chairs sat waiting for them. Another group of young people was already seated to the right. They looked so at home; Gideon realized they must be a delegation of German kids. The Ramon boys glanced with envious looks at the Germans – so well-dressed, lounging with such confidence. "Even here in Baumwald they can be at ease," thought Gideon.

The German group was co-ed. Gideon saw some of its girls cast peremptory glances over his group and then look away. The Ramon boys were not the type these girls would look at twice. His boys met the same flat disregard at home from rich girls from Tel Aviv on their way to a weekend at the Red Sea when they changed buses at the Ramon intersection.

He knew their hurt and resentment when "regular" girls and boys found them invisible. Gideon looked at his boys and hoped they hadn't noticed. Maybe they were too emotional. Tears sprung into his eyes. They had made it to this place together – the boys everybody had written off and he, their principal, who had started as the truant son of a psychotic survivor.

Chords of solemn music from the loudspeakers roused Gideon from his reverie. The ceremony began, and the boys bowed their heads as they had been instructed. A neat woman with a plastic badge marked "Baumwald Visitor Staff" pinned below her white collar stepped up to the podium. Her glance scanned the assembly as she began to speak. Gideon saw his boys straining to catch the words of her German-accented English.

"I am so pleased to announce that today is a special day for us at Baumwald," she said. "Today, we have a group visiting us from Israel. These children from this special country prove the indomitability of the human spirit." She looked at the audience and inclined her head with a smile. "We are honored to be able to host you young people. We redeem our humanity through your eyes. You can return to your brave little country knowing that the evil of the last generation is wiped out and that the new Germany puts its faith in all young people to hold hands and build the new world together."

"And now," she continued, "I would like to call on one of our young Israeli representatives to come forward before us. I understand he has prepared a few words he would like to share on behalf of his group."

Gideon's boys shuffled their feet and looked toward one another from the corner of their eyes. They craned their heads in Gideon's direction, but his face was as puzzled as theirs.

A tall boy from the German group stood forward. Gideon saw his blond forelock fall over his light freckled face as he reached down to pick up a folded paper under his seat.

That's it, thought Gideon; things became clear to him. The announcer didn't understand who was going to speak. It was indeed the German youth who was standing on the podium ready to deliver prepared words. No doubt to add a welcome to the Israelis, to his boys. His Ramon boys had to come all the way to Baumwald to be seen as just plain Israelis instead of delinquents, thought Gideon. But how had the German kids known to expect them?

In heavily accented English, the blond boy began to read from the paper he held before him: "It was an honor for us to have been chosen as the Youth Delegates from Municipal High School Four, Ramat Aviv, Israel. On our way over here from Israel, some of us were afraid to come to Germany – afraid of what we would find, afraid of how people would treat us. We were sure we would feel so different, and also, we expected to feel some anger against the people here.

"But we have been staying with our host families for a whole week now in town and everyone in Baumwald has made us feel like at home. Everyone! In my host family, Hans and Dieter have been so wonderful and warm to us, and I know this has been true of all the host 'brothers' and 'sisters.' We have seen how they live, and the most moving thing is that we discovered it is not different from our way in Israel. The soccer match arranged for us at Baumwald's sports stadium yesterday was a real climax. Before we leave, there is a big dinner in the church social hall and then a dance with their whole high school.

"And this morning, we pay our tribute to the past, to innocent people who passed through Baumwald to even worse places, or who never made it out. But the really important part of our visit to you as representatives of all the young people in Israel is what this means for the present, for the future." The boy droned on, reading platitudes from the paper in his hand.

Gideon's boys stared at the blond speaker. Sammy coughed loudly without covering his mouth. Others took up the cough, too. Momi pounded rhythmically on the seatback in front of him. Gideon tensed. This was not in the script.

Ori began to snap his fingers, with several boys following until the auditorium filled with clicking. The German hostess raised her chin, frowned, and put a thin warning finger to her lips. She was silent, but her eyes blazed.

The blond boy continued, looking away from his paper. His voice was strong and he was smiling. "And I'm looking forward to Hans and Dieter visiting me in my home in Ramat Aviv in the summertime. Yesterday evening, I talked to my parents and they have agreed. I hope to be able to take Hans and Dieter to my soccer training camp near the Sea of Galilee. And I know I'm not alone. Everybody from our class wants to host his adopted German brother or sister who has shown each of us such a warm welcome in Baumwald."

The ceremony ended. Nobody looked at or mentioned Gideon's boys. Rushing and jostling one another, they exited the auditorium.

Gideon's group walked out of the camp in a tight mass, like a fist, their shoulders hunched up and their hands in their pockets. Snowflakes were falling faster, but nobody paid any attention.

They walked down the streets of the town, heads in the wind, not speaking.

Maurice was first. He kicked the tire of a forest-green BMW. Then he gave a big leap onto the shiny hood, jumping up and down and swinging his arms. The other boys began to do the same, running down the pavement to be the first to reach the cars. Sammy grabbed the silver logo of a Mercedes-Benz, twisting it in an attempt to tear it off. Sammy pulled a pen out of his pocket and made a small, quick scratch on the door of a parked van.

As they walked through the spotless streets, they began to bend down and pick up small, loose stones near the graveled storefronts. They tossed them with a disdainful flick of the wrist into empty alleys, then closer to the buildings. They just missed hitting a pet store window. Poodles and parrots stared out at the raggedy band of boys who ran by shivering in their cheap nylon suits.

Halfway to the hostel, the snow turned to rain. The boys' hair was soaked. Some of the dye on the stars started to run in yellow streaks down their backs.

Gideon realized he had to get them into a dry, warm place. He spotted a cafeteria next to the train station and herded the boys in.

The air in the cafeteria was hot and humid. Steam covered the windows. At the head of the line, Gideon ordered 15 portions of hot orange soup with white doughy dumplings and circles of translucent lard floating on top.

Aproned servers handed each boy a tray slick with greasy residues. "Find an empty seat, boys." Gideon gestured to them, and he went up to the cashier to pay the bill.

Kobi and Sammy headed for the same corner seat. Both tried to sit. Neither would yield. Sammy shoved Kobi, and Kobi's tray fell. Oily soup splattered on the clothes of the boys nearby. A few of them grabbed Sammy's sleeve. He gestured backward to Menashe, who came forward, his fists clenched. Kobi and Sammy faced each other, hunched over. They hunched lower, menacing, and began to circle one another. Sammy snatched a fork off the table and held it out in front of him, waving its prongs tauntingly in Kobi's face. The rest of the boys, recapturing a familiar, long-unused ritual, jostled one another into a tight circle around the pair, elbowing their neighbor if he began to block their view. Trays were pushed off the tables. Chairs fell backward and clattered onto the stone floor.

Gideon, putting his wallet back into his pocket, spun around. He felt a shooting pain in his own stomach as he watched the punches begin.

Racing over, arms outstretched, he tried to pull Sammy and Kobi apart, but the circle of onlookers, taunting and hooting, wouldn't allow him to push through their tightly packed bodies. Gideon's white hands fluttered, trying in vain to break in. They kept their backs to Gideon. He called, "Kobi! Menashe! SAMMY!"

Sammy looked up. Gideon raised his arms in besiegement, looking hard into Sammy's face. Sammy's eyes met his. Sammy nodded, and Gideon felt relief. Sammy, the leader, was coming to his senses. The other boys would follow. The craziness would stop.

And then Sammy's head swung wildly around the room, searching. He bent down, picked up the metal cafeteria chair, and hurled it sideways toward the windowpane. The glass cracked and then crashed with a sound like bullets.

Two flushed cafeteria workers cowered in the entranceway to the kitchen. They shook their heads, and the white net caps quivered. They crossed their plump arms and gasped. One pointed her index finger at the boys. "*Arabern*! Arabs!" she whispered to her companion. Her lips twisted in fear and distaste. "They shouldn't be allowed in here to Baumwald."

The cashier rushed over to the phone box. She screamed into the receiver: "Police!"

IRON EAGLE ON WEST 11TH STREET

Reimagining the story of Hannah Arendt and Martin Heidegger

Otto's letter confronted Trude as she left for the Institute. It lay on her doormat with the rest of the day's assortment that Sanchez the elevator man arranged into a paper pyramid. Largest pieces on the bottom – the obligatory *New York Times* at the base, covered by the *Journal of the American Society of Political Science*, with Trude's name in bold on the masthead: Trude Fried, Professor of Political Philosophy. After that, *The New Republic*, Trude's reluctant concession to a weekly newsmagazine. Then the ever-skimpier German-language Jewish newspaper *Aufbau*, to which loyalty alone made her renew her subscription; as the German Jewish refugee community aged and died off, so did *Aufbau's* readership. A small stack of bills and faculty announcements completed the tidy pile.

The mail was as neat and compartmentalized and impersonal as her life, and Trude was pleased to see it lying obediently, waiting for her to slice each envelope with her silver letter opener, then to pull open the little cubbies of her secretaire and file each letter there and in her mind.

But today, Otto's letter lay on top, breaking the harmony. His letters came as regularly as the phone bill, the watery black ink and square Gothic calligraphy unchanged in 40 years.

She had first encountered that scrawled handwriting in the margins of papers she wrote as Otto's student, his almost illegible comments lancing her enthusiastic if sophomoric ideas. She struggled then to puzzle out each convoluted phrase, to piece together the master's voice.

Later, when it was already familiar, if never friendly, Trude found Otto's handwriting in notes folded into tiny squares that he passed into her palm in the corridors of the faculty – the risks that she took left her pressing her back against the wall trembling with anxiety. Some of the notes were on little unsigned slips left by prearrangement behind the chipped flower pot outside the secretary's office.

By then, she knew his sharp, birdlike letters by heart, pecked into the paper with a pen like an angry beak.

Besides, the contents of those terse notes were simpler than his comments on her political philosophy exercises. They bore a set formula: "3:15 in back of Teller's Pub" or "After the lecture at students' entrance to chemistry laboratory." She crammed the notes into the back pages of her Engels or Rousseau.

Scribbled directions for illicit meeting places were the only love letters Otto sent. Trude may have been intellectually precocious, a rising star in the medieval university town, but about the realpolitik of love, she knew much less. Hardly past her teens, Trude stowed each cryptic note in a secret pile in her wooden trunk, tying them up in a ribbon the way that she read in books that lovers' correspondence was preserved. She waited for a love poem, even one copied out of a book. But no poem ever came. Trude contented herself with what she had.

Otto's caresses had the staccato, impatient quality of his letters.

"Why were you so desperate to keep him?" a therapist had once blurted out as Trude sat huddled miserably in the opposite chair twisting her watchband around her wrist.

Was it flattery at being singled out by the august professor? The narcissism of a young woman warmed by the sophisticated gaze of the worldly older man? Had she imagined she could advance herself through an association with Professor Heinemann, even if it was an illicit liaison? She couldn't answer the therapist then, and she couldn't have done so today. The passing years had not unclouded her motivations. She recalled only the irresistible magnetism she felt in Otto's presence when the time for each meeting drew near. The magnetism, and then the void.

Now there was Otto Heinemann's newest envelope lying like an accusation on top of the bundle of mail at Trude's threshold. Trude heard the cartilage in her back creak and felt her bones rub together with a stab of pain as she bent over to pick it up, jabbing the rubber tip of her cane hard against the far wall of the narrow corridor for support.

Trude sometimes found herself wondering if his letters of the last two decades contained nostalgic passages about their old passions or allusions to his prewar lust couched in flowery quotations from Schiller or Heine. She couldn't imagine Otto asking anybody for forgiveness.

But she pushed these reveries angrily out of her mind when she caught herself slipping into fantasies. She had no idea what Otto wrote since he had tracked her down in 1957 via her first published book review in a minor American university press.

For of all the letters that Sanchez or his predecessors had placed on Trude's doormat, she had not opened one single envelope.

True, she no longer tore the letters up in a rage nor threw them into the incinerator chute, hoping to obliterate Otto's echo. In a way, she admitted to herself, she came to count on those letters. Arriving in a steady flow every three or four months, they were a way to mark the seasons for Trude, those cheap brown envelopes with the unremarkable stamps marked *Deutsche Bundesposte*. Since the Nazi defeat, even the German postage stamps avoided calling attention to themselves. No more iron eagles, like Otto, too, had once been.

Ten years before there had been a gap of almost a year. Furious but powerless to desist, Trude counted the number of months the letters were absent. Despite herself, Trude looked out for Otto's envelopes. Trude conjectured that he had given up, gotten over his bad conscience – or been unable to write. She imagined him, gaunt and yellow, lying in a charity ward bed. She wondered how she would take the news that he had died.

She scavenged the political science journals for some kind of announcement. "Otto Heinemann," it might run, "Distinguished Professor of Political Theory, 1926 to 1945, University of Marburg, known for his seminal work linking the pre-Socratic thinkers to 20th-century thought, passed away last month in the Sisters of Mercy Hospital in Marburg..."

The announcement would be a terse one. It would not dwell on Heinemann's cooperation with the National Socialists or the rumors that he had actually become a Party member as far back as '35.

An obituary would not mention his postwar disgrace and isolation, either. It wouldn't have to, for the infamous example of Professor Otto Heinemann was known to every undergraduate student of political science – how the once mighty professor, himself the cause of the hatcheting of so many of his "undesirable" colleagues, had ended up in ignominy and isolation. Indeed, in the field, to call someone a "Heinemann" had become a synonym for an opportunist who blew with the political winds, no matter how unsavory the breezes were. A Heinemann was an opportunist who later paid the price.

Rumor had it that Otto Heinemann had become so poor he was constrained to tutor young boys laggard in their high school studies. Trude imagined that the profession would allow Heinemann back his dignity, at least in his obituary notice. The dates of his sinecure, their end precisely coinciding with the fall of the Third Reich, would speak for themselves.

But then, after several months, the flow of letters started up again in a gush, like a frozen waterfall after the spring thaw.

Trude no longer had the compulsion to destroy them as soon as they arrived. These days she could bear to let the letters rest on her vestibule table next to the telephone until she amassed a bundle of newspapers to carry down the corridor to the incinerator. Even though they pierced her less over time, Trude was never completely at ease when there was a letter from Otto on the table, as if he were again in a position of power, able to drive a wedge into her heart and her life.

Trude had never written down his address, but her eyes involuntarily glanced over the sender's address every time, and it was always the same – still apartment seven on Sebastienstrasse 36 – which she herself had known so many decades before. Trude's heart had always beat harder when she raised her hand to the lion's head brass knocker of apartment seven. Otto's wife, Bette, opened the door a crack, her pointy nose twitching suspiciously. And Bette, of the white-blond plaits, had good reason to suspect her profligate professor husband.

Trude was not Otto's first fling, far from it. Trude knew that. So did everyone. She had heard the open rumors that he made a point of bedding his star students. But with none of the others had history conveniently stepped in to aid Otto in terminating the relationship and returning to Bette's hard blue eyes. Before Trude, Professor Heinemann simply grew tired of this *Fraulein's* moist lips or that one's generous bust, often the very qualities that had made him rage to bed her in the first place.

The professor's tastes conveniently paralleled the semesters: Over the summer, he would lie fallow, trekking through alpine hills with his wife. Then, when autumn came, Otto was fresh to look over the new crop. And invariably, every year delivered into his lap a new batch more appealing than the last.

Otto stood unrivaled. Quiet though he was, the professor was the strutting cock in the political philosophy department of the little university. His reputation as a maverick genius gave him free rein to make rendezvous after rendezvous with whichever delicious and adoring student he pleased. Otto was as successful in the theater of sex as he was in the field of political philosophy. There wasn't a back alley or park bench where Otto Heinemann hadn't embraced one young student or another.

The biggest problem was finding an appropriate venue when his caresses became more advanced. His home was out of the question, and female residences were heavily chaperoned. He was constrained to engage in relations in the office provided to him by the university. His dislike of using the cramped room for his sex acts was obvious; Trude could feel his impatience. He rose quickly afterward from the thin couch on which he had spread an old curtain that he stored balled up in the drawer of his massive mahogany desk, running his fingers through his hair over and over again to make sure it was in place.

Professor Heinemann preferred to keep his intellectual and physical exertions in separate realms. Sitting around the antique oval table in the professor's seminar on Hegel, Trude never felt his glance land on her with anything more than the cool impersonality he showed to all the doctoral students. "Fraulein Fried" he would address her formally in public; thinking back, Trude could not remember him ever uttering her first name out loud. Not even in bed. Their last winter together, Bette's parents died, and Bette went to the countryside to wind up their affairs. Otto installed Trude in the flat the day after Bette left, and had her stay until two days before his wife's return. Enough time to air it out, Trude realized in retrospect.

This year Otto's letters began to arrive more frequently; since July, they came almost every week. Trude pushed this latest envelope with her cane, managing to maneuver it over the threshold and into the apartment behind her. She shut the door and walked stiffly down the corridor.

Trude walked slowly up the long city block to Fifth Avenue. Since her fall the previous winter, she learned to keep her eyes on the pavement ahead of her, looking for the peril of cracks. Trude hadn't regained her old confidence, and she felt trapped in an unfamiliar fragility. Once she reached Fifth, she continued along the one short street north to the Institute.

It was the first day of the fall term and Trude was engulfed by the pliant flesh of young bodies rushing up the steps and across the lobby. She clutched the banister, fearing she might be knocked over by those youths intent upon one another to whom she was no more than an obstacle to be maneuvered around. She plodded on, placing the cane squarely on the floor before every step as she made her way toward the stainless-steel elevator.

Trude had retired from active work on the journal but held on to her full-time teaching duties. For the first few years in America, Trude had to care for her mother. The old lady had become ever more disoriented, talking only in German, in the end thinking they were still back in Marburg. But since her mother's passing 12 years before, Trude had few demands on her time. She was a single woman with no dependents; the Institute became her second home.

When an apartment opened up a few years earlier on 11th Street down the block from the Institute, Trude was quick to take it. From then on, her days were split between her office and her apartment. Eleventh Street became the boundary of her world. Her inner world spread much farther.

The Institute for Political Study where Trude held the senior chair in Political Philosophy now enjoyed a worldwide reputation. In no small part, this was due to Trude herself, whose contribution to the field was termed "seminal and unparalleled" by the chairman of the Academy of American Political Science when presenting Trude with the Korchaw medal. It was the Academy's highest award, globally renowned.

Trude doubted whether those reading the many papers issued from her department would picture the extent of the Institute's drab modern institutionalism. Such abstract hypotheses and theoretical conjectures should by rights have been conceived in the Gothic chambers of her academic youth in Marburg. It seemed incongruous to examine the texts of Kant when below her window she could see the yellow taxis weaving down Fifth Avenue, with nervous shopkeepers looking at their watches and rushing outside every hour to feed change into the meters ticking away beside their parked cars.

Trude stared down at the white stripe painted along the center of the avenue, but she was remembering the medieval cobblestones that paved the streets of Marburg. Marburg was the center of her world, and the university was Marburg's navel. Growing up there, Trude never imagined she could ever leave.

Trude was accustomed to the stares of new students. Until they learned who she was – the "Grande Dame of Political Science," by far the biggest name in this star-studded Institute – she could not avoid the puzzlement in their eyes. She looked out of place among the young students and the professors with serious expressions and manicured beards, rushing to and fro with proposals and documents stuffed under their arms. Last semester she overheard a gape-mouthed girl in the corridor eyeing her and verbally jabbing her vacuous companion: "Hey Melissa, get a load of that bag lady – or is that maybe your granny coming in here to track you down?"

Trude recalled the words and cringed. Standing in the elevator behind two students, she wondered if she, too, had once had such effortless energy. As they hurried out of the elevator, one of the young men gestured behind him toward Trude as she stepped out.

Before the doors snapped shut, he said in a stage whisper to his companion, "Who's that stray old cat?"

And his companion's laughing response: "No idea! Maybe she's just another of those zombie coffin cases who wander in mistaking this ugly building for the Social Security office for the aged." Their laughter ricocheted against the cinder block walls as Trude's cane thumped down the corridor.

Trude made her way down the Institute's Social Science wing on the second floor. She unlocked the milky glass door to her office. It smelled stuffy from the summer's disuse. While she was struggling to pry open the window, there was an impatient rapping on the glass door. Before she had time to respond, Sam Samuels burst in.

"Trude!" he cried, striding over to the window and flinging it open. "Welcome! I've been to your door a dozen times today waiting for you to show up! Welcome to another new year!" Samuels raised an imaginary glass of champagne.

Trude tried to muffle her sigh. Now she would have to listen to Samuels' account of the annual world meeting of the Political Philosophy Society held the previous month in England. It was the first time Trude declined to attend, but her doctor said the hip she injured in her fall was still too weak for transcontinental travel.

Samuels never looked this eager.

"We missed you at Oxford, Trude," Samuels began, settling his body as best as he could on the steel chair the Institute provided for office visitors. "Oh, the conference itself was no great shakes. Was sometimes a chore just to keep awake; I passed the time picking out how many closed eyes I could spot in the audience. Kept looking out the windows like a schoolboy wishing I could escape. Actually, afterward, Marge and I found this great way to tour the Lake District. Did you ever hear of barge trips, Trude? Not at all expensive, even though the rest of England was absolutely *prohibitive*. Marge brought back some nifty brochures, if you want..."

While Samuels droned on, Trude looked at the titles of her books lined up on the shelves behind him, wondering how much of each she really remembered. She had accustomed herself to Samuels' long-windedness and suspected that his monotonous voice and predictable jokes put the students to sleep for real.

"But, Trude," he continued, "you won't believe who showed up there. Absolutely resurrected from the dead." Little beads of sweat gleamed on Samuels' upper lip.

"Take your jacket off, Sam," Trude said dryly, and Samuels smiled gratefully at her and tugged the wrinkled seersucker blazer off one thick shoulder and then the other.

Trude felt the certainty of her premonition and didn't want to hear what was coming, especially not from nosy Samuels. She tried to forestall him. In a wooden voice, she asked, "Wasn't there anything new presented in the lectures? What about some reaction to my work on the changed perspectives in Marxism in light of the invasion of Afghanistan?"

"It was Heinemann. Otto Heinemann!" Samuels plowed on. "Trude, you have to hear this. Nobody had heard a peep out of that old Nazi for over 35 years. And then he just went and turned up in the audience like a ghost. Didn't dare to open his mouth, of course. He wouldn't go that far. That's all anybody talked about for the rest of the conference. Everyone was shocked he even dared to show his face at an international gathering, after all those people he had given the ax to. Warhaftig from Michigan felt the Organizing Committee ought to make some kind of public statement of objection to Heinemann's attendance."

"And did they?" Trude asked, not able to help bursting in.

"Almost, but not quite. The organizers felt that so much time had passed and that by now Heinemann is an old, powerless has-been. He's been blacklisted in the whole profession since the war. By the way, no university press – not one – has published any paper with Heinemann's name on it since 1938."

Trude nodded. She thought of the yellowing article in her file, the file marked *"O.H."* – the last paper Heinemann had published in the *Political Philosophy Annals*, spring issue of 1938, on the link between polytheism and political organization of East African nomadic tribes. The old paper seemed to be crumpling by itself even though the article lay sheathed in a protective acid-free envelope inside the file cabinet. The image of Dorian Gray popped into her mind. Was Heinemann aging as badly as his last published paper? Trude listened closely to Samuels despite herself.

"But Warhaftig had backers," Samuels went on. "Older members remembered how Heinemann had systematically excised all the Jews in the political philosophy departments. Not only in Marburg. No, Herr Professor was such a star that during National Socialism, his word carried weight in all the faculties – Nuremberg, Heidelberg, Dresden."

Trude sat silently, remembering how everyone short of 100 percent Aryan had held their breaths in 1934, 1935, 1936, hoping their own position would be spared. Not one was.

"But the moderate camp led by Stanton-Poole won out," Samuels shrugged. Stanton-Poole made a little speech in an ad hoc meeting of the Executive Committee. Feelings had gone that far just from seeing the legendary infamous Otto Heinemann daring to show his head in public and attend one measly lecture."

Samuels crossed his legs, arranged his pudgy frame, and proceeded to imitate the British peer: "That beanpole Stanton-Poole looked down his long Anglo nose and argued that Heinemann should be allowed to stay, on condition he remained quiet. His position was that if the postwar authorities didn't see fit to put Heinemann on trial for turning his Jewish colleagues in, then it was not the place of an academic organization to do so ex post facto after nearly 30 years.

"Between you and me, Trude," Samuels said, leaning toward her as she found herself pushing her back more tightly against the backrest of her chair, "I just think Stanton-Poole didn't want the conference his university was hosting to turn into a media happening. And you know that if the Society had made a public statement excluding Heinemann, jeez, it might very well have been picked up by the press. Even, God forbid, the television." Samuels snorted. "That would really have made a good story for the news. Just imagine the *Sun* or the *Daily Mail*: 'Old Nazi hatchet man given the boot – Crawls out of professional 'hiding' to turn up at academic meeting – Former chums continue blacklist.'

"So in the end they listened to Stanton-Poole," Samuels said. "Without taking any formal decision or writing down any notes, the Executive Committee authorized Stanton-Poole to contact Heinemann with the utmost discretion. He was to tell Heinemann he could stay if he kept a low profile."

Trude's head jerked up. A low profile. Those had been Otto's words to her in 1933. "Just keep a low profile," he said when bands of brown-shirted SA thugs slathered "Jude" in red paint on the doors of the professors in Marburg known to be of the Jewish persuasion. The paint ran down the door frames in scarlet rivulets.

"As God had marked the Jewish doors before Passover," Trude's mother had prophesized, "but this marking us is an evil omen." Nobody dared remove the paint even after it turned a rusty dark brown. Upon the carved medieval doors of the faculties, they smeared swastikas and the names of non-Aryan professors in the same crimson color.

"You were one of those people Heinemann sacked, weren't you, Trude?" Samuels asked, his nasal voice interrupting her thoughts. There, she felt, he had finally said it out loud, what she knew many whispered behind her back. "Heinemann's protégée turned mistress," they probably said, "and it didn't make a bit of difference. Trude Fried was one of the first that old fascist threw to the dogs."

It had been the shock of her life. For her Otto Heinemann and the Third Reich merged. Trude shied away from serious commitment ever since.

"No, not sacked... not exactly," said Trude out loud. "My thesis had passed through the faculty the year before and I had just been awarded my degree. I was up for nomination to a teaching post – but then we decided to leave Germany, my mother and I."

Trude looked up at her first diploma hanging on the opposite wall, a small rectangle with brown blotches on the yellowing paper – "Discolored, spotted, like my own aging hands," thought Trude. The diploma hung lodged among the certificates and awards Trude had gotten with increasing frequency over the decades, stately in their wooden frames or laminated on gleaming plastic. To any observer, the Marburg diploma was the most inconspicuous, but to Trude, it was the most important. Handwritten in Gothic calligraphy. Every word in Latin, every letter flawless as a Japanese scroll or a Bible. "The President and the Honorary Trustees of the University of Marburg hereby bestow upon Trude Fried the degree of Doctor of Political Philosophy. The year of our Lord One Thousand Nine Hundred Thirty-Three."

Trude's eyes traveled to the blot on that pristine document, a blot added later by a careless and greedy municipal clerk in the police station when Trude the petitioner had come to beg for her freedom. On the bottom corner of the diploma was a tiny green stamp pasted crookedly, partially obliterating the flowery Gothic signature of Marburg's dean. The stamp was adorned with the iron eagle, and over it was the scribbled signature of the Nazi police commissioner of Marburg. This mark of shame was the price demanded by the Third Reich to permit Trude to take her diploma with her when she left the country.

She had to give in to extortion to get the diploma out of Germany. How else would anybody believe her credentials? Nobody at the university in Marburg would confirm the degree of an expelled Jewish academic. The fee for acquiring the little green eagle stamp that allowed her to take the diploma with her had cost almost all the inheritance her father had left them. The rest she used up to book steamship passage out of Bremen for herself and her mother.

Trude's mother had accompanied her, but only in body. When she died in 1954, her mother still spoke nothing but German, and her only interest in her last years was to replay in her own mind and out loud – whenever she could get Trude to listen – their "real" life in the medieval university town.

Trude carried the diploma around from country to country, from address to address, in her black satchel, wrapped in tissue paper and two sweaters to protect it, until she finally got a real teaching job and settled for good on West 11th Street. The first thing she did when assigned her tiny cubicle of an office deep down in the windowless library stacks was to hammer in the nail and hang up her doctorate.

Looking at the diploma never failed to ground her when she felt at sea in the New World, surrounded by ever younger and more innocent faces. And the green eagle stamp never failed to stab her anew.

Trude rose steadily upward in reputation. She felt proud and recalled Otto's terse aphorism, "Cream rises to the top." Her work became celebrated, and with it, Trude moved up the academic ladder. Yet she retained the self-image of a fish out of water – an ungainly refugee with a comical German accent she could never shake.

Although Trude always knew that one day one of her colleagues would bring up the subject of Heinemann to her face, Samuels' words nauseated her. She imagined speculation about her past – What had been the relationship between herself as a young prodigy and the world-famous Heinemann?

Still, she was unprepared for Samuels' gossipy off-the-cuff recitation. Although that was precisely what she ought to have expected from Sam Samuels, Trude realized. She waited for Samuels to leave so she could sort out her whirling thoughts. Her back felt weak, and the pulse in her neck throbbed. Trude leaned her elbows on the desk to try to get relief. But Samuels crossed his plump legs and made no move to rise.

"As we broke for coffee after the lecture," Samuels said, bending forward with a conspiratorial air, "Heinemann cornered me in the hallway. He made a sort of awkward half-bow as if he were a bad actor in a 19th-century melodrama. And he began to beg: 'I pray for your indulgence. Just for the smallest moment, Herr Professor, I implore you to speak to me in private,' he bleated, tugging at my sleeve," Samuels shuddered. "Ugh, his fingers were skinny, like the claws of an old bird. Mottled, disgusting! And looking at me balefully with those rheumy eyes. I felt uncomfortable even being seen next to him – I could feel on me all the eyes of the people in the auditorium. I ducked outside with him. Luckily, I spotted a secluded bench on the side of the building, adjacent to the employee parking lot.

"The thought crossed my mind that he wanted money – he looked that poor. I started to calculate how much I could spare just to shake him off my back.

"But it wasn't the money he was after. It was because of *you*, Trude, because of you he singled me out." Samuels made his announcement as if he thought it would come as a surprise to her.

Trude looked at Samuels, but in front of her eyes was the morning's brown envelope with the tiny German postage stamp, lying crookedly on the parquet floor where she had pushed it with her stick.

"Heinemann must have made inquiries to find out we are both here at the same Institute," Samuels continued. "As soon as we sat down, he broke down, heaved dry sobs. The old man fumbled into his jacket pocket and pulled out a letter. He started to thrust it into my hands – 'For – Professor Trude Fried,' Heinemann croaked out. 'Professor Fried, she is a colleague at your esteemed Institute. You must doubtless be in her acquaintance. You will be back at your Institute shortly – give this to her, I make entreaty of you!'"

Samuels imitated Heinemann's beseeching stance. "He spoke in a funny English. It wasn't only that he was a foreigner. No, Heinemann used old-fashioned phrases you don't hear anywhere anymore like someone cut off from people and even from TV – someone whose knowledge comes from outdated books."

Samuels doing a clumsy imitation of Heinemann's stilted English and heavy German accent was laughable. Trude shifted uncomfortably in her seat, but despite herself, she found herself looking for Samuels to reach into his pocket and pull out another brown letter from Heinemann, this one hand-delivered. Samuels was his usual embarrassing self, yet Trude was shocked to consider the possibility that the haughty Heinemann had sunk so low as to accost a stranger and beg him to deliver his messages.

Samuels went on. "Then – boom, out of nowhere – Heinemann seemed to hesitate. I put my hand out – I really wanted to get that letter – I had a feeling you'd want it, Trude. Was I right?"

Samuels sought to give Trude a meaningful look, but her eyes refused to hold his moist ones. Samuels continued, relishing every word of his recitation.

"But it was no use, something had made him change his mind. Heinemann crumpled the letter into his pants pocket. 'No, Herr Professor,' he whined. 'There is no sense, no hope to send another message. I have sent to Professor Fried already dozens. Answer has not come, not for any one.'

"He put his yellow face up to mine. I could see the swatches of white hairs sprouting on his cheeks where the razor had missed. I tried to back off, but he put his eyes close to mine, and I saw milky gray blotches on his iris. His eyes were empty, but they frightened me. They had the color of November leaves. Hah!" Samuels laughed, "I didn't know I had it in me to be poetic."

He paused, waiting for Trude to respond to his witticism. When she did not he shifted in his seat and went on. "You know, I heard about Heinemann. Believe it or not, he was considered a fast number in his time. How could he have had the reputation as a lady killer? What could any woman have seen in that old windbag – excuse my bluntness, Trude."

Trude searched her empty mind for some response, but Samuels didn't pause.

"He begged me to intercede with you: 'I know I could never deserve absolution.' Honest, Trude, those were his very words – *absolution*. 'But if only she would recognize me again – would suffice one word. Would prove my life's work worth something: to have been an influence on the thinking of Trude Fried. The great Professor Trude Fried!'"

As Samuels plowed on, Trude tightened her lips. She didn't want to think of Otto old and broken, cataracts preventing him from seeing where to pass the razor blade. Not that she pitied him. No, not pity. Not one drop resembling sympathy for the man who had cut her out cold soon after the National Socialists came to power.

Long before the Nuremberg Laws of '35 made cohabitation between Aryans and non-Aryans illegal, Otto Heinemann expelled Trude from the faculty room in the university, from weekly departmental gatherings, and from his bed. Each expulsion pierced Trude's scarred memory.

Still, she rationalized to herself that in a strange, perverted way, Otto Heinemann might have saved her life. If he hadn't thrown her out so early – way back in 1934 – she would have no doubt stayed on in Marburg like the others. Stayed until the last possible minute. Then it might have been too late. Maybe she would not have been able to get a visa. By then there were too many expelled Jewish academics desperate for a country. So in a bitter sense she had been lucky to get the boot early. Heinemann's cruelty had done her a service.

By 1937, she was already in Washington Heights enrolled in night school and learning English. She had been hired to teach one class at City College, although in those days, she was not sure her English was comprehensible to her young American students. They were unfamiliar not only with heavy European inflections but with classical references as well. To her shock she discovered that even doctoral candidates – even, God forbid, full professors – were almost universally lost not only in Greek but in that basic of all basics, Latin.

It was when she took that subway train back and forth to the immigration office, begging them to extend her visa, scrounging for witnesses to support her endeavors and vouch for her worth to the United States of America – just to get a legal identity – then she despised Otto fiercely for bringing her down so low.

Trude went deeper into her reverie. She looked up to see that Samuels had finally stopped talking and was giving her an inquisitive look. Samuels was pushy and obnoxious, but he was chairman of the department nonetheless. Even though Trude was at least 30 years his senior, he held the higher administrative title, and she knew that by academic protocol she owed Samuels an answer. Besides, in his blunt, bearlike way, Trude knew, he felt he was being friendly to her.

Trude spoke in a slow voice. She looked past Samuels to the wall of books behind him. "Listen, Sam, what I have done in my life I have accomplished despite Otto Heinemann, not because of him," she said. "Otto Heinemann threw me out. He threw out many others, too. Most of them died. I might have, too. Otto Heinemann cannot earn my pity now, no matter how pitiful he has become."

Trude thought she detected reprobation in Samuels' look. "Ever the iron-hearted one, aren't you, Trude?" he asked. "But I can't say I blame you. None of us could have been tossed in the gutter like you – and in danger of your life – and gone on to become what you have." Samuels gestured at the wall bearing her diplomas and certificates. "Well, I hope I haven't been too forward. But I thought you'd want to know that you are still in the thoughts of the legendary Otto Heinemann of Marburg.

"And I wanted to prepare you too, Trude. I wouldn't be surprised if you yourself may be hearing from Heinemann directly one day."

After Samuels left, Trude picked through her office correspondence. Her hands were shaking, and she willed them to stop. But she knew today she would not regain the concentration to read. So she contented herself with looking through the invitations to upcoming conferences, marking in longhand on her calendar the dates of the events that seemed of interest.

Trude waited until 2:30 and then locked up her office. She hadn't had the heart to stay waiting for the fresh inquisitive students to knock with naïve questions about reading lists or begging to be let into her overbooked seminar. Today she could not put on a professional expression and tend to mewling undergraduate scheduling conflicts.

Trude avoided entering the faculty lounge where she heard voices, laughter, clinking dishes – the staff was having their first coffee klatch of the season. Their cheery first-of-the-year chatter floated above her as she plodded down the corridor, the rubber tip of her cane placed carefully on the industrial speckled linoleum. She imagined her armchair beckoning to her. She wanted to sink into it and look at the red coleus plant winding toward the light on her windowsill and sip an infusion of tea brewed in the iron teapot-for-one she had discovered at the Japanese import store. Trude was relieved; she would soon be home.

As she walked to 11th Street and then crossed west toward Seventh Avenue, Trude was remembering Marburg and her walks around the old, cobbled streets, from the faculty to the library and back again, day after day. She had never been back, never accepted any invitation to speak in Germany, but the place was hardly out of her thoughts for a day at a time.

Trude couldn't shake off Samuels' description of Otto's cloudy irises, the eyes that used to be so close to her own, that looked off into space with a perspicacity she had never met since. Eyes empty like November leaves, Samuels had called them. And Samuels was not a poetic man. She ought to feel glad at the description of Otto as so shabby that he looked destitute, Trude told herself. Instead, she saw before her the eyes of how he looked in the olden days – so slim and elegant in his tapered jacket, and with his hair already turning salt and pepper in his 30s.

Trude would be 72 in two years and herself reach mandatory retirement. Now that she was an old woman, she told herself, she ought to find it in her heart to forgive. After all, Otto hadn't turned *her* in to any authorities – he had just shunned her out of his life and shunted her out of the department. Otto was a man who lived in the rarefied academic retreat; he hadn't made any of the policies or even had an influence on them. And for going along with them like everybody else? Otto had paid his price – the brilliant mind ignored for over a generation, not allowed any forum – no podium, no journal, not permitted to give a single university lecture. Otto had suffered the worst punishment a scholar could have – banishment from the world of scholars – the only world that would count to him.

Otto Heinemann was 14 years older than she was. That put him well past 80 now, not an age for being destitute and alone. She wondered how he had found the strength – and the funds – to make it to the conference in England.

As she proceeded down the block, her resolve, frozen for decades, cracked. Her heart raced as she felt herself changing her mind. Trude determined to help him just a little. Perhaps she would send a check, a one-time shot in the arm. Her salary was generous and her honoraria plentiful. And she had no dependents. Trude calculated that her bank account would hardly feel the loss of $1,000, $1,500, or even $2,000.

As Trude walked, she had to admit to herself that it was not only humanitarianism she was feeling. No, revenge had its part. Maybe a big part. To be the one to send the legendary Professor Heinemann money to keep him out of the poorhouse – Trude tasted the sweetness of it.

She was impatient to reach her apartment house. She pictured Otto's letter lying on the floor where she had pushed it with her cane in the morning. Everything fell into place. The letter was a plea for money, for support; that's what he had been sending all along. Now she understood why the letters' frequency had increased of late. Otto needed the money more now. The way Samuels described him, Otto was desperate.

She stepped into the street on the corner of Greenwich Avenue, oblivious to the red light, and was startled by the angry honking of the taxi that screeched to a halt before her. The driver leaned out of the window and barked, "Lady, if you're blind as well as lame, better stay home!"

Trude was breathless when she reached her building. She tottered to the entrance and reached for the brass door frame. The doorman rushed over and propped her up under her elbow with his thick gloved hand, escorting her to the elevator door.

"Feeling under the weather, Professor?" he asked. Trude had only the strength to shake her head. "Now you look out for yourself." The doorman tipped his hat as she hobbled into the elevator. He said to the elevator operator, "Take the professor up real gently now, Sanchez." He glanced at Trude for appreciation of his joke, but Trude didn't respond. Even after all these years, the unaccountable familiarity of Americans still caused her discomfort and made her stiffen. Besides, the only thing Trude was thinking of was the letter in her hallway.

She got out her keys as she rode up the elevator, fidgeting with impatience as the car creaked up to the tenth floor, its steel cables and pulleys whirring inside the walls.

Trude transferred her handbag to the arm that held the cane as she unlocked the door and then dropped the cane on the floor as she bent over double to snatch up Otto's envelope greeting her as she stepped in. The wooden cane clattered against the parquet. So many letters had come over the decades and not one had she opened, she thought with irony. Now the time had come. In her heart of hearts, she had known it would.

She had pushed him away for years; now she could not bear to wait even one more minute.

She wondered with which words Otto had chosen to approach her for help. Depending on how desperate his tone was, Trude decided, that's how she would decide how much money to send. Should it be a lump sum, or a series of small payments, just enough for him to buy more heating oil and a few extras?

Trude carried the letter across the room toward the window. Painfully, she raised her thin arms to push the drapes open as far as they would go. Then she eased her body onto the armchair and reached for the silver letter opener and extra glasses that lay on the inlaid wooden table beside the chair. Settled, she turned over the envelope and sliced it open.

Trude greedily unfolded the sheet inside with her knobby fingers. There was only one page. Cheap, white, wrinkled paper. Her eyes were drawn first to the large irregular stain of dried coffee on one corner. No date, no heading, no paragraphs. Trude took in the scrawled black letters, and her mind began to make sense of the German words. Her head began to swim. Her eyes skipped among the disjointed phrases, written in crooked lines scattered about the page in demented graffiti. "Fat swine of a thief." "Your crime should be exposed to your beloved academic world." "...stealing my ideas and sucking blood from them like a bastard spider." "My hatred of you grows bigger as the years pass as I follow every hollow so-called advancement of yours..." "I count the days until your denouncement will come... When you are exposed – that is the day I will be content to die."

Trude dropped the letter. Something gripped her throat preventing her breath, just like it had the faraway morning in Marburg when she found Otto's note commanding her to get out.

She put her elbows on the armrests, pushed her torso up to stand. Trude groped for her cane, but it was lying far away by the doorway where she had flung it when she came in. Nausea was rising in fast waves from her stomach to her mouth.

In panic, Trude crouched down, painfully lowering her knees on the floor. Then she scuttled across the living room on all fours, a crippled crab, feeling the parquet splinters needling into her palms, and praying to make it to the bathroom before the vomit came.

GERMAN LESSONS

Mordechai Taubman is the oldest student in the overflowing beginner German class in Tel Aviv. Glancing sideways at his classmates' taut cheeks and shining hair, Mordechai calculates that at 46, he is about double the average age.

They look normal to each other. But he worries that when they look at him, they probably see an old man.

The first evening the teacher sweeps into the classroom and suggests they go around the oval table introducing themselves. The first is a young man in a cutoff T-shirt who looks like a manual laborer. But looks are deceiving – he has enrolled to study medicine in Frankfurt next year. Another in an olive army uniform has landed a job for Israeli airport security in Munich after his discharge. Two or three, reddening, admit they have come because of German boyfriends or girlfriends or are exchange students or summer volunteers. A girl says she met *"mein Mann"* at a beach kiosk in Netanya; she looks embarrassed, but Mordechai thinks she is also showing off. He wishes there was a woman waiting for him at home to ask about his progress in German Level One.

When his turn comes, Mordechai clears his throat. "My company plans to send me on business trips," he says. "To Germany, maybe to other German-speaking countries."

It's only a white lie. Mordechai has already mentioned to his supervisor at the bank that he is a registered student at the Goethe Institute. He fantasizes himself fastening his seat belt on Lufthansa, leaning back and meeting the eyes of a smiling stewardess, glimpsing at Dusseldorf through clouds, sipping a beer in a crowded hall with mirrored walls. Who can tell where this new language will lead him? For now, the German lessons will fill his Tuesday evenings.

Archetypes begin to emerge. They have their class clown, their dreamer, the one who is always late, the one who never does his homework, and one girl they have nicknamed "Miss Dictionary" because her vocabulary is far beyond the rest thanks to an Austrian grandmother living at her house. Mordechai runs his hand over his thinning hair and worries; he suspects they may be dubbing him *der Alte*.

After his father stopped recognizing his mother and had to be transferred to the around-the-clock-care nursing home, she took to telephoning him seven, eight times a day. He thought he heard the snickers of the other workers when the phone rang at his desk; the line was normally so silent.

Mordechai started to go over to his mother's apartment during his lunch hour to check up on her and then once again after work. After a few months, it seemed natural to move back in. When she died 18 months ago, he considered transferring into the big bedroom and maybe renting out his little room to a student, but he has not gotten around to it. He continues to sleep in the small back room in his boy's bed with the frolicking bear cubs carved into the wooden headboard.

Since her death Mordechai has had time on his hands. For the last year, Mordechai has been canvassing Tel Aviv for a friendly place to go, a place where he will be recognized, maybe smiled at.

Sabra though he is, Mordechai cannot face the boisterous Israeli establishments. He did give the chess club a try, but the incessant background chatter while he was concentrating on his moves distracted him, and the loud, familiar bantering made him more tongue-tied than usual.

Mordechai has always felt more comfortable with foreigners. They don't automatically ask how many children he has or make it obvious they assume he is married. They don't ask what his job at the bank is. With them, he feels it's OK to be shy.

Even ten years before, in his 30s, Mordechai's Friday afternoons were spent in the American Cultural Center library. When budget cuts closed its doors, it was like losing a friend.

Once, walking on a wet winter afternoon on the seaside promenade, he went on impulse into the British Cultural Center's coffee shop. He loved its name: *Shakespeare*.

"English tea," he said happily to the waitress, wondering if they served Twinings or some other brand normally unavailable in Israel.

The waitress stared blankly.

"Tea with milk, the way the English drink it," he said. "It's called English tea."

The waitress shrugged.

She brought him a cup of hot water with a tea bag beside it on the saucer. By the familiar W on the tag, Mordechai knew it was the regular Israeli variety. She had forgotten the milk.

He tried to get her attention, but the waitress was primping in the reflection of the mirrored wall beside the register and firing away in Russian into her cellphone.

When Mordechai forced himself to try *Shakespeare* again, he arrived to see the building half-demolished. On a big construction barrier around the block were signs for a soon-to-be-erected luxury apartment house.

He decided the French Institute in the heart of the old business district was inconvenient to reach by bus; besides, the French made him feel about as self-conscious as the Israelis did. He wondered if the Italians might have some kind of center, but he couldn't find it in the phone book.

So although he hadn't thought of it first, or even second, Mordechai was more than happy to discover the Goethe Institute.

Mordechai finds himself looking forward to Tuesdays. The class laughs as it sweats, trying to remember the avalanche of rules. Surprise complications compound them at every turn. Masculine and feminine were not enough – German has managed to throw in neuter, too. Every part of speech seems to transform itself according to the context, like those fantastic medieval beasts that could change their shapes and yet remain the same. The sentence structure hops around in puzzling ways, and he has to hold his breath until the very last word to understand what's going on.

Mordechai's mouth gropes to form the new sounds. Every phrase seems complicated. A chopped-up sentence emerges from his lips, with long pauses between each jerky word. When he says, "What time is it?" or "I wish to order a beefsteak with potatoes and a glass of beer," the teacher beams like a mother watching her toddler walk. She never so much as winces at the verbal slaughter.

Mordechai arrives early to catch a seat adjacent to one of the girls; he doesn't care which one. He loves looking at the smooth skin of their arms on the table as they write new phrases in their clean notebooks.

Four months into the course, he can count, he can buy tomatoes in the virtual market, he can ask his student partner for directions to the dentist's office. The course books are witty and clever, designed for grown-ups with a sense of humor. The state-of-the-art syllabus is multimedia, aiming at sophistication.

He soaks in the camaraderie of the group. They support each other and encourage each other's progress, not like the underhanded competition he recalls from high school. When the teacher praises one of his answers, Mordechai basks in the others' admiration.

Every lesson, right before the break, the teacher dims the lights and presses the buttons on the TV in the corner. Bavarian beer melodies fill the room as pedagogic videos come on the screen. Some are semi-pornographic. Heidi and Dieter – young, beautiful, and semi-clothed – hold conversations in bed, illustrate the use of the familiar form of "you," teach the terms for "shower" and "marmalade." Heidi and Dieter have lover's quarrels and then make up with a kiss and, all the while, as if by chance, enunciate words like "motorcycle" and "computer programmer." The other students make catcalls and jokes. Mordechai is quiet, intent.

During the break Mordechai goes out into the bright fluorescent light of the lounge and unwraps aluminum foil to eat the roll spread with sardine paste he prepared for himself at home. He listens to the other students joking and flirting. He wants to pull a chair into their midst and join but doesn't, telling himself he will when he knows them better.

He manages to strike up an acquaintance with one person – Meir, the man who operates the coffee bar, closer to Mordechai's age than his classmates are.

While other countries seemed to be cutting back on their overseas cultural services in Israel, the Goethe Institute continues to cater in full force. Mordechai finds a well-stocked and user-friendly library with a series of rotating exhibits and cultural programs. Now, from a poster tacked on the wall beside the coffee bar, he learns there is a German film screened every Wednesday evening. Mordechai reads the flyer: "Free and open to the public. Next attraction a classic! 'The German Lesson.'"

What Mordechai likes above all is the smiling staff, leaping up at the slightest beck and call, asking if they can help. He suspects that in Israel, the Goethe Institute is on best behavior. The first German word the teacher taught his class was how to say "excuse me." What an unexpectedly passive choice for this sanguine race; he concludes the Germans feel they have to lean over backward for Jews now wherever they possibly can.

Mordechai is satisfied; the Goethe Institute is pleasant and well heated, and good for him in the bargain. But not everyone sees it that way. "German! Why *German?*" Mordechai is asked incredulously at work by the man at the desk next to his. He finds himself groping to justify his choice. He cannot admit he comes for company.

The excuses he makes are not entirely external. From time to time the inevitable dark shadow flickers in front of his eyes, so quickly he hardly notices it. Deep down, he knows German can never be a neutral language, even for him whose relatives had been in Israel for 80 years, safe from the slaughterhouses of the Reich.

In the Goethe Institute, posters of Nuremberg hang cheerfully on the walls. In class, they learn to conjugate the verb *arbeitet* and practice the pronunciation of *Konzentration* without batting an eye. But in Israel, no German word can be so innocent that it does not reverberate with implications. The class makes embarrassed macabre jokes about *Polizei* and *Wehrmacht*, and Mordechai senses a little shiver of guilty fascination run through him with each overlapping insinuation.

In Tuesday's lesson, the teacher recommends the upcoming film. The language of "The German Lesson" is not complicated, she says encouragingly, and they may surprise themselves by understanding a great deal.

In the lounge during the break, Mordechai sees an empty seat at a round table, between Miss Dictionary and the future security officer. He takes the plunge, sits down. They go on with their conversation, discussing the pros and cons of attending the film. They don't address Mordechai specifically, but nobody looks unkind. Hearing their words flying over and around his body, he feels included. He nods to show he is listening.

The students decide it will be a lark to attend the film. The future medical student, the future security guard, and three girls spend the rest of the break figuring out when and at which entrance to the Institute they will wait for one another.

Mordechai cannot wait for Wednesday to come. Instead of eating his sandwich at lunch hour, he goes to the kiosk at the corner and chooses an assortment of sweets. He pictures each student, trying to imagine what each will prefer. He fills a bag to overflowing – chocolate-covered peanuts, caramels, sesame bars, licorice, honey drops, rolls of mints, and fruit toffees.

The movie is screened at seven on an evening when no classes are held. Mordechai arrives at the Institute early. He whistles under his breath, anticipating, wondering who will arrive first.

Entering the auditorium, he hesitates about which seat to choose. Should he place himself near the entrance to make sure not to miss them, or nonchalantly in the middle? He compromises on a place on the aisle in the center of the auditorium – the best row – and rehearses motioning to his classmates when they enter. He is glad he came early so he could get the best pick. But ten minutes before show time, his heart sinks. The auditorium is still four-fifths empty.

He keeps his body twisted backward, his neck craned toward the door. He watches as people enter. He looks at his watch. The film is due to start in six minutes, and this being a German establishment, he expects it will be on time.

Nobody from his class arrived.

Tonight Mordechai suddenly finds himself half the age of everyone else. The crowd reminds him of the residents of his father's nursing home. He watches as they struggle into the auditorium, worn-out remnants. Hobbling on canes or leaning on one another, they work their way down the aisles and lower their bodies into the seats. Less than two dozen, wearing the dull browns and heavy tweeds of European pensioners, glaringly out of fashion, they nod greetings to one another. Clearly, they are the Wednesday night regulars.

Mordechai has fallen upon another insiders' club; this time he is a gawky bird among a rigid flock of retired refugees.

They peer at him curiously, critical eyes magnified by bottle-thick lenses. They whisper to one another, frowning.

Mordechai listens to them chatting as they remove their ancient overcoats, musty scarves, and unfashionable felt hats and lay them at precise angles on the back of the seat or upon thin thighs. They murmur to one another in German, with a few Hebrew words sprinkled in. Their voices are quiet and gray, lacking the peppy inflections he is used to from his teacher. Mordechai strains to catch their words.

"Colder than last week, more humid," he makes out one old man saying to no one in particular."

"*Ja, ja*," several heads nod assent.

Down his row, a man inclines his stiff head toward a woman with a wobbly chin, "Where's Wolfie?"

Mordechai understands the tremulous reply: "Wolfie? Still in bed with angina." Mordechai's class learned medical terms in the last lesson, so he leans closer, eager for more words he might understand. But seeing his stare, the conversants glare at him and lower their voices.

It is 7:15. The film has still not begun. Not one student has shown up. Mordechai gets up and walks up the aisle, on his way to slip out before the movie starts.

He hears a voice calling, "Hello, hello!" It repeats insistently, unmistakably in his direction. He looks up to see one face he knows.

Meir, the coffee server from the lounge, is in the back center aisle setting up the reels for the film. He seems to be having trouble threading the celluloid through the teeth of the projector. But Meir doesn't look stressed, and the audience does not seem impatient. They go on prattling, or sitting sunk into immobility, waiting. Meir stops fiddling and smiles at Mordechai's obvious surprise at the audience.

"The old folks?" he says. "Oh, they come week after week. They don't care what's on the program. They watch whatever film we show them. They sit through police flicks and weird modern movies *nobody* could understand. Those mummies sit there without blinking and without complaint."

Meir places a hand on Mordechai's back; it feels heavy and foreign. "Don't pay these has-beens any mind," he says. "Do yourself a favor. Next time, bring a friend – the films are sometimes really good. And with the prices of movies these days, the Goethe cinema is the best deal in town!"

Mordechai shrugs his shoulders. Now that Meir has spotted him, he cannot very well leave. He slips quietly into a seat in the back row next to the side and hunkers down. Meir seems to be accomplishing his task; he bends up and down next to the projector, looking like he means business. Mordechai gazes around the room at the aged audience.

So here he is, introduced to the Goethe Institute's "other" public, Mordechai thinks, aghast. Out of Germany half a century or more, none voluntarily. Had they lived out their lives as they foresaw, they would still be sitting with straight backs in their drafty foyers in Berlin reading beloved poetry. Instead, starving for those guttural phrases of their youth, this little fortress of German has become their beacon. What do they want here, watching films of the nation that destroyed their lives, sitting in the heated library leafing through glossy newsmagazines, hungry to hear the pure unspoiled accent of the German staff?

"Doesn't this immersion reopen your wounds?" he wants to inquire. "Isn't it like revisiting the beloved who betrayed you? Isn't it better to be isolated than humiliated?" But he knows if he dared ask, they would dismiss his question with the impatient wave of an arthritic finger.

"*Ach*," he imagines them muttering beneath frowning gray eyebrows "How can you – a *youngster, an outsider* – even hope to understand? Who are you, comfortable since birth in your own homeland, how can you even presume to ask?"

After the lights dim and the crackling film has been on for five minutes, Mordechai sidles out of his seat and up the aisle. He scurries out of the Goethe Institute. Under the yellow light at the bus stop, shivering and solitary, he unwraps a peanut caramel. Its sticky sweetness coats his teeth. He pushes cold hands deep into his pockets and waits for the Number 11 to take him home.

LOVE OF THE LAND

I was that invisible tag-along euphemistically known as "accompanying spouse." That's how I got to Israel – on Joe Fein's coattails. It was July 1974, the summer after the disastrous Yom Kippur War, and it was thanks to that war that Joe, our toddler Mara, and I were there.

After its existential scare, Israel sent out the urgent word to its universities: Lure over Jewish physicists. It didn't want to ever risk a repeat of Egypt's surprise attack across the Suez Canal.

Israel's Academy of Applied Science reached out to recruit Joe straight from Caltech. They offered Joe his own lab, a guarantee of five years of employment, and a research grant so large that it didn't appear in any official budget. Plus a rent-free house for as long as he and his family stayed.

After he accepted, the Academy headlined Joe on the first page of its English language bulletin, the one mass-mailed to potential donors: "Professor Joseph Fein (USA) and his lovely wife and child will be joining us in Rehovot. Professor Fein is one of the brightest upcoming minds in applied physics. His genius will help our country develop crucial detection systems."

In short, Joe was supposed to prevent annihilation.

Joe was told that we'd be met at the airport and escorted to our apartment in Rehovot near the Academy. But as the other passengers dispersed with their luggage, Joe and I found ourselves standing on a blasting hot furnace of a sidewalk in the shabby airport. Around us, a cacophony of horns blared. We were buttonholed by sweaty men grabbing Joe's elbow, urging, "Taxi, Jerusalem? Taxi, Haifa?"

A corrugated tin roof protected us from the blinding sunshine, but brutal heat radiated through. We held Mara in our arms, as we always did when away from familiar settings, shifting her back and forth between us. She was small for a two-year-old, but her leg braces made her heavier.

Finally, I spotted a short curly-haired driver holding a burning cigarette in one hand and fanning himself with a brown cardboard sign with the other. The cab's front wheels jutted into the pedestrian crosswalk. He stood with one dirty sandal resting on the bumper. After three or four swipes across his moist face, he held up the cardboard with a desultory gesture. I made out the crooked crayoned words: "family fine."

I nudged Joe and stuck my chin toward the fellow. "Do you think that means us?" I asked.

It was. What passed for his taxi was an old once-beige Peugeot with a crooked antenna and broken wipers. Hand-painted on the side were Hebrew words, and underneath: "Shmulik Capelluto. Taxi all occasions."

I didn't think I'd ever get past Shmulik's looks. His sweat-soaked nylon shirt gave off a pungent smell, and a hairy belly peeked out from above wrinkled pants. Salt-and-pepper stubble shadowed his heavy cheeks. He wore a giant, faded red straw hat dotted with holes where the weave had worn through. A hat you might expect from a pineapple picker in the tropics, not on a driver in Israel sent to pick up important guests. Incongruously long sleeves covered his arms, even in this heat.

"This is the guy they sent as a reception committee?" whispered Joe.

But when the driver saw us holding Mara, her legs in braces dangling down, he did a double take. He extracted a handkerchief from his pocket, waved it behind his ear, and pulled it with an elegant flourish. The handkerchief became a bunny rabbit. He held it out to Mara, and her tired eyes lit up. Her arms jerked up, trying to reach the bunny, and Shmulik extended a chocolate toward her hand instead. How could he be expected to know that Mara was unable to grasp? I took the chocolate, broke off a tiny piece, and put it in Mara's open mouth. Shmulik repeated the rabbit trick every time we hit a red light, turning around in his driver's seat to face backward, and Mara laughed as if every time were the first.

On the dashboard, in the spot usually reserved for a radio, balanced a beat-up plastic cassette player held together with grimy masking tape. As Shmulik careened through the roads, he fiddled with a cassette with one hand until he succeeded in inserting it.

I expected to hear Hebrew songs like they played at bar mitzvahs in Milwaukee – songs like "Hava Nagila." Instead, they were melodies in a language I didn't recognize.

"What's that?" I whispered to my husband. "Turkish? Greek?"

Joe whispered back, grinning at his pun, "It's Greek to me."

"So where you are from?" asked Shmulik. "Brooklyn, no?"

"We're arriving from California, but we both are actually from Milwaukee," said Joe.

"Is that in America? Milwaken?"

"It's the city where your prime minister is from! Golda!"

* * *

Joe and I met when we were midway through college. My roommate at the University of Wisconsin told me one day about a talk.

"Might be interesting," she said. "The speaker is an old guy called Abe Fein."

She didn't have to give him more of an introduction.

Abraham Fein was a name familiar to all Jews in Wisconsin – at any rate, all the ones like me who had been sent to Sunday school. His memoir *Out of the Inferno* was required reading for us all.

Abe Fein was a teenager in eastern Poland when the Germans overran it in 1941. He survived the war fighting with the partisans in the forests of Belarus. That's where he learned to shoot guns and fight under the worst conditions. When he learned that all his four sisters and parents had been shot by the Einsatzgruppen back in '42, he vowed to keep avenging Jews wherever the need arose.

At the war's end, Fein made it out of Soviet-controlled territory to a Displaced Persons camp in the American zone in Germany.

Without much optimism, Fein registered his name as a survivor on the lists that were being drawn up. But a great uncle who had moved to America in the 1920s found him. The uncle sponsored him, and Abe Fein arrived in America in 1947.

That's where Fein's story should have ended. Nobody would have heard of Fein had it not been for what he did next.

A year later, Abe Fein turned around and volunteered to help Israel in its War of Independence. Fein went to Palestine in 1948 and joined the Jewish army brigades made of up foreign volunteers.

Abe wrote daily letters home to his fiancée in Wisconsin. The collected letters had just been published by the university press. He was due to speak on campus about the book and his experiences.

I was never much of a joiner, and I had never been to Hillel, the college's Jewish club. I can't say that I was enthusiastic to go, and if it hadn't been to hear famous Abe Fein, I wouldn't have.

Fein was middle-aged and bald, but his words were thrilling. Fein volunteered two weeks after Israel declared independence and was immediately attacked by Arab armies.

"That's where I met my best buddy, Jacob Emmanuel," Fein said. "The infant country had no army to speak of, and Jacob was a US Army vet. We fought on the road to Jerusalem near a monastery at Latrun, in a unit side by side with other foreigners – a bunch of starry-eyed novices from Toronto and Cape Town. Jacob had seen combat in Normandy. I had 'graduated' the partisans in Poland. We considered ourselves experts.

"So after the battle in Latrun," Fein recounted, "Jacob and I sneaked away from our volunteer unit. Jacob talked our way into a platoon of local Israeli soldiers on their way to Jerusalem. Things like that were possible in those days when the country was just being born and the rules were being written as the days were lived. Besides, Jacob could talk anybody into anything.

"There were no uniforms to speak of, and the rifles they gave us were rusty old surplus from Czechoslovakia. But nothing before or since has ever given me more of a thrill, or more pride, than to help in the birth of the Jewish state," said Fein, his voice reverberating through the hall. "Especially after what I had seen over in Europe.

"When I came back to Milwaukee, I got a hero's welcome. One thing blackened the story. I returned alone. In the battle for Jerusalem, Jacob took two Jordanian bullets, one in the throat and a second in the lung. He bled to death next to me.

"I carried two identical boxes home with me. I brought Jacob's parents the posthumous medal Israel had awarded their son. Here's the other." Fein held up an olive box, unclasped its gold hinge, and held up a bronze medallion and purple ribbon nestled in the velvet. We craned our necks to see.

Fein invited whoever wanted to remain afterward to continue in an informal discussion. I stayed in the group clustered around Fein until the very end, until everybody had drifted off except me and a boy.

And that's how I met Joe, Abe Fein's son.

The first time we went out, Joe and I sat in the pizza place talking and talking. The crusts of our deep-dish pie got cold and stiff; the ice melted and diluted our Cokes.

"How come you went to my dad's talk?" Joe asked. "What's your special connection to Israel?"

"Well," I admitted hesitantly, "it's sort of because of Golda Meir. She grew up in Milwaukee just like me." I was embarrassed to confess that my heroine was an old lady with a gray bun, orthopedic shoes, and a cheap black handbag.

"You're telling me!" Joe exclaimed. "They never let us forget that in Sunday school. How our fair Midwest city spawned Israel's founding mother. I used to think that she looks like somebody's immigrant grandmother. How did she get to sit in the prime minister's chair in Jerusalem? But then I heard her talk once on TV while she was addressing the UN. Boy, was she some whip. She spoke so deliberately. Hell, she was smarter than everybody. You just couldn't beat her logic – slow but inexorable."

"I loved Lake Park when I was growing up," I went on, seeming to change the subject. "It was so gorgeous, the winding paths like a fairyland. I'd take my roller skates and spend the afternoons there, fantasizing that I was on white figure skates and that my figure eights were so graceful they would land me in the Olympics."

"What's the connection?"

"I read a biography of Golda that the Sunday school handed out as required reading, and… "

"They gave that to us, too! You actually read it?" Joe broke in, laughing. "Remember the blue-and-white cover with Golda's photo in the center of the Israeli flag? You could say Golda was the Jewish jewel in Milwaukee's crown."

"You're so right. I guess I was the kind of kid to buy into the legends they fed us," I continued. "So when I read about Golda's childhood, it said that Golda used to visit Lake Park, too, whenever she could, that she would escape there from her family's poor home, from her angry father who wanted her to quit school and go to work, and she would imagine getting an education and becoming somebody. And then later, how she started to dream of settling in Palestine, where there was some cockeyed experiment called a Jewish homeland. I mean, she went to Palestine when it was a really hard, courageous thing to do.

"It was the Golda connection, I guess, that started me caring about Israel. Knowing that she had loved the same park I had, knowing that she had dreamed her dreams there, too."

I stopped talking, knowing how corny I sounded. I suddenly remembered how I had learned about the Holocaust from another book the Sunday school had handed out: the book by Joe Fein's father.

But Joe was beaming. "Roz," he said to me, "I was born into Zionism, raised on it. All my dad's stories, you know. He taught us that the State of Israel is the miracle answer to the Holocaust. It's great, sort of amazing, to hear how you came to it on your own."

"I never knew anybody before you who would have been interested," I said.

Joe and I married the summer after I got my degree in speech therapy. Then we moved to Joe's first job as a faculty member at Caltech. I got pregnant after the first semester.

Our Mara was born in California. The delivery room nurses said it was the longest labor they remembered. In the neonatal unit, they told us to expect that Mara might never walk or talk.

Our location in Pasadena made Joe and I feel a little bit less unfortunate – it had the country's foremost expert on the development of children with cerebral palsy caused by birth trauma.

Mara was espoused early by Dr. Rose's team. The physical therapists worked with her day in, day out, and Joe and I sang to her by the hour. Did fate know what was in store for me when I chose speech therapy as a profession? By the time we left for Israel, 22 months later, Mara was tilting her head back and forth to "Old MacDonald," singing out a recognizable "e-i-e-i-o." We looked forward to her taking her first wobbly steps.

* * *

After I got married, I followed the example of my parents and went to temple once a year. That's where Joe and I were sitting during Yom Kippur services when the whispering began to spread throughout the hall: "War, a war's broken out." "Israel's been attacked!"

In October 1973, there was no lightning victory as there had been in 1967. For several weeks, it seemed Israel's continued existence was a touch-and-go proposition.

Joe and I took that danger to heart, and it heightened our excitement when the offer came the following spring from the Israel Academy of Applied Science. It would mean we would live our Zionism, and it would also give Joe a continued first-class scientific environment. He'd be in the Middle East, but that wouldn't hold him back from developing professionally.

For me, it was another story. What kind of demand could there be for an English speech therapist in the Israeli provinces? I put myself aside, partially because in those years it was still the accepted – and expected – thing for a wife to do. In all honesty, though, I, too, was excited at the prospect of living in Israel.

However, there was one thing we couldn't ignore: What facilities would be available for Mara?

"My parents will be thrilled," Joe told me confidently. "We'll call tonight."

When his parents answered, both listening at once on separate extensions, Joe delivered our news.

"They just finished fighting a war, for gosh sakes," Abe Fein exploded. I could hear him pounding his fist in Wisconsin through the telephone receiver.

"And it won't be the last war over there, not by a long shot. I know what war is," he shouted. "I've seen it up close. Too close. War is not a fireside talk at the University of Wisconsin. No reason my only son has to raise his hand and race over there."

"Dad, you did your part. I've been hearing about it all my life. You helped defeat the Nazis. You helped create the State of Israel. I want to help it stay alive."

"Dammit, Joe, it's not like you are a soldier. You wouldn't know which end of a gun is up. And I'm glad about that. Don't flatter yourself: They have enough Jewish brains over there.

"And besides," Abe said, pulling out his trump card, "when I went to Israel, I went alone. I was sure your mother was safe back in Milwaukee. But you, you want to up and take your young wife along, too. And not only her – your defenseless little girl. Mara, Joe, think of Mara."

My parents were dead set against the move, too. "Imagine the danger you'll be putting yourself in," my father dubiously.

But it was mostly Mara's future that weighed heavily with my parents.

"It's a struggling country, Roz, you know that," my mother begged. "Much as they would like to, what kind of resources can they afford to allocate for handicapped children?"

I hated to hear that word – handicapped.

Later Joe said, "When you talk to her again, remind your mother how advanced Israel is in science. It goes to reason they must also put an emphasis on medical development."

"And besides," I said as the thought occurred to me, "Jews love kids. Children are the most important thing for them."

Joe's mother cautioned that Mara would be facing enough hurdles learning English. Why subject her to another language?

"Think of the great things we've heard about Hadassah Hospital," Joe countered.

"Right," I agreed, "and how caring a totally Jewish staff will be to our little girl. Still, it will be hard to top what she's getting here in Pasadena."

Mara made great motor strides in the first 18 months of life. But her last half year had been strangely stagnant. We didn't mention this out loud, as if not verbalizing it proved her lack of progress was just in our imaginations. She docilely repeated the arm movements she learned, making circles in the air, reaching out toward a lollipop, but there was no improvement to speak of. Dr. Rose's unit kept refining the exercises and trying new machines, but there was no change. I told myself either Mara has reached her limit or she needs a dramatic switch.

Maybe that's why we didn't inquire into specifics about Israeli care for children like Mara. We wanted to make a leap of faith. We wanted to believe Mara would be in good hands, maybe even better ones that would turn her around.

Joe and I talked and talked, wavering back and forth for weeks. I was the more hesitant one.

"What if, instead of progress, Mara might regress in an unfamiliar environment?" I worried out loud.

Israel in its hour of need seemed to be beckoning to Joe personally. And frankly, he was flattered by the attention. We were young. My husband had all sorts of brilliant ideas in his head. But unspoken and most of all, I think it was that old father-son paradigm. Joe didn't want to forever be thought of as "the son of." In his mild-mannered way, Joe wanted to duplicate the contributions of Abe Fein.

We decided to go.

Joe eased in well. Everybody in Rehovot in 1974 was solicitous of the American scientist. They looked upon him gratefully – someone who had come to pitch in. His mentors had trained in top universities; all the research papers were in English. So it was natural to conduct his work in the lab in English. Besides, science was an international language.

Joe even got a kick out of practicing his Hebrew at the staff cafeteria.

"Wow, Rozzie," he laughed. "My mistakes must sound so dumb. You should see how patient they all are with me."

The Academy was an oasis. It had a sprawling campus dotted with trees and buildings donated by Holocaust survivors abroad. Joe joked that the royalties on any discoveries in his lab should be shared with the Ronya and Simon Karchmar Memorial Fund in Philadelphia. Sprinklers sprayed water across wide lawns. A rarity back then, there was a sparkling swimming pool for the staff and their families. The welcome shock of air conditioning beckoned in every building.

My life was a different ball game. I had crashed into the chaos of a sweaty, rowdy Israeli town. Into a baffling maze of cultural barriers. Into sand traps of misunderstanding. The spaces weren't the same. Noise intruded non-stop from loud voices and nonexistent acoustics. No matter if they acted friendly, I couldn't get a handle on the people. The very air I breathed felt different: stiflingly hot, humid, and smelling of stale cooking oil and boiled chicken.

In their invitation, the Academy described our apartment as a ten-minute walk away but didn't mention the 90 degree plus temperature that turned every living thing to an overheated brick in minutes. Joe was assured we had only to pack suitcases with our clothing because the apartment was outfitted with furniture and conveniences.

The conveniences turned out to be very inconvenient – an ancient fridge, with a freezer unit on top caked with crystals that was hardly big enough to hold an ice tray. The motor crooned an unending, plaintive ballad 20 hours a day. When the fridge switched into its abrupt silent phase, we sat terrified it had conked out for good. While we waited for the motor to restart, we heard the diesel buses below and people shouting hoarse words in the street. The couch was a hard foam-rubber affair upholstered in swirls of orange and brown, and the beds threw me back to the cots in Girl Scout camp. Among the plain furnishings, we found two rusty fans, one in our bedroom and one in the L-shaped dining room/living room/kitchen. There was a black-and-white television with spotty reception, which didn't bother me since there was only one station to watch, spouting a language I couldn't understand.

I suspected the Academy was skimping on our housing. But when Joe's colleagues, even his superiors, invited us to join them for Friday night dinners or holiday gatherings, I found their apartments just as basic. It was another world from faculty teas in California with their heated pastries and pewter serving sets.

Our building was an old, three-family home, each apartment one flight above the next, linked by steep stone steps. We were on the top floor, which meant Joe or I had to carry Mara three full flights each time we left or came back.

The neighbors seemed friendly enough when we passed them, but there seemed nothing to converse about after a quick hello. On the main floor was a taciturn elderly couple who mumbled to each other in German. The second floor held an exhausted-looking man and wife. The Yanivs were both postdocs and besides their studies and lab work, they had several children. Exactly how many and whose kids were theirs I never knew exactly because assorted neighborhood children were continually bounding up and down the stairs, dribbling balls and screeching in raucous Hebrew. Both Yaniv parents were mostly absent, probably fleeing the tumult into their labs.

Mara and I faced the long days together. I was dogged about continuing her speech exercises. But singing the "ABC" song in Rehovot seemed irrelevant, and "Old MacDonald," with its oinks, bowwows, and moos, felt even more out of place.

We found almost zero facilities to help our daughter develop. After the head of Joe's department intervened as a special favor, they promised to hold an opening for Mara in the Academy's preschool when she turned three. I was to stay in the classroom to assist Mara.

"But they have nothing special for her, not even physical education for her motor development," I pointed out. It's unbelievable. If I knew..."

"Let's try the pediatric clinic," Joe suggested. "The Academy's arranged for us to get National Health."

I took the bus to the other end of town and waited with Mara at the local public health branch for our number to be called.

"You're asking for therapy *every other day*?" I was told.

"Sorry," said the nurse went on, not sounding sorry at all, "the sick fund covers one weekly group session. If you want more than that, you'll have to go privately."

"But back in California, my daughter got..."

"This isn't the golden land, lady," the harried nurse snapped. "Our rehabilitation centers are overflowing with neurological cases from the war, with soldiers relearning to walk with one leg or trying to strengthen arm muscles to push themselves in a wheelchair because both their legs were blown off next to the Suez Canal."

Was that supposed to make me feel understanding? Or patriotic? The health system was stretched thin and they were doing their best to accommodate everybody. I couldn't rationally blame them.

In fact, I was the one at fault. I could understand maybe, or accept, if fate had meted it out. But Joe and I ourselves – Mara's own parents – had taken her out of the rehab institute in California, away from the best experts in the world. Why did my Mara have to take the punch? Especially at this crucial time in her development.

It was wrenching my guts. I didn't see a way out. Whenever there was something I felt Mara needed, I came up across a brick wall – those ominous words "not covered," "not available," "only privately," "needs to be specially imported from abroad."

It was eating at Joe, too. Every day he came home, his first question was, "How'd our girl do today?" Unspoken between us was the knowledge that although both of us had wanted to come, it was Joe who had championed diving in.

"Mara is just getting accustomed, slowly, like us," Joe said, convincing himself. It was in line with his optimism, his general faith that things would work out. Besides, he loved his work at the Institute.

I began to resent both the country and my husband.

I started to make weekly withdrawals from our bank account in California, transfer the dollars to Bank Leumi, pay sky-high fees to convert the funds into Israeli currency and use them to hire a physical therapist twice a week. Because even though the Academy was compensating Joe generously by its standards, the salary covered only our living expenses. Certainly no frills or luxuries such as a car. Or giving our child an extra push.

But nothing. Despite more therapy, Mara stayed at the same level she had been during those last months in California. She sat hour by hour in front of the grates to the balcony, wet curls plastered to her neck, looking up at the roofs and the clouds across the street, her thin legs spread out in a V, seeming to enjoy the cold, stone tiles.

We were lucky to have a telephone with our own line in the apartment. Even so, transatlantic calls were a big deal back then. We communicated by thin, blue aerogram letters. I glossed over the difficulties, especially where Mara was concerned. Having a crippled grandchild was painful enough. My parents didn't need to hear the details.

The carriage changed everything.

A British scientist planning to immigrate had brought it over in his family's lift. When the family threw in the towel and went back to London after three years, they shipped their furniture back with them. Since their babies had outgrown it, the carriage was left behind.

"Come on down, Rozzie," Joe called up from the street one evening to my open balcony. "See what I brought for Mara!"

I looked down, and my jaw dropped.

In front of my eyes was a pram meant for British royalty.

The enormous wheels were thin-spoked. Silver glinted below the rust. Underneath an old protective blanket, the inside was lined with soft satin. The regal exterior was white enamel, its name embossed with metal lettering saying "Silver Cross"; underneath was stamped "Made in England."

It was a wreck, but it was glorious.

"Apparently, they imagined Rehovot might have a place like Regent's Park suitable for elegant prams," Joe laughed. "A place with nannies and pinafores... I knew you would love it." I could tell that even plain Joe from the Midwest wished that the Holy Land had turned out to be a little more upscale.

Joe scrubbed the rusty wheels with steel wool and polished the chassis until it shone. We parked it under the stairwell behind our German neighbors' rickety shopping cart with its old plaid plastic cover cracked from the heat.

The carriage jump-started my walks.

Mara was so big, almost two and a half, much too old for a carriage. I was afraid people would laugh when they saw her propped up. But I tried not to care. It was much better than a wheelchair. And by October the merciless heat had lifted.

Mara beamed every time I put her in. She held on to the sides of the carriage and smiled her crooked smile at the motor scooters zooming past. A princess in a satin coach.

I ventured farther each day. Farther and farther, until I left the Academy behind. I continued on the two-lane road as it left town, walking by the side of the road with the traffic to my back.

I came upon a white road sign with an arrow pointing straight ahead. Under the Hebrew words, I was relieved to see an English translation: "Nes Ziona. 7 kilometers." I recognized the word *nes* from Hanukkah in my childhood. I remembered it meant miracle.

"Nes Ziona. Miracle of Zion," I told Mara.

Every day as we left the town behind and I strode along, I repeated in a singsong, "I'm gonna Nes Ziona! Nes Ziona. Nes Ziona, here I come."

Every day, I went farther afield until the buildings thinned out and orchards encompassed me to my right and left. Orchards as far as the eye could see. Green, shiny leaves and straight, proud trunks planted equidistant from each other.

I walked down off the road over the caked dirt and pushed the carriage toward the trees. To my surprise, the trees were not fenced in. At first, they looked like a monolith, but when I came closer, I saw that fruit hung from each branch – dozens, no hundreds– on each tree. I wondered how I could have missed it. Then I realized the fruit was still green and blended in with the camouflage of the leaves.

The orchards became our daily destination. Mara lit up when we left the asphalt and the ride over the dirt became bumpy. She jiggled in her throne seat and mouthed, "Ney, ney, ney."

I joined in: "Nes Ziona, here we come."

One day as I was walking, I heard a faint whining. I thought it was an airplane in the distance, but as it got louder, I realized a motor was approaching from a nearby lane of trees. I froze. How could I explain the crazy picture Mara and I presented? I was a blatant trespasser.

A tractor came into view, the back loaded with a jumble of empty wooden crates. The man in the driver's seat veered to the right and the tractor lurched to a halt. A raggedy red straw hat obscured his face.

"What! Aren't you... the taxi driver?" What was this guy doing here on a tractor?

Shmulik looked as surprised to see us as I was to see him. He recovered quickly.

"Taxi business slowly," he told me. "In little weeks will come harvest. In winter, I am working with oranges, and the fruit of grape."

"Fruit of grape?" I laughed. "Oh, you mean grapefruit."

With gestures and pidgin English, he motioned Mara and me up on the tractor. I would've been reluctant if Mara hadn't shot both her arms up toward Shmulik. She made happy sounds, bouncing up and down so hard that the carriage lurched, and I fumbled to steady it.

He picked her up gently, careful not to grasp around the braces.

I climbed in and sat up front next to Shmulik. Shmulik parked the carriage in the shade of a big tree at the end of a row. Holding Mara on my lap, we had a guided tour through hundreds of lines of greenery. As we went from one lane to the other, Shmulik spoke in his brand of English, calling out the name of the fruits: clementina, mandarina, tapuz Jaffa, fruit of grape.

At afternoon's end he deposited us back at our carriage. Shmulik made ready to head off, but, looking at me struggling to push the carriage over the dirt, he scrambled off his tractor once again, hoisted the carriage onto the back, and lodged it between the orange crates. He drove back into town, the ochre walls of the Academy on the right. The tractor went slowly, and cars sped by us right and left. People stared at us from the curbs. Some children pointed. But we didn't care. We were queens of the road.

When we arrived, Shmulik jumped off and wrapped his arms around Mara to let her down.

That's when I saw it, the purple number tattooed on his forearm – ugly, incandescent, almost psychedelic, standing out on his pale, freckled skin. I saw it just that once; he pulled down his sleeve so quickly that I almost doubted it was there.

But Shmulik didn't let the moment pass. He said, "Yes, I have seen so much suffering that now I love every beautiful thing in this world double strong. And I want helping everybody I can to get most from life. Like here your little girl, God blessing her."

Every time after that, Shmulik wore long sleeves buttoned at the cuff, no matter how hot it was. I never dared to ask about Shmulik's tattoo – Who had he lost? How was he saved?

From that day until the rains started two months later, and afterward, too, on dry days, Mara and I were private guests on Shmulik's citrus coach.

He didn't speak much. Just bowed with a flourish when he hoisted Mara up. "Princess Mara," he called her. He always brought his handkerchief, and the bunny appeared at the start of every ride. We watched the fruit turn light green, then take the hue of yellow for lemons, pinkish yellow for ruby grapefruit, and shades of orange for clementines and oranges. I learned the different strains of oranges: Jaffa, Washington, Valencia. My love was the blood oranges, with their deep magenta pulp and their sweet and sour taste.

I fed little sections of ripe fruit into Mara's mouth, and the juice trickled down her chin. I hoped that the warm Mediterranean sun and the nectar would work a miracle with her body. I wanted to be able to write that in an aerogram to my mother and father. I longed to take a photograph of Mara walking on her own in the furrows.

On every ride Shmulik's cassette recorder serenaded us with those mysterious lilting tunes.

One day, as he switched on a song, Shmulik told me, "That's from old home. I come from beautiful island, the island named for roses – the island of Rhodes."

He turned to little Mara.

"One day, Mara sweet, you will hearing about Maccabees. My people lived in Rhodes a long time, maybe since those days. Since the Maccabees, until... But we now talk about happy things, about oranges and princesses."

Turning to me, he said, "The music is my old language Ladino, the language of all us Sephardic from the Mediterranean. It's a mixup from all around our wonderful mother sea – from Spanish, and more from French, Italian, Turkish, Arabic, Hebrew. Ladino enough big to hold all."

That's as far as Shmulik ever opened up.

There were small victories for Mara, and we held our breaths. But no leap came.

My determination evaporated. Too hard for too little recompense. Darling Mara was treading water. Then the truth hit me: Mara wasn't stagnating. She was falling backward.

When Joe opened the door, I shot out, "Don't you see it? While you are flowering, our Mara is sinking. I am not willing to sacrifice her, not for any idea of Zionism."

Again, Joe tried to urge me to give it more time, but his words had become half-hearted.

The Academy wanted him to stay on, kept upping its offer. Then the University of Minnesota offered Joe a chair – and the American-size salary we needed to help Mara.

We threw in the towel. We departed Israel two years after we arrived.

We left in early spring. The trees were in bloom, their waxy green leaves at their shiniest among clusters of delicate yellow-white blossoms. On the way to the airport, I unrolled the windows of Shmulik's taxi and inhaled. I held Mara up and the sweet wind blew her hair. I felt she knew we were saying goodbye. Whenever I've seen orange blossom perfume since then, I've bought a bottle. But not one has ever come close to the paradise of the real thing.

We vowed to return. And we did – to visit.

In between visits, times when I felt nostalgic, I put on some music. Always in Ladino, the melodies I grew to love on Shmulik's tractor, the language of the orange groves.

Joe kept up his ties with the Academy of Applied Science. For the first few summers –five, maybe six – he came back to resume his research in Rehovot. Mara and I came with him. Always Mara, Joe, and I, a perennial threesome.

Shmulik met us every summer, and every time the bunny welcomed Mara, long after it would have seemed age-appropriate. Joe and I began to look forward to that bunny, too. It became part of the package, just like Shmulik and his dust-streaked Peugeot. Shmulik was Mara's first grown-up friend, her first champion. When he maneuvered his taxi to be closest to the pickup area, it was as much to welcome back Princess Mara as to escort Professor Fein and his accompanying spouse.

During those visits, as Shmulik drove us south from the airport, my heart leaped as we passed through dusty, sleepy Nes Ziona. Soon, soon, I would see it. I craned my neck until the green ocean arose to our right and to our left, stretching on to the horizon in both directions, parting only wide enough to let our car through.

It was the trees, their white blossoms, and their golden fruit I loved about Israel. It was what I never stopped missing.

* * *

As the time approaches for Joe's retirement, we decide to come back to Israel for a final sabbatical. It's been many years since we've been, 20 at least.

This time it's not only Joe who's invited, it's me. Israelis are anxious to hear about the techniques I've developed in teaching postoperative throat cancer patients how to regain their speech. I have a full schedule of lectures in the ENT departments of all the major hospitals.

"Dr. Roz Fein spent some time with us in Israel in her youth," an Academy biologist brags at a cocktail party to the director of a teaching hospital.

"I believe you were here at the Academy?" an oncologist says, draping his arm familiarly around my shoulder.

The Israelis we meet assume we will want to move to Tel Aviv or at least to Jerusalem. But all Joe wants is to be set up with a lab again at the Academy.

I, too, opt for Rehovot. At first, when I met Israelis in the US, I rushed to tell them about my beloved citrus groves. But they looked at me with such a bemused expression, almost condescending, that I kept it to myself. Now I'll be able to go back to the trees.

We land in the late afternoon, so by the time we are on our way, the road to Rehovot is in darkness. A young driver in an air-conditioned Mercedes whisks us southward.

The apartment they give us is nice, airy, modern. No trace of the old "conveniences." There's an elevator, of course. I remember carrying Mara up those three flights of stairs. Now it is I who is glad of the elevator – I am almost 65 after all.

The first thing I do when I set down my bags and open the windows is to phone Mara at her apartment at the independent living facility in Minneapolis.

But she is out. I reach her roommate and leave a message.

Mara manages the bus by herself in her mechanized wheelchair, traveling all over, including her part-time job at the library. For many years, we would never have dreamed of spending even one night far from Mara, but now Joe and I hardly worry about her anymore. Mara is her own person; she is what the experts call semi-independent. All through the years, Joe and I put away our excess earnings for Mara's needs. And if I had to describe her, I can honestly say our Mara is a happy person and a joy to our lives even through the obstacles.

"Almost all the faces at the Academy are new," reports Joe after his first day. "But guess who's head of the immunology department? Remember the graduate students who lived in the apartment under ours the very first time? The noisy ones?"

"You mean the Yanivs? Wasn't the husband's name Amos, or maybe Aaron?"

"It's not the husband who's chief. It's the wife, the frazzled one who was always screaming at her kids. She's the big cheese. Rinat Yaniv.

Everyone addresses her as Professor, and I swear it looks as if they almost incline their heads when they speak to her."

The first week, while I am walking down the street a stout woman plants herself in front of me. "I remember you!" she declares, her pointy finger almost touching my chest.

I recognize Rinat Yaniv. I mumble a hello.

She has become effusive. "I remember how you used to carry your little girl downstairs and how you both looked so happy when you wheeled out the carriage from under the stairwell and started out for your walk. You were celebrities in the neighborhood!"

I want to say, "Then why didn't you stop to talk to me?" But I hold my peace.

Yaniv keeps me for almost half an hour – peppers me with question after question about Mara, seeking the details of her progress. And she comes right out and asks, "Did you have more children?"

I shake my head.

"And Shmulik," Yaniv continues right on, "well, everybody saw him escorting you and the child on his tractor. The people who didn't see it pretended they did. So that he became a local icon. So much they insisted to get Shmulik as a driver whenever they called the taxi service."

"Is Shmulik still in business? Where is he today?" I burst out.

"No idea. Haven't seen Shmulik around for several years. The Academy uses all new drivers now."

"Yes, it figures, so many years have passed. Shmulik must be retired, or..."

In Rehovot, the old smells are gone. Nobody hangs out laundry on the service balconies. Falafel stands have been replaced by coffee bars. On the streets, French with a Moroccan accent has been supplanted by Russian.

I go to the 24/7 store and buy staples. The products are better. I look in vain for the unwrapped loaves of bread thrown helter-skelter on the shelf and eggs sold singly from open cartons.

One thing hasn't changed: the contrast between the bedlam of the main street and the serenity of the Academy.

I am waiting for one thing. After a week, my jet lag has passed and I've organized the apartment. I'm ready.

I catch the bus out of Rehovot. The destination sign on the bus announces "Nes Ziona." I sit by the window up front and rehearse how to ask the driver to pull over and let me out when we reach the orchards. The way looks strange. The two-lane road has been replaced by a multilane thoroughfare.

Before I know it, I see we are pulling into a bus depot. It turns out we've arrived at the central station of Nes Ziona. Already? How could I have missed the trees? There must have been more buildings constructed adjacent to the roadside.

I scramble off the bus and hail a taxi back toward Rehovot. I manage to give directions: "Turn left. About ten minutes before the entrance to the Academy, that's where the orchards start."

But when the driver does so, we come upon signs pointing to Technology Park. I must have forgotten where to turn. I find myself surrounded by a stark new development. Everything is paved over. Like Brasilia springing out of the jungle. Block after block of postmodern pastel gray and pink buildings, all with underground garages, with glass doors and signs above the entrances: Comtech, Optik, Logicon, New Directions.

There is hardly a soul outdoors. A few straggly trees droop halfheartedly beside shadeless pavements.

"Pull over," I say to the driver when I see a pair of young men carrying computer cases and walking toward one entrance. "Where are the orchards? Can you please direct the driver to them?"

"Orchards?" The men look blank.

I tell the taxi driver, "Let's go back to the main road and ask at a gas station."

The worker at the pump shrugs. "Go see the manager in the office, maybe he knows."

An old man is sitting on a broken swivel chair picking his teeth with a toothpick, wearing a faded navy parka with the gas station logo. The man is clearly an old-timer, so I take a chance.

"I knew a man – a taxi driver – about 15, 20 years ago – name was Shmulik. He wasn't only a driver, he used to moonlight on a tractor harvesting oranges." I struggle to describe Shmulik, but I can't think of anything but the hat. "He wore a raggedy old straw hat–"

The man's expression changes. "Straw hat – you mean that old Holocaust survivor?"

"Yes, that's him! Where is he? Where can I find him?"

The old man shakes his head. "No more, no more," he mumbles, and gestures as if the past had flown away, his bony fingers fluttering. "I knew him well – I could even call him a sort of friend. Always filled up his taxi and his tractor in my station. And he helped whoever he saw in need. Helped everyone, no questions asked. He was some guy, some guy."

"And?"

"I heard his heart gave out," the man says. "Wasn't so old. Only 62 or so. They said he never got over the shock of the war – the damage to his insides from the cruel deportation from some island he came from. All sent straight to Auschwitz. They said he was only one of a handful who survived. Shmulik didn't have any family left. He loved the music of where he came from. And here he loved the land."

He makes a dismissive gesture with his hand. "Shmulik, gone. Orchards, gone too. Ten, maybe 15 years already."

I swallow hard. I don't want to talk anymore or ask anything.

A customer has come unnoticed into the office behind me. A heavy man, he holds a can of Fanta and a bag of pretzels, waiting to pay. He jumps enthusiastically into the conversation, addressing me in native English: "It wasn't profitable to keep the citrus. Exports dried up. Those Europeans, they prefer to buy from Morocco, from Spain. The costs of production were too high. So they gave it all up. Didn't even try to grow something else."

I picture the heavy clods of sienna-colored loam that coated my soles after we returned with Shmulik, the earth perfect for planting.

"You wanna know the real reason, lady? The land around here became too expensive for plain old agriculture. In the last few years, the graduates of the Academy have been founding start-ups right and left: computers, medical research, you name it. They have ideas galore. The obvious place to put the labs and offices is near their alma mater. Some continue to teach there part-time. Matter of fact, I work with the Academy, too, I supply lab equipment to it. I'm official importer of American..."

"But orchards?" I break in. "Where can I find citrus orchards?" I feel a pounding desire to walk in furrows again and to remember Shmulik.

"You looking for oranges? You'd be best to go to the supermarket. There's one about a kilometer down the road, on the lower level of the new mall. You can't miss it."

He exhales and enunciates slowly, as if to a child. "The signs are in English, too, lady. No problem. You'll find lots of oranges there. More than enough."

MY MUSICAL EDUCATION

I went to the tomb of President Ulysses S. Grant almost every Wednesday, needing to calm myself down before my piano lesson with Pania Rutka. The mausoleum had no heat, but it kept out the humid wind that froze my cheeks when I stepped down from the warm cocoon of the Number Four bus. The tomb standing at the entrance to Riverside Park was my refuge from the cold hurtling across the Hudson onto Riverside Drive.

I never thought of it as an actual tomb, holding a long-dead president, a president we learned about in school but who lacked any emotional pull. Standing alone and majestic on Riverside, it offered a convenient haven for me to spend a solitary hour.

I wasn't the only one. There were interesting people in Grant's Tomb, unexpected people. It sheltered love-struck couples from the Theological Seminary holding hands through their woolen gloves. Kids played hooky from the local public school, running circles in exuberant hide-and-seek among its marble columns. Doctoral candidates wandered down from Columbia University with furrowed brows, their exceptional minds deep in the crevices of enigmatic equations. But mostly it was totally empty, just me and the spirit of Ulysses S. Grant.

Music divided my week in two. After my lesson came three or four good days when the next Wednesday seemed far off and I was safe to leave the wooden door on the piano shut tight. But as days passed, guilt goaded me to return to my untouched arpeggios and my simplified extracts. The two consecutive nights before the lesson, I raced through them 20, 30 times, my fingers on the keys, my mind on what I planned to do next, and my eyes on the lazy hands of the clock on the mantel across the room.

Actually, my lessons near Grant's Tomb came late in my musical education. But they fit the pattern. Pania Rutka was the last in a series of musical refugees whose pedantic English and Old World pedagogy were foisted upon me in my parents' insistence to instill classical music. These *panias* hardly ever spoke a word unconnected to the business of notes and measures: how many times to practice a piece, how to set the metronome, how far to sit from the keyboard, how to keep my fingers curved. There were little more than perfunctory hellos and goodbyes exchanged between us. Opening the door, they surely noted my glum expression.

To them, I was an alien girl-child of their adopted country, and like that country, I was to be held at a distrustful distance. Between us – the disappointed musician living in bewildered transplantation and me, the unwilling student constrained to put in my time practicing scales – there was a gap never to be bridged. They taught me without bothering to care who I was, and I made it worse by confirming their lowest expectations.

Pania Henia was my first teacher and the best. She and I shared the piano bench and played simple duets in her sunny room. Her warm bulk took up most of the space, but she didn't edge away when I rested against her. Pania Henia smelled of milk and baby oil. She didn't seem to mind my mistakes. Maybe she didn't hear them. As we played, she kept her ear cocked toward her infant in the next room. He summoned her every time. At the sound of faint whimpering, Pania Henia would bolt up from the piano bench. No matter where we were in a piece, she dashed out to attend to the baby. In those frequent respites, I looked at the boring illustrations in my beginner piano book as long as I could and then got up to watch the ritual of Pania Henia cooing musically to her drooling infant, bending over his bare bottom to rub him with an excess of baby oil and love.

By the next year, when the baby had learned to walk, Pania Henia had to give up lessons except for a few pupils squeezed between his erratic naps. I was one of them. I didn't mind playing accompanied by the toddler scurrying around under the piano and banging on the legs with his blocks. Once, though, my mother arrived early and observed. I found myself transferred to another teacher.

Pania Marishu came to our house for the lesson, so I could never be late. During the two years I played with Pania Marishu, I was only saved once, by a four-week transit strike. Pania Marishu lived somewhere far out in Queens. When the subway was out of commission, so was she. Ever since her era, "Fur Elise" is accompanied in my mind by the sounds of Pania Marishu gobbling Lorna Doones and slurping tea made pale with lemon that my mother would reverently bring out to her on a lacquered tray covered with a paper doily. Pania Marishu's face lit up for the tray as it never did for my music. Her only smile was when my mother appeared in the doorway. She never refused the snack. During the week, moist Nabisco crumbs sometimes tumbled out from between the pages of my music.

Then Pania Marishu announced, "My husband 'Engineer Janek' is invited to West. Invited by USA government." She alluded to a mysterious project getting underway in Southern California. "Tops secret," she said in a stage whisper. Pania Marishu was the first person I knew who would be setting foot in that exotic paradise called California. She rose in my sight.

Pania Marishu left Queens and our lessons ceased. I received the departure with joy, preparing to be granted a lifelong pardon from the piano.

I imagined myself outfitted in stretchy gray jodhpurs and black riding boots, cantering around Central Park on a speckled gelding. But my hints, and then my pleas, for riding lessons went unheeded. Similarly, my requests to join a ballet class, where a group of my classmates hurried off to on Tuesdays, giggling and whispering in their pink leotards and tights, were ignored. How I longed to slip into buttery-soft black leather ballet slippers and adjust the elastic over my instep.

My delusion of reprieve was short-lived. Not all musical refugees had rambunctious toddlers or were summoned out West.

I was therewith delivered to the dark lobby of Pania Rutka Krakovsky, the last and most dour of the brood. As I ascended to her apartment, the gloomy light of the elevator bulb set the tone for the dark mood upstairs. The childless Krakovskys split the apartment for teaching their respective pupils.

Pania Rutka was married to a not-quite-famous pianist. He was well-known only within refugee musical circles, where his past, like theirs, was not viewed as exaggerated fiction. They remembered who Pania Rutka's husband had once been. From time to time, my parents received invitations to his sparsely attended concerts at the Y or a community center out in New Jersey.

Pan Edek Krakovsky had begun as a stunning child prodigy in Warsaw. It was said his musical career, stunted by its uprooting, never fully recovered in the rocky soil of the Upper West Side. He was one more transplanted postwar refugee musician trying to pry open the doors of the American establishment. But for every one Arthur Rubinstein, there were ten Edek Krakovskys.

For this, everyone around him took the brunt, but his fiercest glare was aimed at the dumpy figure of his receding wife as she led a reluctant pupil down the dark corridor in her thick-heeled brown shoes with their silent crepe soles.

Yet if Pan Krakovsky had not attained success as a concert pianist in the New World, his precision and technical mastery made him valued as a teacher. His master classes were jammed, and piano prodigies lined up to audition to become his student. Having studied under Pan Krakovsky was considered a ticket into the classical music world.

The first time I was towed in to be introduced to Pania Rutka, my mother and I were ushered from the dark hallway into a magnificent living room full of light. The far wall was all windows from floor to ceiling, looking over Riverside Park and the Hudson. You could gaze down onto the dome of Grant's Tomb across the street. The room was dominated by a shining Steinway, its wing open like a majestic black bird.

Pania Rutka grasped my elbow and steered me into the narrow kitchen where she planted me in front of a stained enamel sink and gestured toward a bar of Ivory soap. "When you're finished washing your hands," she instructed, "come back and exhibit us what you know."

I sat on the edge of the velvet-covered double piano stool. My hands, though still damp, managed to sweat. I raced through an abridged, simplified minuet. I knew Mozart had composed it when he was younger than I. Pan Krakovsky was there when I began to play, his arms crossed around his chest, but when I looked up at the end, only my mother and Pania Rutka remained.

It was the first and last time I ever played on that great bird of a piano. The next week, when I arrived for my first real lesson, I walked straight into the living room, but Pan Krakovsky, who was sitting on the stool with a thin boy bent over the keys, looked up and glared at me.

"Rutka," he called loudly, "show your student where is she to go!"

I learned the rules. While the star pupils of her husband played Chopin overlooking the park, Pania Rutka's students had to walk down the narrow corridor lined with a row of indistinct drawings in faded red ink. We were received in the drafty room next to the pantry.

The piano there was a plain brown upright. Plain as Pania Rutka. Weak yellowish light came from a lamp perched on top. The room faced an air shaft in the building's rear, the curtains always drawn. The room was meant to be a second bedroom – the one for a child, or a maid.

Pania Rutka favored loose gray cardigans with tissues tucked into the sleeves. Her features are indistinct in my memory except for her small pupils magnified through the inside window of thick eyeglasses and sparse black hairs sprouting above her upper lip. I assumed she had always been like that, born mousy and brown, like an illustration in a children's book of a forgettable background character.

So I was unprepared for what I heard when I was grown up, ages after my lessons had ended. My mother and I sat in the back seat of a taxi as it sped down the Henry Hudson Parkway. As it exited onto Riverside Drive, I stared as we passed Grant's Tomb, its neoclassical white columns rising with majesty near the verdant trees.

I turned to my mother and asked, half resentfully and half in real puzzlement, "Why on Earth did you pick that nonentity as my teacher?"

"Which teacher do you mean?" she asked, bewildered at my out-of-context query.

"You know, Pania Rutka, the piano teacher, the one who lived near here on Riverside."

"A nobody? *Pania Krakovsky*? She came from the best family in Warsaw! Benefactors of the arts. And she was their only daughter! She could have married anybody she chose. *Anybody*."

My mother didn't stop talking as we sped downtown. She told me the Krakovskys' story, the part she knew. I'm still turning it over in my mind, trying to reconcile the brown mouse I knew with the beloved only child.

Pania Rutka, my mother said, came from a line of aristocratic and emancipated Jews, the intellectual elite of westernized Warsaw. A shy and promising student with dark hair and luminous eyes, Pania Rutka, like many in the conservatory, had fallen in love from afar with Edek, the rising star of their musical world.

Edek toured Europe; he performed in Paris and Vienna before he was much past 20. There were rumors that in these capitals he enjoyed art deco night clubs, imported American jazz, and dancing with sultry bohemians at midnight parties following his triumphant sonata recitals. Edek fanned the rumors, bragging about his exploits when he came back to the quiet oak-lined street of residential Warsaw, where the loudest sounds were the chords of Beethoven symphonies from windows opened to let in spring air.

But, as usual, marriage was another thing. My mother sighed. It was well-known that Edek made a smart match with Pania Rutka, whose doting parents set them up in a large flat downstairs from their own. She was their only surviving child, her beloved older sister having succumbed to pneumonia while a teenager. After the wedding, the bride's parents gave Edek their Bechstein.

"A *Bechstein*, you understand," said my mother, "a Bechstein was worth more than a Steinway."

Five workers were hired to carry it down to the newlyweds' apartment. "And," said my mother, "I heard that her father stood at the top of the stairs like a lieutenant to make sure its legs must never scrape the ground. The whole town knew the story! That piano was almost as precious to her parents as Pania Rutka was."

Before they could settle into the anticipated pattern of their life, war erupted and drew its curtain across the past. Pania Rutka's parents were among the first to perish and Pania Rutka prepared herself mentally to follow them.

"What happened to Rutka and Edek?" I asked.

"Edek's music saved them."

Thanks to his concert tours, Edek had influential admirers high in the French musical world. Laissez passer were secured to France, and from Vichy, they obtained visas to Portugal. Traveling in haste, the young couple fled from Lisbon by boat to Argentina, and then on to Chile.

Pania Rutka was pregnant, but the child was lost. They spent a stupefied three long years in South America until they received permission to enter the United States, where they found themselves among the core of displaced, educated Central European Jewry between Broadway and the river.

"And she never had more children?" I asked.

According to rumors, my mother heard, there were two more miscarriages during their disorienting transitions. No more pregnancies followed.

"When they started, Pania Rutka was on top," my mother sighed. "But fate overturned all. Everything she had handed Edek – family, wealth, social status – all was erased. The only thing that remained to Rutka in America was herself. Not enough, not enough."

Those details, which might have made me feel something toward my wooden teacher, all had been kept from me. Childhood so often meant being told only the boring things. That's what I thought in retrospect upon hearing my mother. But what, after all, could this melodrama have meant to a reluctant child whose concerns were far, far away from pianos and piano teachers?

In New York, Edek and Rutka lived for the next three decades in their cavernous rent-controlled building on Riverside Drive.

As I was shepherded past their living room, I glimpsed red sunsets over ice chunks floating down the freezing Hudson. On snowy afternoons, when cottony flakes swirled past the high casement windows with their thick glass, the room took on a white luminosity. The grand piano's ebony lacquer was polished and oiled to a mirror shininess, the name Steinway unmistakable over the keyboard in the gold letters.

The star pupils went to Pan Edek, the talented young students in black turtlenecks aspiring to Juilliard. His wife's days and years were filled with a stream of the uninspired offspring of the immigrant middle class, sent for a few seasons of mutual suffering until their lack of talent and interest was too evident to ignore. The other bread-and-butter pupils and I were relegated to the upright piano in the back room.

In the silences between my discordant bars, as my clumsy fingers groped for the notes of the next chord, I heard rippling trills wafting from the Steinway in the front. Pania Rutka never turned her head nor ever acknowledged them. Her stiff shoulders never diverted from a painful concentration upon my mistakes. She tapped her index finger rhythmically. Every measure or two, she stopped me. In a flat and precise tone, without anger or censure or hope, she repeated what had once again gone wrong.

Each time before I started to sweat over a new piece, Pania Rutka took my place in the center of the piano bench to give me a demonstration. I stood sullenly beside her, looking over her shoulder. She took her time to adjust her distance from the piano, cock her right foot above the pedal, and cup both hands a fraction of an inch above the keys. Then she focused her nearsighted eyes on the sheet music and played the music straight through without hesitation.

As I stood fidgeting, the music lamp over the piano illuminated her thin raven hair pulled back into an iron bun. I saw with repugnance lines of pale white scalp peeking from underneath. As she played, Pania Rutka's body remained stiff, but her yellow hands with translucent short nails returned to some long-forgotten life of their own. The music startled even me; it could be moody and soft and then turn crisp, the chords reverberating inside their wooden home. If I closed my eyes to block out the dull room and its dull mistress, we could have been in the light-filled salon overlooking the Hudson.

Pania Rutka was not happy with my stumbling, although she never used any harsh words. Her lips stayed pursed, the corners turned down.

Pan Edek was a blurry shadow, in his early 50s I guess now, his puffy white face hemmed in by its own Old World snobbishness. If I bore him scant interest, he bore me none at all. He was often in the living room as I arrived, greeted by an agitated Pania Rutka opening the front door with a silent twist of the handle and with her finger up to her lips. I glanced at him as I passed into the hall, seated on the piano stool before the kingly Steinway, his lumpy behind pressed against the slim, seated figures of nubile prodigies. In the rare instances he opened the door himself, he seemed annoyed and hardly looked at me, gesturing roughly backward toward the corridor. Pan Edek was too haughty to greet a mere child, especially one of his wife's second-class pupils.

I don't remember Pania Rutka or I ever smiling during the three years of our acquaintance. She and Pan Edek never spoke to each other, except sometimes when my metronome ticked too loudly and he called out a gruff order to shut the door. Rutka slid noiselessly off the bench and darted to obey.

I smiled after the last lesson for the season each June as I waited for the wrought-iron elevator to deliver me down to a two-month respite from Schumann. The rest of the year was filled with too many Wednesdays.

So whenever I arrived at my bus stop before the appointed time for my lesson, it never crossed my mind to go upstairs. Where could I wait except in the corridor of the faded sketches?

That's why I used to spend the time trying to keep warm in Grant's Tomb across the street. The monument was my temporary hideaway.

One afternoon in late winter, as I sat shivering on a marble bench outside the portico of the tomb, I looked up to see the outline of a couple in embrace just behind the line of Doric columns. The young woman stood facing me with her head thrown back, her auburn hair fanned out against the white wall, eyes trembly closed, pink mouth slightly open. I was so close I could see the pulse in her white throat fluttering. In front of her unbuttoned jacket lurched the back of a man in a heavy woolen overcoat. I saw thin strands of pepper-gray hair over the collar as he nuzzled his weight against her. I was hidden by the columns but too close to move away unnoticed. I was forced to watch.

When he broke away, hoisted up his trousers, and wiped his open mouth on the back of his woolen sleeve, I heard him say in the unmistakable clipped staccato of the Polish intelligentsia, in those funny, not-quite-right American phrases learned from diligent study of outdated textbooks used in night school: "We ought to better get upstairs now in a jiffy. With your slow progress, we risk not to be ready on the ball for our duet at the Brooklyn Academy."

I listened numbly with the shocked morality of the young. "Tawdry" is a word I learned later. They didn't see me as they left, and after a few minutes, I followed them out of the park and upstairs.

Pania Rutka opened the door, once again with a finger to her lip. "Juliette Steele," she whispered, gesturing toward the young woman with the white throat and black leotard playing a fanciful fragment of Mozart on the Steinway. "Juliette Steele, who won the Young Artists' Competition. She is practicing with Pan Edek for joint appearance. He is her sponsor for big career. Next week, invitations are ready – I shall save and give your parents. Soon, in next year, you will be old enough as well to come to Pan Edek's evening concerts."

As I passed into the corridor, I tried not to look into the living room, but I couldn't stop myself. I saw Pan Edek's gray head standing at the window, languidly tapping a cigarette ash onto an ashtray, facing the dome of Grant's Tomb and the river flowing behind it.

For the next few weeks I tried to polish my two sonatinas to perfection. I rushed into Pania Rutka's apartment without glancing at the virtuoso or his students playing the grand piano.

But my attempts to bring some light into the eyes of Pan Edek's wife with my puerile chords proved futile. And although she had to stop me only once or twice for minor infractions of rhythm, Pania Rutka no more reacted to my efforts than she had to my mulishness. My achievements were of no interest. Pania Rutka's straight back remained stiff and inert, and I soon reverted to my usual lassitude.

That spring my parents saw the wisdom of allowing me to give up piano lessons for good.

THE RIGHT TO HAPPINESS

When Gamal Abdel Nasser began to strut and menace Israel in the spring of 1967, Hilda was unprepared for her high-strung reaction. First, Nasser got rid of the UN observers stationed in the Sinai Desert who were meant to keep the Israelis and Egyptians apart. Without these peacekeepers, Hilda fretted, who would be there to make sure Egypt kept away? She wrung her hands when she heard that Egypt was blockading Israeli ships. Shows of strength, threats, step-by-step escalations – all were familiar to Hilda.

Suddenly, she felt an astonishing interest in Palestina and a growing hysteria worrying about its existence. "Palestina" – that's how her father and mother used to refer to Israel when she was growing up in Germany, and she still thought of it this way. She lost her taste for matinees. She neglected to pick up her alligator handbag in repair for its broken clasp even though Mr. Scaparetti called three times to remind her it was ready. "We changed also the lining, Mrs. Gruenstein, it was too frayed for such a special purse," he oozed. "And we refreshed the leather. You'll find it better than new!"

Every morning, Hilda awoke fearing to hear that while she slept, little Israel had been wiped off the map. She rushed to turn on the radio before preparing her coffee. She pored over the news reports and commentaries in the *Times*. She flipped through the television channels searching for coverage.

As the days passed, one word began to repeat itself over and over. It beat drum-like in her head: war, war, war. She found herself concentrating on faraway personalities whose names she had just learned. A retiring fellow named Levi Eshkol headed the State of Israel – roly-poly and balding, he looked as harmless and ineffectual as an aging schoolteacher. Eshkol reminded her of Hindenburg in the Germany of her youth, that aging leader hoodwinked by Hitler.

She learned to pronounce the names of others, like pirate-like Moshe Dayan, a one-eyed general appointed to head the Israeli army. The papers sang his praises, although he appeared too extravagant and swashbuckling for Hilda's taste. The news showed lean, tight-lipped men striding in rocky fields, diplomats ducking in and out of limousines, and spokesmen delivering curt communiqués in heavy accents.

One person was head and shoulders above everyone else. When she first heard the bell-like British voice and elegant phrases, Hilda was not sure whom she was hearing. An eminent Jew from Great Britain? A member of the British Parliament? An adviser to the Queen?

It turned out the beautiful voice with its eloquent defense of Israel emanated not from London but from Jerusalem, from the heart of its government. Despite his bizarre foreign name, Foreign Minister Abba Eban was an Israeli who spoke like a member of the British royal family. She heard him in broadcasts from Jerusalem, his voice strong, clear, and mellifluous above the static of the radio. She followed his progress when he was dispatched to France to beg Charles de Gaulle for support and detected the bitter disappointment in his voice when de Gaulle declined. When Eban flew first to Washington and then to New York, Hilda tracked all his moves.

"*Ja*, he is the new Churchill!" Hilda told her friend Margo, who nodded in agreement.

Anybody who heard him had to become convinced of the rightness of his cause. There were surely others like Eban in Israel, people of culture and refinement, helpless before the threat.

She phoned her friends to share her worries about the Middle East. Would America support Israel? Would Europe make some move this time to save the Jews?

Now, on the second of June, Hilda sat perched on the barstool in her kitchen drinking double-strength black coffee and nibbling a biscotti with small, sharp bites. Her hands were making the gesture they performed of their own accord whenever tension built up inside. One palm caressed the back of the other hand, and then her hands switched. It was as if she was washing without water.

Hilda's gaze focused on the swirling eddies of the Hudson River in the distance. Flowing water soothed her. It always had.

As a teenager walking the promenades beside the canals in Berlin, she and her brother, Philip, kept a respectful few paces behind her parents, watching them huddled arm-in-arm as they exchanged anxious words. In Hilda's Cuban years, the azure Caribbean gave solace. And her New York apartment won her heart at first sight for its multiple views of the river spanned by its majestic bridge. Fifteen years had passed since she moved to Riverside Drive in 1952. Now it was 1967, and she had never yet tired of watching the river.

Hilda's eyes passed without interest over the row of dusty cookbooks on the nearby shelf. The books were house gifts from well-meaning dinner guests at her husband's firm who assumed Hilda would want to learn to bake pecan pies with lattice tops, macaroni and cheese casseroles, and meat loaf with ketchup crust. Everybody chipped in to turn Hilda red, white, and blue. Hilda had never opened one.

Propping up the books stood a copper-colored faux bronze Statue of Liberty with a glued-on room thermometer, the red gel inside congealed to read a perpetual 62 degrees.

The Statue of Liberty was arrayed amid other patriotic mementos her son, Phil, brought home over the years. Phil arrived bearing garish souvenirs unfamiliar to Hilda – a miniature triangular felt pennant with the puzzling word "Giants" stamped on it, or decals of brown bears dressed in scout uniforms with "Smokey" written across their chest.

Last year on St. Patrick's Day, coming home from the parade on Fifth Avenue, Phil dashed in, yelling, racing over the waxed parquet. From his pocket, he fished a rabbit's foot keychain dyed a lurid green. He held it out to her, perplexed when Hilda recoiled.

This year, Phil considered himself more mature. "Momsie, I found you the best, best gift!" he said. Out of a brown paper bag he extracted a heavy glass beer mug imprinted with an emerald shamrock.

Although she kept every single one of Phil's gifts, Hilda was remote from her son's clichéd memorabilia. She had never considered taking the ferry to visit the Statue of Liberty. Like the other monuments of her adopted country, it was meant for the natives and their gum-chewing, baseball-cap-wearing children. Everything Phil knew of landmarks. he garnered from class trips or Boy Scout outings.

Hilda could count on the fingers of one hand the number of New World institutions she embraced with any enthusiasm. The classical music radio station WQXR was one. Now, she recognized the violin concerto filling the apartment and anticipated Vivaldi's every bar. As always, WQXR's master recordings formed the backdrop of her morning.

She walked purposefully to her room where girdle and stockings lay ready on her chair; on a nearby hanger were her Italian knit skirt and matching silk blouse. Standing tall to her full height,

Hilda hardly topped five feet one, but her energetic movements made her appear bigger than her diminutive dimensions.

She maximized her appearance. Much as she tried to avoid the thought, next year she would be 50; yet in Saks, she marched straight into the express elevator and rode up to the eighth floor to the children's department. She passed unseeing by the layette and toddler department to the section marked "Girls 7 to 14". She had discovered it was the best place to find Scottish wool pants and sweater outfits to wear in their country home in Vermont. Girl's size 12 was usually a perfect fit. Even the best quality children's clothes were so much more economical. Thrifty Hilda always bought the best, but she loved getting a good price. Never waste, her mother cautioned her as a child, and she lived by that motto.

Imagine a middle-aged woman of 49 wearing a girl's size 12. She didn't care. When she topped the outfit off with a designer scarf imported from France, nobody could guess her outfit's secret.

Hilda was a scrupulous dresser. But today, in her haste, she couldn't be bothered with the buttons on her cardigan.

"*Ach Liebchen,* you are a *perpetuum mobile,*" her father had dubbed her so long ago in Berlin. "My little *perpetuum mobile.*" He called out using the Latin phrase. "Yes, Hilda you are a machine constantly in motion, he said as he watched her twirl through their apartment to the strains of her brother practicing a Straus waltz. But Hilda thought she caught her mother's glances that seemed to say she wished her daughter's features were as delicate as her movements.

Hilda had never been pretty. To others, she seemed to brush aside her looks and occupy her fast, efficient hands with whatever needed to be done. They did not suspect it, but Hilda looked after her own person with meticulousness paid to every detail.

Her homeliness diminished with age. Or at least it was less painful to Hilda. She more or less made peace with her small, nearsighted eyes and bulbous nose. Yet the sting of her looks never completely healed. She avoided mirrors unless it was to see if her slip was showing or check if her collar was straight.

One American alone she considered a soul sister. A stab of recognition hit when she heard about ugly duckling Eleanor Roosevelt's one wistful childhood wish: to have been called just a little bit pretty.

Usually, the determined, nervous movements of her compact, barrel-shaped figure contrasted with the rippling trills of a Chopin prelude or a lively Beethoven scherzo. Hilda did not actively listen; the music formed the indispensable backdrop to the start of the day's activities, like snapping up the Venetian blinds to reveal the park outside her window or vigorously brushing her short, coarse hair, the hair she had touched up Inky Midnight every six weeks on the button.

Until now this spring of 1967 had been glorious, but this year Hilda hardly noticed. Hilda was distracted, every day more so. She couldn't remember the last time she felt so jittery.

This morning, the second of June, even Vivaldi seemed irrelevant. Uncharacteristically, she switched away from WQXR and tuned the dial to the all-news radio station.

Had Nasser backed down from the Straits of Tiran? Would he call off his embargo on Israeli ships? Hilda strained to catch every word. But instead, there was no good news at all. Nothing optimistic. The announcer called it a hardening standoff and reported ominously of the mounting fever toward war.

Hilda was used to hearing about armies, bombs, and threats. But this last month had been different. She was terrified that war would equal annihilation of the Jewish state. That's what Nasser was promising. The words jumped in her mind, flashing behind her eyes: annihilation, gone, wiped away.

She could not explain her extreme anxiety.

Hilda had never visited Israel. She had no plans to go there. She did not make donations. She never considered buying an Israel bond. She did not follow issues involving Israel or feel that the Jewish country represented her. She had hardly paid any attention to the Suez hostilities a decade earlier.

But to think that its people might be driven into the sea, as Nasser threatened to do? That it might be wiped off the map? That it could be the 1940's all over again?

Suddenly the doorbell's shrill buzzer startled her. Most unusual. Unprecedented, in fact. Nobody was let upstairs without the doorman calling first from the lobby to see if they were expected.

She opened the door to find herself facing two girls scarcely into their teens.

Their faces looked familiar. One held a school clipboard against her chest. What was this all about? Under no circumstances did their building allow soliciting. The girls were the first uninvited individuals who had ever rung her bell. Behind them stood Jimmy the elevator man, a tentative expression on his face.

Hilda shot Jimmy a stern look.

"Mrs. Gruenstein, ma'am" – coming from Jimmy's mouth her name sounded like Greenstine – "this here is the Dresslers' daughter from 6G and this other is the Adler girl who lives in 3B," he explained hastily. "Their parents gave them permission to go through the house collecting some kind of signature."

Jimmy's words were a go signal for the girls.

"Sign our petition to support Israel!" chirped the girl holding the clipboard, thrusting it toward Hilda.

Hilda recoiled a half step backward into her apartment.

The other girl, more outspoken, added: "We're collecting as many signatures as we can get, and my parents will mail it to Mayor

Lindsay and our congressman. Maybe even to the president! So far, every single person we asked has signed!"

"But... shouldn't you be in school?" blurted Hilda irrelevantly.

"Oh, we got the morning off."

"Yeah," chirped in her companion. "The principal said this petition would be a life lesson."

Hilda peered down at the list of signatures on the upside-down page in the girl's hands. She had never signed a petition in her life.

The girl turned the page right-side up and held it close to Hilda's face. Hilda took a step back and read: "DON'T LET LITTLE ISRAEL FACE HER ENEMIES ALONE! NEVER AGAIN ENDANGER INNOCENT JEWISH CHILDREN! URGE CONGRESS TO SUPPORT ISRAEL!" The text continued, but Hilda stopped reading.

She grasped the pen held out to her, scribbled *Mrs. Hermann Gruenstein*, and without a further look at the girls or the elevator man, closed the door.

Hilda went into the living room, lay back on her chaise lounge, slipped her feet out of her black pumps, and stretched her legs. She put her hands to her head and moved her fingers through her hair, over and over, the red nails making furrows through the recently brushed strands.

Hilda mulled over the bizarre incident, the affront to her privacy. Ringing doorbells? Where would it end? She reached for the phone to call Hermann. She would ask him to protest to the building's management.

On the other hand, the girls showed pluck. So young and yet clearly involved. And their optimism – albeit naïve – that their activism could influence outcomes. They were pushy, yes, but they had something to admire.

She started to dial, then let her hand drop. Hilda felt disequilibrium down to her joints. She hadn't experienced this feeling of dissolving since she and her mother were spirited out of Germany nearly 30 years earlier. And yet, she asked herself, why did she feel such panic, such *personal* panic?

Although they were paid-up members of Temple Emanu-El, neither Hilda nor her husband ever went. Her son, Phil, had not stepped inside since he finished the Reform temple's kindergarten.

Now, a dozen years later, Phil was focusing on high school graduation. That's where he was today, at his commencement rehearsal. His mind, she knew, was on parties and his part in the class play where he snagged a supporting comic role. And on how he would spend his last "free summer" – as he put it – living it up before beginning the grind of Dartmouth.

Dartmouth, that had been a battle Hilda lost. She had always assumed Phil would go to Columbia.

"But our Columbia, one of the best universities in the world!" she protested when he told her he was applying for early admissions to Dartmouth. "And such a fine faculty – cosmopolitan." For Hilda, cosmopolitan was the code word meaning Europe. She had once attended a lecture by a lady archaeology professor with a French accent, and she heard that a refugee from Berlin was a professor at Columbia's law school.

But Phil insisted, "Momsie, you just want Columbia because it's nearby!"

Hilda didn't admit it, maybe not even to herself, but Phil was right. Separation from Phil, even if only five hours away in New England, made Hilda uneasy.

"But think, Phil, Columbia is known all over the…"

"I am tired of living at home," he shot out. "And I don't plan to take that same old 104 bus to school for the next four years. All those years at Columbia Grammar School were enough for me. It's unbelievable you want me to go to college as if I were still in junior high school! I deserve freedom – freedom like everybody else! It's not like you both can't afford it. And Dartmouth is the tops, just the tops. *Everybody* in my class is going to an out-of-town school, and I will, too!"

And as usual, Phil had his way.

He treated spring semester final exams as a superfluous nuisance. Hilda perceived that what really mattered to her son was what people wrote in his yearbook, the solid heaviness of his new class ring whose weight he loved feeling on his finger, and the welcome escape from the tedium of high school.

Hilda propped Phil's graduation invitation on the semicircular entrance table just inside the front door: "Convocation Exercises, Class of 1967: With Pride and Honor." With pleasure, she studied her son's name halfway down the list of graduates: Philip Gruenstein.

Her anxiety rose when she thought about the emptiness of the fall when the apartment would be silent until Hermann came home. But September was still months away, Hilda told herself, and she would find a way to cope. She always had.

She didn't actually take care of Phil anymore. It was just knowing that he would be coming home in the late afternoons, even if only to fling down his school blazer in the hall and then shut his door to call his friends or listen to rock and roll at top volume. Her days after he left for college would continue, filled as they were now with bridge games, social functions, enrichment classes, and frequent vacations.

Her Phil was one of the boys, Hilda marveled. She loved how that phrase rolled so easily off her tongue as if to be one of the boys was the most natural thing on earth.

His integration seemed nothing less than magic. Bundled up in her beaver coat the color of dark chocolate, her nose reddened by the cold, Hilda attended his track meets, standing apart from the chatting mothers in their shiny rainbow-hued parkas.

She admired the complicated English texts she saw carelessly tossed next to Phil's blazer: Chaucer and Donne and Melville. Hilda herself tried to read a book he had been assigned in his junior year – "A heart-wrenching tale of displacement and devotion – unforgettable," Hilda read from the blurb on the cover. But though her literary skills were high, try as she might, Hilda could not understand the puzzling vernacular of John Steinbeck's poor Oakies in *The Grapes of Wrath*.

How could Phil so easily make that verbal transformation? To have such a native son! It was to Hilda a source of secret smugness. Americans, expecting all as their due – and then getting it after all. Phil was like that to a T. But it made Hilda nervous – could such privilege go on indefinitely?

Hilda pampered him. Her Phil, named in memory of her brother, was the apple of her eye.

But rarely she could not help but erupt.

Like a few Saturdays earlier when Hermann had to go into the office to deal with a client emergency. The city was at its sparkling best in May. It was the perfect morning for taking a drive up the parkway and across the bridge, then north towards Bear Mountain. She and Phil would make a day of it, she decided. What better way to have one of their last twosome days before he went off to college? She would introduce him to the lunch buffet in the converted mansion overlooking the river. As soon as they were ready to leave, she planned to order the car delivered to their building from the parking garage a couple blocks away.

Starting at nine, Hilda began waiting for Phil to rise, looking at the clock and cocking her ear for noise from behind his bedroom door.

Finally, at 11:30, Hilda burst in. Phil lay sprawled in bed, deep in sleep among the tangled sheets. Hilda flung open the windows, muttering her favorite German proverb: *"Morgen, morgen, nur nicht Heute, sagen alle faulen Leute"* – "Tomorrow, tomorrow, just not today, all the lazy people say."

Phil groaned and buried his head under the pillow. To shut out the light, if not his mother's voice.

By then, it was too late to start out. Instead, Hilda went alone down to Riverside Park with the paper.

Their apartment hung four floors above the park; the treetops across the narrow avenue seemed about to brush the windows. In late spring, the foliage was at its thickest, and between the sycamore leaves, Hilda barely made out the loden waters of the Hudson River streaming past the throbbing city toward Liberty Island.

Today, Hilda's eyes blinked faster than usual. She paced from one tall window to the other. The placid scene outside on Riverside Drive contrasted with the buzzing inside her head.

The international crisis hit the headlines in a puzzling escalating series of events. When Nasser closed Israeli passage through the Red Sea, international ricocheting began. May had passed without violence. But it was already June 2, and the crisis was growing more dire by the day. Hilda's heart began pounding when she heard reports teenagers were mobilized to pile up sandbags in Tel Aviv.

Hilda turned her attention back to the radio.

The news items continued in descending order of seriousness. The radio announcer left the Middle East behind. A jackknifed tractor-trailer truck was snarling traffic on the Cross Bronx Expressway; an electrical outage was stalling the C train at Chamber Street. Reports that were of complete indifference to Hilda, they might as well have been talking about a foreign country.

It became apparent that the international news was done.

Hilda twirled the radio dial back to its usual location. Debussy's evocative chords filled the room.

Music calmed her, as it did during her childhood when she heard her brother, Philip, practicing the piano in their Berlin apartment as she pored over Latin declamations.

In her mind's eye, Hilda saw the embroidered cushions in the window seat embraced by the heavy maroon curtains where she nestled to study Caesar's Gallic wars, then as the years went by to tackle Virgil and Ovid. And to listen to Philip play.

Beside the piano stood the dense mahogany table, its midsection covered with a white triangle of French damask starched to impeccable stiffness, a crystal vase exactly upon its center. The vase never stood empty. In spring, it contained furry yellow balls of mimosa, in autumn, waxy chrysanthemums. Sensual peonies appeared in July, their heavy blossoms drooping down toward the table, soundlessly shedding petals upon its polished wood. In deep winter, when no flowers bloomed, Hilda's mother saw to it that the vase was filled with sprigs of evergreen.

Hilda's favorites were the fragrant lilac blossoms of late spring, so heavy the stems soon gave up supporting their weight. The first time she came across a row of lilac bushes in Riverside Park, Hilda's heart raced. Their beauty was the same – pale purple and delicate – as they had been in Berlin. But the New World lilacs somehow lacked their perfumed odor, as if they were fashioned out of silk or paper. Here, lilacs, too, were an imitation of life.

The best thing about the table of her childhood was its curved legs ending in lion paws. As a young child, Hilda made the cool, dark space under the table her private sanctuary. She crouched underneath hidden by the tablecloth and ran her finger along a leg's smooth waxed sheen, down to the curved knobby ends perched upon the Turkish rug.

That same table still stood intact upon its four lion's paws, transplanted like Hilda to an apartment in the New World overlooking the Hudson River.

Hilda's mother was on the new continent, too. No longer the imperious countess of assimilated Berlin Jewry, she leaned on a cane as she hobbled into the elevator in her gabled apartment building in Kew Gardens where she lived with other German Jewish émigrés for neighbors.

* * *

In 1939, her father announced to Hilda that she and her mother were to be sent on ahead.

"Why not send Philip instead of me?" she protested. "He's no longer really interested in the piano. He hardly practices anymore. He's always sneaking out to see his friends. Why can't you and Mother admit it?

"And if you send me away, my violin studies will be interrupted – thrown away – as if the dozen years I've played since the age of eight didn't exist at all!

"And Papa, Papa," she admitted the real reason. "I don't want to leave you!"

"Don't fret, not at all, Liebchen," her father told her. "I am not worried. You remember how I taught you to tie your shoes? How I always told you to make a bow and then to go back and pull it tight – otherwise it would unravel? It's the same with my business, with our house affairs, with the staff. I need only to tie all the strings here into sure bows, and then your brother and I will be at your doorstep. Dear Hilda! Only 20 but so mature. Responsible since you were a little girl. I can count on you to help Mother to set up our new lives, to prop her up. You will be my ambassador."

"But what about you and Philip? The radio – those speeches?" she asked, shivering at the barking oratory of the Nazis prophesizing the cleansing of Germany.

Hilda dug her fists into her eyes. She wept so bitterly that her shoulders shook.

"Oh, my little Hilda, you are so young still – you will learn speeches are always exaggerated," reassured her father. "Just to persuade the masses. If there is any war, we Himmelsteins can always get out."

Indeed, the Himmelsteins lived in a bubble of privilege. Hilda hardly remembered any Jews in her childhood. The only ones she saw were the unappealing, poor-looking groups in unfashionable homemade clothes she glimpsed congregating next to cheap food stores and charity kitchens. Women with shawls and men with comical black hats, either with big brims and flat tops or tightly fitting beanies hugging their scalps. None of them like the elegant woolen bowler hats worn by her papa and everybody else.

Behind her parents' backs, Philip mimicked them, bobbing his head up and down with his hands on his hips and imitating their ugly language with its whiny singsong that sounded like bastardized German. Hilda covered her mouth to stifle her giggles.

As her parents pulled her away, Hilda stared backward at the ugly assemblage. Who were they? People like them didn't exist in Berlin!

Refugees, her parents told her, refugees fleeing the Bolsheviks, newly arrived from Russia. "They are Jews," her mother said. "But different. Not Jews like us.

"They are *eastern* Jews," her mother continued, lips curling.

From then on, the favorite pastime of Hilda and Philip was to play what they dubbed the Refugee Game. Hilda would pull a black girdle of her mother's upside down on her hair; Philip draped one of his mother's white shawls over his head and shoulders. They danced around one another, squinting and pulling imaginary coins out of their pocket, pretending to run to catch a train or hawk wilting vegetables. Outside in their building's enclosed courtyard, Philip dared to imitate their strange babble and then stroke comically on imaginary side locks. Hilda erupted in laughter.

Then, incredibly, Hilda found herself forced to be a refugee for real.

In the spring of 1939, no lilac blossoms filled the vase in their salon.

On the eve of war, in the last heavy days of June 1939, Hilda and her mother arrived in the New World, not via Liberty Island to New York, but more than a thousand miles south in humid Havana.

In Cuba they waited in limbo for a visa to enter what they thought of as the real America.

Her mother darkened the room in Havana in the vain hope of keeping out the heat. She passed whole days fanning herself and rocking on a rickety cane chair.

Hilda walked through the markets in a dream, grazing past pungent guavas and swollen plantains. Wild green parrots streaked overhead, landing on the crests of lush trees. But Hilda could not shake gray Berlin from her thoughts.

Where did her father spend his days now that he had been barred from the bank? Did he sit and listen to Philip practice piano? She hoped Philip would understand to give him that pleasure. What Hilda would give to sit in the window seat watching Philip's fingers on the keys and hearing her father's purposeful steps approaching.

Letters arrived in thin, cheap envelopes, with stamps picturing the talons of Nazi eagles.

The news was never good. They were forced to give up the piano. And after that to relocate. Her father explained away the changes in delicate phrases: "We are much more comfortable in a smaller place, your brother and I, especially since we have no woman's touch to help.

"And we are lucky, Philip has been put to work in an armaments factory. That's fortunate. He has become classified as a worker essential to the war effort. It will keep Philip safe."

Fortunate? Hilda was appalled. She recalled Philip's delicate fingers that the family had protected so carefully for his piano. Philip was always excused from any task that might endanger them, however slightly. They didn't even allow him to put logs on the fireplace for fear an ember might jump out. She recalled bitterly the special cashmere-lined gloves his parents had ordered him from England, ashamed to have felt jealous.

"Not to lose hope, Liebchen," her father's letters ended. "Philip and I will rejoin soon. In the meantime, I am counting on my little perpetuum mobile."

Two words shouted out, repeated themselves in every letter: "Still waiting, still waiting…"

In Cuba their finances, which had seemed so unshakable, began to dwindle. Bank transfers from Berlin became infrequent, then abruptly ceased. Hilda had to scrimp.

She considered going to work, something that had never been in her future. Hilda began to calculate. What could she do in Cuba? Perhaps give violin lessons? She wouldn't need to do much communicating in Spanish for that.

It proved unnecessary.

Hilda was just beginning to achieve a stumbling fluency in Spanish when the American visas came through for her and her mother.

Despite herself, Hilda had been lulled into the rhythms of the tropics, palm trees against a red twilight, swaying women carrying sugar cane stalks in baskets upon their heads and calling out in singsong tones: "Two pesos! Sweet as a baby's kiss! Only two pesos!" Every day, Hilda bought a red-green stalk, sucking the sugar out of it.

And the music! Everywhere, on the streets, in cafés, beside the port. People singing, strumming, dancing. It opened a world of sensuality and rhythm.

Her mother booked passage to quit Cuba one week to the day after the permits arrived.

"Why so hasty?" asked Hilda, stunned by her mother's boundless energy after two years of immobility and by her frenzied commands to pack and leave.

"I've learned one lesson: not to rely on anything, never to delay," her mother answered. "One of the last things your papa told me: Don't delay!"

"But the American visa states it is valid for a whole year," protested Hilda. "And we can't leave now – this is the only address Papa knows! If we leave, he won't know where to find us. Papa is counting on me to wait for them here. I am his ambassador!"

But her mother would not budge.

"Never can we be fooled again to depend on this world being the same in the morning as it was the night before," she replied. "Any new emergency, any new bewildering regulation might appear overnight and imprison us in this Cuban oven forever. No, we get out now. Right now. Papa and Philip will find us; they will follow us to New York."

Displacement, Hilda realized, had taught her mother the last thing she was capable of learning: life was arbitrary, life had no rules, one must act quickly as soon as one had the chance.

* * *

Hilda's memories of the ship journey – their predawn docking in Norfolk, Virginia, their transfer to the passenger train for the trip to New York – were a jumble of blurry images.

Hilda was dry-mouthed, her eyes burned from the stale air, her feet felt numb, her ears throbbed from the dissonance of the wheels, and she felt nauseous from the starts and stops as the train bumped northward on a special temporary route to Grand Central Station. The long, monotonous journey over Delaware flat lands, shabby Maryland fishing coves and scrubby New Jersey farmland culminated in New York.

She remembered that moment with the pure sharp mega awareness that illogically accompanied extreme fatigue. When the train pulled into platform 5 at Grand Central under the bowels of Manhattan, Hilda felt the surging power of the new country. The ground reverberated around them.

Hilda and her mother emerged from the moist, subterranean darkness of the train platform up into the vaulted station, light streaming in from its immense skylight windows. "Like a cathedral," Hilda whispered.

It was the marble hall of Grand Central with its magnificent high ceiling, curving staircases, round portals branching out to the city beyond, that forever symbolized Hilda's American welcome. It was her real arrival.

Grand Central felt as cosmopolitan and comfortable as the majestic train stations of Germany. Her feeling of familiarity was somewhat diminished by the station's rainbow assortment of servicemen – chubby sailors in white looking like bewildered rabbits; blasé Army Air Force men in blue with cigarettes dangling from lips; rowdy recruits in khaki barely out of their teens; cool Marines striding across the polished floor as if assigned to protect it. But the crowds – purposeful, urban, oblivious of one another – were refreshing. Coming up for air in mid-Manhattan, Hilda felt almost at home – in another great metropolis.

So the Statue of Liberty never symbolized Hilda's America. Ellis Island conjured up heavy-legged peasants wearing babushkas, not young ladies awarded medals in excellence from the Berlin Violin Conservatory. No, Grand Central Station was her America.

And within the station, one symbol stood for her idiosyncratic osmosis into the new country: the big bronze, four-sided clock in the middle of the great hall, its bland moon-like countenances bearing indifferent but omnipotent witness.

As she gasped and groped for some tether amid the scurrying multitude of bodies, she fastened her eyes on the station clock looming like a sentinel in the middle of the floor. She looked at the translucent white face and bold numerals. Here, in the most unlikely of places, a messenger from her disappeared home. And it had not one face, but four, one pointing in each direction.

The looming clock was a giant replica of her father's waistcoat watch, his beloved Schaffhausen, the watch that every day of his life so elegantly hung on its silver chain. The New World could not be all bad, all foreign, all uncouth, if it boasted a timepiece that mimicked her father's.

* * *

If Lady Liberty was no beacon to Hilda, Grand Central retained its magic.

Whenever she found herself – however infrequently – at the terminal to see Phil off to summer camp in the Berkshires or to accompany Hermann and their navy blue Lincoln on the auto train to their annual summer holiday at Maine's Golf in the Pines resort, Hilda surrendered anew to the awe that had washed over her in the vast marble cavern on that first morning.

In later years, when Hilda found herself on the way to the optician on 42nd Street to have the arms of her tortoise shell frames tightened, or heading toward the tobacconist on the corner of Madison to replenish Hermann's English pipe tobacco, she liked to cut through the big station instead of walking outside on the street.

Hilda loved Grand Central most at Christmastime, that holiday of gifts and snow and music and spicy gingerbread sweetly biting the tongue. The crowds ballooned before Christmas, all in a rush to celebrate, to shop, to recreate once again the miracle of the baby in the manger.

Every December, the Hanover Nursery truck – "New Hampshire's Finest!" – stopped in front of the service entrance to Hilda's building. The driver checked his clipboard: "Gruenstein: use service entrance." When he opened the back hatch, the perfume of evergreens escaped into the gritty city air. He untied the rope around the burlap protector, and then Hilda's tree – Class A+, Color A+ – was rolled out on a dolly. "Gruenstein, Apt 4A" read the yellow tag attached to the base of its trunk. A trail of needles dotted the sidewalk as he ferried the tree up to Hilda's apartment.

Realizing to whose apartment the Christmas tree was delivered, some tenants nudged each other and eyed her in the elevator. Hilda could feel it. Harvey Gelbman's son from 7C stared at her in the lobby.

This past December, a week after the tree was delivered, she and Hermann exited the elevator and passed Rebecca Kimmel and her brother as they waited for the Ramaz School minivan to pick them up. As she and Hermann turned up the street, she was almost sure she heard the girl whisper to her brother, then laughter.

"Did you see those children?" Hilda snorted. "So badly behaved, so badly brought up! Ach, well what can you expect, after all?"

But as usual, stolid Hermann was in his own world and gave a small shrug of his shoulders, more to acknowledge that he heard Hilda speak than to agree or disagree with what she said.

Let parochial Jews turn up their noses at them. Hilda didn't care. It was the least she could do to bring back the joy of her holidays in Germany when her parents' mantel had borne a dwarf tree studded with candied fruit and hung with golden balls.

During the Christmas season, Hilda detoured to Schmitt's German bakery way over on Second Avenue where traditional Christmas cookies could be found. Holding the white box tied with red and white twine on her lap on the crosstown bus home, Hilda sniffed the confectioner's sugar that coated the star cookies and the triangular pine trees whose crinkly sugar was dyed bright festive green.

She set out the sweets during her weekly bridge game.

"Those winter holidays, the beauty of them, were my best experience, ja," Hilda said, her head bobbing up and down with vigor. "It was the best time for me.

"'Our miniature tree is a strain developed by horticulturists at our city's world-famous Ornamental Gardens,' my papa used to tell his guests who came to toast the holidays. They raised heavy crystal glasses filled with dark ruby port. And I still hear the voices of my mother's and my two aunts' first soprano, second soprano, and alto mingled in the crescendo of 'Silent Night' that they sang in high German."

"*Christmas?*" burst Henrietta, her steady bridge partner. "I understand if your family wasn't religious, fine, so you didn't follow traditions. But how in the world can Christmas still be that important? Especially after everything. In our house, we turned on backs on everything German after what happened."

How could Hilda explain that her family ceremonies were almost holy, even though the Christ child, Mary, and Joseph held no more religious meaning for them than the ancient Greek deities of Apollo or Athena?

How could she explain that keeping whatever she could of her old home helped blunt the trauma?

* * *

At 24, Hilda found herself adrift in the New World. With polished French, eight years of intensive Latin, and four of Greek, she could quote Racine and Goethe and Ovid. But of English, Hilda knew not one word.

Hilda's first New York months were bitter. She managed to find a job composing advertising copy at the offices of *Aufbau*, the weekly German Jewish newspaper. The notices all had the same depressing theme, differing only in the particulars. Either they were placed by other German-speaking refugees seeking work, or they were appeals for information about missing relatives.

"Seeking whereabouts: Family Knoll. Deported October 1941 from Grunewald Station, Berlin. Call TRafalgar 7-4144."

"Seeking information about whereabouts Hans Wilhelm Goldstein, age 27, birthmark over left eyebrow, last seen Genoa, Italy boarding steamer for Shanghai, September 1938. Contact Aufbau, refer to Notice #742."

The wordings said "whereabouts," but everybody knew that was a euphemism for "fate." If any appeal was ever answered, Hilda was unaware of it.

Noontimes, she descended in the clanking metal service elevator and exited the overheated building. She found space on a bench in the Broadway' central divider, flanked by old women holding canes and walkers. She was alert for weaving drunkards. She recoiled from homeless men in filthy, tattered rags. Unwrapping the lunch she prepared at home, Hilda ate her pumpernickel roll with a slice of salami so thin it was translucent.

As soon as they arrived in New York, Hilda went to the post office to mail a letter informing Papa of their address. The clerk took a look at the destination – Germany – and raised his eyebrows.

"I doubt this letter will go through, Miss," he said. "It has to travel via Sweden, and mail ships in the Atlantic these days are few and far between. And if it doesn't arrive, you will never know. Best not waste money on the stamps."

Hilda didn't know if the clerk had been right, but from Papa in Berlin there descended an ominous silence. Letters that had arrived in Cuba via the Red Cross stopped entirely when they were in New York.

Then came December 1941 and Pearl Harbor.

Hilda panicked. She made the rounds of the refugee boards, the international aid committees, anybody she could think of. She had to get word to Philip and Papa and tell them where she was.

Everywhere the answer was the same.

"Lady," they'd say, "our country is at war with Nazi Germany and their Jap allies! There are no more cables, no more lists from the Red Cross, no more consular connections. Give thanks to God you and your mother made it over."

Hilda returned agitated and angry to reproach her mother.

"I told you! I was right!" she rebuked. "We should not have left Cuba. Surely, Papa is still trying to reach us there. Maybe he is asking for our help, for us to notarize documents for him and Philip. To facilitate their exit papers. I am certain: Papa is trying to contact us! And we've abandoned them."

Her mother stared back in stolid silence.

"No hope, no hope, Liebchen," was all she would say.

"Of course there is hope!" screeched Hilda. "Somebody will get them out! The Himmelsteins have connections all over the world!"

She continued her tireless, futile knocking on all the doors.

Hilda returned home at dusk from her job at the newspaper to find her mother wrapped in a black shawl on the upholstered chair in their furnished studio in the apartment hotel on Upper Broadway. Her mother's mind, also wrapped in a black shawl, never recovered from their dislocation. To the end of her days, even in later years when Hilda visited her mother in her dark apartment off Queens Boulevard, her mother ordered Hilda to close the blinds against the tropical Cuban sun. She never stopped dolorously insisting they were still stranded in Havana, awaiting the magical visa to America eternally on the verge of arrival.

Four evenings a week, Hilda sat perched on child-sized chairs at the local elementary school, where she tackled learning English in night school. The classes bulged with immigrants. Hilda listened in vain for strains of German in the halls; she never exchanged a word with anyone.

Hilda hardly glanced at the newspaper headlines about battles in the Philippines, Burma, or the jungles of Indonesia. The war in the Pacific was of indifference to her except insofar as it might influence what was known as the European theater.

The struggle against Germany and Germany alone held her undivided attention. She felt as if she herself were landing on the beaches at Anzio. She lived through the amphibious invasion of Normandy. She was breathless and goose-bumped for a week during the final glorious liberation. She never drew a clear breath until after VE Day.

She waited for her father and Philip to emerge and reclaim them.

But Papa and Philip had not been lucky. Confirmation of their death came to Hilda and her mother privately, without headlines, about three years after war's end.

The official lists they received stated that in the summer of 1942, Hilda's father and brother were deported to Theresienstadt. There her father died "a natural death due to disease." A year later, Philip's name appeared on a transport list from Theresienstadt bound for Auschwitz. Nothing further was available.

Even then, Hilda and her mother could not bear to give up their Christmas celebrations. Even after Hitler, they wouldn't – couldn't – renounce the flickering candles and the exotic indoor scent of pine.

Papa and Philip would have wanted that.

Through the black years of the Nuremberg trials, the doctors' trials, the Rosenberg trial, the Eichmann trial, Hilda and her mother, as ever supremely insulated and unpolitical, recreated their prewar Noel rituals.

Hilda and her mother exchanged boxes of Yardley soap, exquisitely wrapped atomizers of Arpège, crocodile purses, kid gloves.

To Hermann, Hilda presented dress shirts from Sulka, cologne from Dunhill, once a Steuben Glass paperweight embedded with a flurry of snowflakes. Hermann accepted them politely, indifferent to the ornaments and the singing, yet humoring Hilda her eccentricities. Yearly, he bought US savings bonds for Hilda and Phil, $100 each.

Hilda's mother handed Hilda $25 in cash every December and every time repeated, "Go to FAO Schwarz and buy Philip a new Pullman wagon replica for his model train set."

Hilda tried to protest that the model train tracks sat collecting dust in Phil's room. But her mother repeated with conviction, "All boys love trains."

Hilda arranged riding lessons for Phil in Central Park. She loved walking over from Riverside and sitting on a bench next to the bridle path past where the lessons would take her son. Phil did not notice her small figure holding a newspaper up to her face as he cantered past beside his instructor, concentration on his face, endeavoring to hold the reins properly and keep his heels down. Hilda swelled with happiness and pride.

Phil begged to buy a horse of his own.

"We live in the city!" Hilda said in exasperation.

"Claremont Stables boards private horses," Phil answered stubbornly. "Charlie Summers has a horse, and also Peter Hayes. You could call their parents, ask them…"

"Out of the question," Hilda replied. "Private riding lessons in Central Park are luxury enough."

The unsatisfactory conversation was repeated every year until Phil was 15 when he abruptly announced he was tired of horses. From then on, he spent his time out roaming the city with his friends or in his room with the door shut.

The language of her new home remained Hilda's Achilles heel – heavy, slow, and accented as thickly as the lenses of her glasses. Even though she never ceased feeling she knew better than they did, that she dressed with more taste, and gestured with more finesse, Hilda hesitated before asking questions of natives. Especially of officials, even minor ones like postal clerks or librarians.

Speaking to the information operator on the telephone was a formidable penance avoided at all costs. Better not to call, better to wait until someone else could find the telephone number. She pushed her son in front of her if they took a bus route not completely familiar.

"Phil, you ask, ask the driver if he goes through straight to York Avenue," Hilda would prompt in a whisper.

But she kept her head high and her eyes focused on her bag or her gloves or the vitrine across the street as if it were from a position of strength that she did not talk to public employees. Nobody would say that Hilda ever looked diffident. Hilda made up for her public silences by holding forth at home.

As for the Jewish holidays, they came and passed without a nod. Only if the solemn day of Yom Kippur fell on a bridge game or a matinee day did she refrain from participating in her activities. Without a rational explanation why, it would not have passed Hilda's standards of propriety to appear at public festivities then.

One year, she planned a large dinner party for Hermann's fellow directors at the investment firm. She penned the invitations with her fountain pen in emerald green ink in her flowery slanted script. Envelopes were stacked in a neat pile on the hall table for Hermann to take to the office for his secretary to seal, stamp, and mail. True to form, Hermann double-checked a calendar and discovered that their party was scheduled on the eve of the Jewish New Year.

Luck was theirs that he had prevented this faux pas. Three-quarters of the firm – Hermann surmised even a higher percentage – would not have come. Worse would have been the loss of face. However nominally Jewish was the investment firm of Kohn & Altschuler, it would never want to risk offending wealthy clients. As Hermann explained to Hilda, all the leading firms were considered either 'Jewish' or 'Christian'. To be neither was to court raised eyebrows.

As the firm's internal accountant, Hermann was largely invisible to clients but indispensable to every partner. Nobody made a move at Kohn & Altschuler without first asking Hermann to crunch the numbers. Numbers were Hermann's best friends. He felt most at ease surrounded by numerical columns – the longer the better.

Hermann had another quality, crucial both at home and at work. He was unflappable. Both by numerals and by people. Hermann was used to frantic calls from enervated partners, men deep into middle age unnerved when the million-dollar bottom lines of expenditures stubbornly and mysteriously surpassed their conjoined twin – income.

Smiling benignly, Hermann pulled up his seat beside a rosewood table, laid the white stack of paper reverently upon its polished surface, hunched over, and happily began his slow, inexorable, and methodical investigation. It never happened that Hermann failed to uncover the errant loan, interest, or investment that somehow managed to escape proper book entry.

Hermann was an invisible cog in Kohn & Altschuler, but not one of its employees had any doubt he was the mortar that held it together. Once, a partner proud of his verbal acuity leaned toward Hilda over a martini and crowed, "Hermann puts the balance in the balance sheet."

Hermann's paycheck, bonuses, and stock options reflected his indispensability to Kohn & Altschuler. Although it was hard to discern from his retiring demeanor, Hermann was among its five highest paid executives.

Hermann reacted with similar equanimity when his secretary passed him anxious calls from Hilda.

"The water is running rust-colored in the bath!" she would cry. "I buzzed downstairs, but no one answered. Finally, I asked the elevator man, but he didn't know a thing. Imagine, the super is on his lunch break – the elevator man doesn't know until what time."

Hermann was called upon for electricity and antenna emergencies. "NBC is fine, but ABC and CBS are showing just gray static," she would say.

Or to avert crises in their social life. "Bonwit Teller telephoned that its head tailor has influenza and cannot supervise alterations on your black suit in time for the benefit."

Untangling every problem, unflappable, calming Hermann was ballast to Hilda's storms.

* * *

Hilda's Jewishness was an uncomfortable suit, a blazer pinching the insides of her arms with every bend of the elbow, the sharp stitches of the tag making a red spot on her skin. The too-tight waistband cutting into her stomach. She could not figure out how to put it on to sit right.

She never prayed, fasted, lit candles, or engaged in any faith-related ritual. Hilda had never been inside a temple until she came to the United States, and then fewer times than she could count on the fingers of one hand. Those other words for a house of worship of the Jewish persuasion – synagogue, *shul* – were so ethnic that the thought of uttering them made her cringe.

About liturgical or theological literature, she was completely in the dark. She was familiar with only one piece of Jewish literature, a translated story she heard read aloud by chance at a session of one of the adult enrichment courses Hilda took every Wednesday at the New School.

If Hilda had known Yiddish stories would be included in Origins of Modern Prose, she would have thought twice about signing up.

But she was not in the habit of reading syllabi. Hilda picked courses by their titles. She had enjoyed Russian Literature from Pushkin to Tolstoy, and then The Rococo in French Royal Décor. Best of all was Sculpture in Medici Florence.

The New School never disappointed. She loved to climb out of the subway onto the gray pavements of 14th Street, to bypass the mix of bohemian art students and poor housewives in shapeless coats on their way to finding bargains at Kleins in Union Square, and then enter into a rarified world of the 19th, 18th, or 17th century. Better yet the Renaissance. Hilda always chose courses about Europe.

Who would dream a New School course would deign to include authors whose very names had an embarrassingly comical ring – Sholom Aleichem, Mendele the Book Seller? People so far from what literature was meant to be.

If Hilda had guessed the origin of the story listed solely as *The Golden Orange*, she might well have skipped class and walked over to the galleries on Madison. Afterward indulged in a coffee crème at Rumplemeyer's. Made a stop for stockings at Albert's Hosiery. In short, made productive use of her afternoon.

Instead, she found herself far, far downtown, nowhere interesting to go but back up, trapped in the middle of the row of the overheated lecture hall. On the podium, a student borrowed from the Theater Department began delivering a dramatic reading of a story about Jews. From Eastern Europe, no less.

The text was a translation; the story was written originally in Yiddish. Written by and about people Hilda had no common language with, uncultured people with embarrassing rituals, nasal speech, outlandish clothes, and foreign customs. Most annoyingly, complete strangers that the world lumped as her brethren.

Hilda turned her head to the left, and then to the right; the seats on both sides were all taken. To climb over others' legs and have them shuffle and move aside books and bags would focus attention on her. She reluctantly decided the course of least resistance was to suffer through.

An impossibly provincial and destitute family in a poor village, the story recounted, received the gift of an orange in the midst of unheated winter. The orange was treated with reverence, considered miraculous. "Note how the fruit itself becomes a symbolic messenger for the Messiah," intoned the faculty coordinator in his unctuous introduction.

* * *

Golden oranges – the words triggered a memory of youth. With a jolt, against her conscious will, before Hilda's eyes passed the image of a rough wooden crate of oranges standing in their foyer in Berlin. Four, maybe five years before the end of their German life. It had been shipped to them by a client of her father. The unfinished wood full of splinters was itself exotic. The crate was stamped with export certificates in bright blue ink – "Port of Jaffa – Passed Agricultural Export of British High Commissioner" and an import certificate in red – "Port of Hamburg: Grade A Citrus; Safe for Human Consumption."

Helmut, their chauffeur, was summoned inside with his toolbox. He kneeled on the carpet upon which Hilda's mother hastily placed a protective sheet. Helmut pried open the wood.

Oranges lay exposed in ordered rows, like swollen jewels. Each was wrapped in waxy parchment paper embossed with the pale etching of a camel. The camel's bridle was held by a master with a black mustache and cylindrical fez atop his head. The fez was colored in faded crimson; a black tassel hung down its side. Below the drawing, the words "Product of Palestine" in a curly typeset mimicked a fanciful ancient alphabet. The dozens of camels side by side in the box looked like a caravan arriving from afar.

Her mother directed that the oranges be stored in the cool larder beside the kitchen. They remained taut and juicy for weeks and perfumed the apartment with hints of citrus.

Five at a time were set out for display on the baseboard of the foyer leading to the dining room. Arranged like a squat pyramid, the oranges' rich color was reflected in the prisms of the cut crystal bowl. Four formed a square, and the fifth, the most perfect specimen, balanced on top of them. The bowl was set on their beige tablecloth of Belgian lace. Every night as dinner came to a close Hilda's mother split an orange into sections and divided them onto four white porcelain dessert plates with gold trim around the scalloped edges. She handed the first plate to Hilda's papa, then Philip, then Hilda, and finally herself. After they finished, they dabbed their lips, then rolled up and replaced their individual cloth napkins into the initialed pewter napkin ring beside each place for use the following evening.

On the walls of the dining room, hooded eyes of dark bearded men in 18th-century portraits stared straight ahead. Their thin lips were set in a grim line. The surprising bright spot in each picture was the bizarre, white ruffled collar that reminded Hilda of the fans she made by creasing a sheet of paper backward and forward, forward and backward. And in the midst of this usually dour room, the startling color of oranges, carrying with them the memory of camels and exotic riders.

Hilda remembered her mother cutting into the fruit with a filigreed silver-handled knife, but she could not recall tasting it. The oranges remained static and luminous, untouchable and unchangeable, like the peaches on the white tablecloth by Cézanne hanging in everlastingly suspended animation on the same corner wall of the first room on the second floor of the Museum of Modern Art.

But if Hilda couldn't remember the taste, she did not forget her father's novel words. "These were grown in citrus groves in Palestina," he said. "What is more amazing, they were grown by people just like us. Our people who moved to a faraway place. Before they left, they were just like us."

"Not by men wearing a red fez?" asked Hilda.

Her father laughed. "Not at all. They are just the transporters. The farmers used to live in our country. They spoke German. They played piano. They knew chess. They studied Latin. And now they have earth under their fingernails as if they never learned past the third year of school. The son of the pharmacist Walter is one."

"And the engineer Rolf," interjected her mother. "The one who married Isolde the nurse. They left everyone behind. And everything. Isolde's mother told me they refused even to take their wedding linens. Now they have become land workers, agriculturists. Isolde, so fair-skinned, of all people standing out in the sun. Probably full of freckles. She writes twice a month, but still, she has broken her poor parents' hearts."

"Farmers. German Jewish farmers," her father continued. "Who could imagine such a bizarre world? And to think, once they were just like we are."

Hilda tried to picture her father wearing overalls and holding a rake like the gruff man in the public park who collected shriveled dead leaves. Or her mother with a coarse cotton kerchief holding a heavy load of round oranges in a checked apron. Maybe her father would look like the camel rider. Did the German Jewish growers trade in their homburgs to wear a fez?

Palestina, inhabited by people who had once been like her parents. Maybe underneath their clothes, they still were. Her brother told her he knew some acquaintances who had left for that faraway place – university students disillusioned with anarchy, who had lost hope that the old corrupt society of Europe could ever be improved

– students who termed themselves idealists before they started calling themselves Zionists.

Zionism became their new religion, Philip told her, and the boys were fervid converts. Hilda lost the thread of Philip's story. She had little interest in Zionists. She was never attracted to the fringe.

* * *

How ironic so many years later to find herself a virtual hostage to a story about Palestina in the auditorium of the New School. A story about an orange in a village? How unlikely!

"The last, ja, really so, the last thing I could want to listen to," Hilda almost blurted out loud. She was a cosmopolitan, a Berliner transplanted into a Manhattanite. Her son was a new American who bore no evidence of having former refugees as parents.

The poor, unrefined, untutored, unaware, uneducated Jews of the East – of Poland, Russia, Estonia, Latvia, Yugoslavia, Romania – all those countries beyond the crisp, clear, orderly borders of Germany, over the borders where no perfect geraniums grew on perfectly white windowsills framed by perfectly repaired and painted-green wooden shutters. Where hungry cats roamed the streets to forage in the offal, or to take the easy pickings that had spilled out onto the street. That had nothing to do with her.

Some nostalgic, sentimental story was not at all what Hilda had signed up to hear. A story that would twist poverty and turn it into quaintness, turn vulgarity into a bemused view of the world, redefine what was desperation into new-found determination.

Hilda would not buy into listening to a sanitized lie. Let those babies believe the story if they would, those Americans who are so coddled since birth that any fiction from the "Old Country," no matter how farfetched and lachrymose, brings a satisfied lump to their throats.

And to think they would concoct some story about oranges from Palestina. Well, Hilda was sure, those paupers could not have had the hard cash to buy one single orange even if they had heard they existed.

No, imported oranges had been destined for dignified dining rooms in Berlin. Dining rooms like her family's, the Himmelstein's. A spot of light in a sea of total harmony.

Hilda sat perched on her seat in the auditorium, the softness of her beaver coat caressing her knees. Her hands began their washing gestures, as if of their own accord.

As the story unraveled, the annoyance she had been prepared to experience burst into bloom. Jewish children were charmed by the exotic fruit. "Exotic, foo!" Hilda thought. "For these backward people a painting, a newspaper – goodness knows, even a pencil – might have seemed special."

* * *

Then suddenly and unpredictably, during the month of May 1967, Hilda felt that same constriction growing in her throat. The same tightness in the chest, the same sense of dread turning on the radio, the same stabs of panic that had weighed on her during the days and nights of the war. Her war.

As May wore on and attack upon Israel seemed more and more inevitable, Hilda ate less. She felt anxiety as soon as she awoke. She had nightmare visions of savage horsemen trampling through citrus orchards on galloping stallions, torching homes as they swept onward to victory.

Her involuntary involvement surprised her. Not only did she have no direct contact with Israel itself, but when she did think of the new country. it was with aloofness. In her eyes, Israel was a place built by Eastern European peasants and North African barbarians.

"Making the desert bloom." That cliché might be true, but even so, a desert would always be nothing more than desert.

* * *

From the beginning in America, her social ties were exclusively with other German Jewish refugees. Refugees who had enough luck, connections, or financial reserves to live in New York – the Jerusalem of the New World.

Every Tuesday and Friday. she met Gerta, Henrietta, and Margot for coffee and a slice of Linzer torte at the neighborhood Kuchen Pastry Shop, where everyone, including the owners, conversed in German. At Kuchen, they might as well have been on the Unter der Linden. On Wednesdays, they enjoyed small, elegant lunches at each other's homes. Then, arm in arm in tight-knit twosomes, they walked downtown to a Broadway matinee. Always a drama, never a musical.

Hilda returned home from the theater by bus or subway. Her upbringing did not countenance extravagance. Elegance by all means, but waste, never. Her son was more comfortable in taxis than she was.

* * *

Despite her unprepossessing looks and an overbite accentuating a receding chin, Hilda was married two years after the war to Hermann, he, too, the son of a financier, and transplanted to the New World thanks to Hitler.

The match was concocted by Uncle Otto, her father's brother. Otto appeared so quintessentially German that he lived openly in Berlin throughout the entire war and reported for work daily as a civilian provisions supervisor in army headquarters. No one, not even senior Nazi officers, thought to question his papers.

After the war ended, Otto returned to his brother's street to inspect Hilda's old apartment building. Otto found the building unscathed; it had escaped Allied bombings. He approached the beautiful oak doors with trepidation. Surely, the apartment would be denuded of its contents.

"But I found it almost completely intact." Otto wrote to Hilda and her mother. "Down to the heirloom furniture, exactly as your family lived with.

"I cornered the janitor. He told me that after they threw out your father and brother, the apartment was awarded as a prize promotion to a high Nazi official and his family. They slept under your quilts, ate on your porcelain. They pulled the cord on your curtains. Only the drawer that held the monogrammed silver cutlery was empty. That and Philip's piano. There is a sad gap in the salon with a faded spot on the carpet where it stood."

Otto had contacts. He arranged to have the Himmelstein's furniture and valuable items shipped to Hilda and her mother in New York.

Hilda's mother said bitterly, "Otto was able to save himself. He was able to salvage carpets. But he was unable to do anything to save Papa and Philip."

Otto moved to London shortly thereafter. He wrote again to Hilda's mother, a letter Hilda read when her mother stared at it without moving her eyes down the page. "I have found a perfect potential groom for your young maiden. Somebody to do honor to my late brother. Hermann Gruenstein's family is not from Germany," he admitted. "They were Viennese. But close enough. Rest assured, Hermann is *unsere* – one of us."

So influential and reputable was the Himmelstein family aura that it survived the war and had just enough life in it even in 1947 to ensure Hilda's nuptials and guaranteed financial comfort.

Hilda gave up her job at the *Aufbau* newspaper. She no longer needed to work.

Most important for the family honor, Hilda remained in the tight circle of their kind of people, not breaking ranks, keeping away from the vulgar, the raucous, the nouveau riche merchants with their Miami Beach vacations and their beach club cabanas.

After Hilda's marriage to Hermann, Hilda's mother told her, "Now there is only one Himmelstein left, Uncle Otto in London. Only Otto remains of your papa's venerable family! The Himmelsteins, whose name shone on the bronze plaque of their private bank in Berlin for generations."

Hilda's mother went on recounting her lost world. "In the prosperous early years of the century before the Great War, the bank expanded to branches in Düsseldorf, Munich, and Cologne," she said.

Every Christmas, Otto sent his engraved card and a holiday basket of plum pudding from Fortnum & Mason. But in 1960, Hilda instead received a cable from London followed by a mailed announcement in Gothic letters bordered in black. Uncle Otto had passed away – and the Himmelstein name expired with him.

Hilda's marriage to Hermann rescued her both from having to earn her bread and from the need to make a true foray into America. She stayed on the sidelines – on the chaise longue in her apartment with legs wrapped in an angora throw, on the plush seats of their Lincoln Continental. Twice she luxuriated in the first-class lounge of the ocean liner *Ile de France* on voyages en route to summer in the French Alps.

She considered it a coup to have been chosen to serve as a volunteer at the Hollenberg Art Foundation, advising them on acquisitions.

Hilda met her friends and arranged dinner parties for foreign clients from Hermann's firm. She glittered in German and French and over the years picked up passable Italian.

After Hilda left Havana, she had no cause to speak Spanish. But she understood much of the loud language that the Puerto Ricans called out to each other on the side streets outside the rundown brownstones of the West Side. Sometimes she sat down on a fire hydrant, ostensibly to fix her shoe, and listened to the Latino melodies and drum music emanating from open windows.

And though she listened to classical music without interruption on the radio, Hilda found it too painful a memory to attend live concerts. She herself never picked up a violin again after she left Berlin.

* * *

Some might posit that her son, Philip, named after her beloved brother, was almost an afterthought. True to the outward modesty stressed by her upbringing, Hilda did not tout her son out loud.

Nevertheless, he was the apple of her eye. She admired him from birth, watched him endlessly in his crib, bought him imported woolen blankets from England and knit rompers from Italy. She never stinted on Philip, spending a small fortune on sailing camps in Massachusetts, on winter ski outings. She knew that boarding school would offer the most outstanding education, but she could not bear to part from her only son, so she picked out for him one of the city's prestigious private boys' schools.

In fourth grade, her son announced that everybody in school called him Phil and that he would only answer to that name from then on. The child was stubborn and stuck to his guns, not turning his head when Hilda tried to keep addressing him as Philip. So Philip became Phil. Hilda never tired, though, of looking for resemblances between her son and the brother she had lost, and of trying to find a hint of Philip in Phil's expressions. Phil, though, showed no affinity for music.

Phil had friends. He did passably well in his studies. And he fit in. That was paramount to Hilda.

* * *

Hilda heard that Jews in America were offering refuge to relatives in Israel. She did not have one relative or acquaintance in Israel. Hermann, though, had distant cousins there. Grandchildren of his grandmother's brother. The brother moved to Palestine after the disgrace of failing his matriculation exams for the third time. It was the scandal of this failure in Hermann's family that bore the retelling, this black sheep who decamped from the Austro-Hungarian Empire to make his life in the wilds of the desert. She had once heard their new name, something she was told had the word "lion" or another wild animal in it, something they might have adopted from the Bible.

She found herself imagining her family hosting a valiant couple, chauffeuring them from the airport as they arrived with farmers' clothes and a violin case, hearing them gasp at the skyline as they approached Manhattan over the bridge. She and Hermann would put them up until the danger passed; they would save their lives.

But Hermann had no idea in which town the people lived, didn't even precisely recall their names. He would have to write letters to cousins in Europe, make inquiries. Who knows how much time it would take to track them down? And, Hermann pointed out, who knew how many children they had? Would there be room in the apartment?

Hermann was interested in the Middle East crisis, of course; all world events concerned him in that they had the potential to affect the firm. But his smiling face remained cheerful and unruffled as he went forth freshly showered and cologned to meet his days.

He reminded her that he would have a heavy schedule in June as the firm was due to receive a visit from three generations of one of its leading investor families. "Steel people from Pittsburgh," he called them. Hermann would be tied up for the two days they would be sitting in back-to-back meetings, and he and Hilda would be among the hosts for the dinner reception at the Four Seasons one night and a Broadway musical the firm had booked the other.

Well, Hilda thought, maybe it's all the better. How would they have managed to talk to these remote cousins of her husband's? She imagined the state of numbness in which they would arrive and could not picture how she, Hermann, and Phil could relate their lives to those of rural people so unlike themselves, even if they were fleeing advancing war.

In any case, Hilda had only a hazy idea of the geography of the Holy Land. The only place names that popped to mind were Jerusalem and Nazareth. She recognized the rocky wilderness in which Moses, Jesus, and various saints were pictured from paintings at the Frick and the Met.

The end of May and the first days of June boasted the most perfect weather of the year.

But Hilda was glued to the news. She went out only for the most necessary of appointments. On the first of June, she went to the hairdresser for her touch-up. Six weeks had passed and there was an unmistakable, if faint, line of white on her scalp contrasting with the raven black of her hair.

This morning, the second of June, after the petition girls left, Hilda wandered around the apartment, fretting about the ominous news.

But she would not permit herself to let any day pass without accomplishment.

Mid-morning she forced herself downtown to pick up her bag, even though the season for wearing brown alligator had passed. If she left it in the shop any longer, Mr. Scaparetti might assume she was no longer attached to it and not keep it stored in the best location safe from humidity and sunlight.

The phone rang as she was leaving.

"I am out of the door, Margot," Hilda told her friend, "headed for downtown."

"Enjoy," Margot said. "Enjoy this beautiful day. Our New York is so lucky for walking. And if you by chance pass Carnegie Hall, can you take a glance at the posters outside? I heard a rumor Vladimir Horowitz plays Tchaikovsky in October."

"If he is, tickets surely will be so hard to achieve."

"Impossible!" laughed Margot. "Still..."

"I will," Hilda promised.

Margot was right. Hilda saw no reason to waste a bus fare on such a beautiful day. She was a firm advocate of brisk walks. A walk had to do her good.

She cut across 57th Street, a good opportunity to look at the book titles displayed in Rizzoli. As she mingled among the elegant, fast-paced pedestrians walking past the Russian Tea Room, Hilda tried to imagine how she would feel among a crowd in Jerusalem, the Jewish capital.

But she could not picture it. Who would have the heart to go about daily business when the adult males had all been mobilized? The news reported that teenage boys the age of Phil were being called upon to direct traffic and deliver mail.

Her Phil, she knew, was attending a rehearsal for his commencement exercises and was then due to pick up his rented tux for the senior prom.

* * *

In the weeks before she and her mother had left Berlin, their life supposedly continued as normal. Each morning, she went to the music theory tutor to continue preparing for the admission audition to the advanced Conservancy program in violin, even though it had become a program she was barred by law from attending.

When she came back mid-afternoon, Hilda found her mother at the window seat in their Berlin apartment looking through the translucent white curtain at the familiar street below, heavy with premonitions of displacement.

Every evening, her father told them in tones he tried to make reassuring that the visas were sure to come through very soon, imminently as a matter of fact. He and her brother would follow as soon as he could ensure the transfer of their capital, of their artwork, and of their gold bullion to a safer location in Europe. He mentioned in particular Austrian Prudential, his bank's London branch where Uncle Otto later secured a position, and where her husband's Viennese father and grandfather had been honorary directors.

In those last weeks, Hilda's father strained to seem normal. He put on a clean white shirt every morning, pressed stiff, and his mother-of-pearl cufflinks, the ones with the bluest sheen. He shined his shoes, shoes he hadn't walked on enough to accumulate even a thin film of dust. Then he sat immobile for hours by the telephone waiting, waiting – for news, for visas, for salvation. There was no work left. The white shirt was a sham. The shined shoes were a sham. But they went together with his life. As long as he lived his life, it had to retain its veneer.

The night before their departure, Hilda took a scissor out of her mother's carved sewing box and cut off one of Philip's bone buttons from his winter coat. She sneaked into her parents' dressing room and pocketed one of her father's mother-of-pearl cufflinks. She put the button and cufflink together with her watch in its soft felt case and saved them through her days in Cuba and their resettlement in New York. The cufflink and the button would rejoin their owners when they were reunited, Hilda told herself. Now they lay in the very back of her jewelry box. Hilda rarely took them out of the felt case, but she never forgot they were there.

Hilda left Berlin angry. Those last months in Berlin might have been a defense against reality, yes, but they were a grotesque parody. Having afternoon tea from the pewter tea set, strolling arm in arm in public gardens on Saturday afternoons, watching dancing stone nymphs among the jets of the fountain – it was all a pretense.

* * *

Perhaps those same sentiments now engulfed families in Israel. In Israel, where despite the cacti and the sand they undoubtedly also had entrance exams to a music conservatory, and Saturday outings to public gardens, maybe even fountains.

A girl of 20, the same age as she had been in 1939, might be rushing down the street, anxious not to be out in the open, shielding both her head and an amber violin, afraid that an Egyptian MiG bomber might streak overhead. Or anxious that the bomb sirens would start to scream and the doors to the public shelters slam shut before she had time to descend from the trolley.

Now, in 1967, the circle seemed to be starting again. There was no threat to her, not here in Manhattan, Hilda knew that, but she could not push away her apprehension by the force of pure logic.

Hilda walked down 57th Street, ignoring the men's seersuckers and women's silks in store windows she usually would have admired. Stores, she was fond of thinking, that would have been to her father's taste.

Deep in thought, Hilda was already at the corner of Fifth Avenue when she realized she had passed Carnegie Hall without stopping to check the concert schedule for Margot. Her feet felt too heavy to retrace her steps, not even on the opposite side of the street, where she normally enjoyed looking into the windows of store after store.

Of all New York streets, wide 57th Street reminded her of Berlin – its mix of stately neoclassical public buildings like the Art Students League and impressive retail stores like the Steinway piano showroom. Its unassuming but famous white-tableclothed restaurants and upscale jewelry stores with glittering emeralds. It was where Hilda ordered their imported sheets and had hand-stitched monograms affixed, two interlacing H's tastefully bracketing the G: Hilda, Hermann, Gruenstein. Yes, 57th Street was unpretentiously pretentious.

Hilda saw with dismay it was already 12:30. Live television broadcasts of Middle East developments from the United Nations were to begin at two o'clock. Abba Eban himself was scheduled to address the General Assembly.

She hurried toward the handbag store.

Turning the corner onto Fifth Avenue, Hilda saw a swarming concentration of people halfway down the block. A white blotch was in the middle, twisting and writhing like a moving creature. As she got closer, the white spot turned out to be an ordinary bedsheet, an enormous one. The sheet was suspended horizontally, waist-high above the sidewalk. Each corner was held up by an adolescent boy dressed identically entirely in black: knee-length black wool coat, black oxford shoes, brimmed black hat pushed back on the head, black glasses, wispy strands of first beard sprouting on faces red with exertion. Their necks glistened with perspiration, their bony fingers almost as white as the sheet they held.

"Give money for Israel!" one wheedled in a high-pitched voice. "Be generous, generous – save the Jewish children of Jerusalem from Arab murderers! Money for Israel here!"

Another held a megaphone into which he shouted a repetitive chant: "Gen-er-ous! Gen-er-ous!" With his other hand, he beat on his thigh in rhythm to the syllables.

A youth in a black skullcap with a dough-like white face held up a banner with the blue Star of David, and under it printed in red block letters: "Help us live!" He danced from foot to foot so that the sign rocked from side to side like a banner at one of Phil's basketball games.

Pedestrians stared at the unheard-of spectacle on the street flanked by luxury brands like Tiffany's and Harry Winston and Elizabeth Arden. Passersby reached into their pockets or drew wallets out of purses and tossed money into the sheet. Getting closer, Hilda saw the sheet was weighted down with hundreds – maybe thousands – of jingling coins. The boys shook the sheet as they hawked out their appeal, tossing up the money in a jangling display.

Approaching closer, Hilda noticed many green bills floating inside. Hilda's stomach turned. Conflicting thoughts raged inside her. She felt acute embarrassment, even anger at this spectacle. Who had the bad taste to organize this shameless hawking in the heart of elegant Fifth Avenue? But at the same time, here was finally a chance to perform some action besides worrying and watching television.

She dug into her bag and, in a once-in-a-lifetime gesture uncharacteristic of her frugality, yanked out the entire thick wad of bills inside and pitched them all uncounted into the edge of the sheet.

Two ten-dollar bills missed the target and wafted down toward the sidewalk. The sharp-eyed bearer of the nearest corner of the sheet swooped down, snatched up the two tens, and launched them like paper airplanes, one after the other, where they both landed gracefully in the center of the sheet on top of the mound of money.

Hilda shivered with dismay and embarrassment. Thank goodness, nobody was looking.

Then she heard it, the high-pitched teenage voice booming over the megaphone. "Follow this good woman's lead, people. Give gen-er-ous."

The chant began anew. "Gen-er-ous! Gen-er-ous!"

The youth nearest her cried in a voice so loud that the crowd fell momentarily quiet. "Lady, lady, thank you for your help!" he said. "A real Jewish heart. This lady looks like a *shiksa*, no? But when the chips are down, she stands with her fellow Jews!"

The people in the crowd – office workers in their shirtsleeves, shoppers swinging glossy shopping bags, models, tourists – craned their heads to focus on Hilda.

"Ladies and gentlemen!" he called. "You've just witnessed an example to the Jewish people here in exile!

"Lady, lady!" he said as he sidled up to her.

Hilda avoided his glance. She strode toward the periphery of the throng.

The young man in the black outfit made to follow her. "Tell the people to be like you, *nu*. What's your name lady? Lady! Missus!"

She managed to evade him.

Finally, the boy gave up and switched tacks. "Better listen to the news today, ladies and gentlemen," he said.

As she fled, Hilda heard him boom into the megaphone: "The smart money says there's a big breakthrough coming up. An important development. Maybe even the president will help out. In the meantime, be generous, save your people. *Never again!*"

Hilda was rushing now, walking rapidly, hugging the inner edge of the sidewalk, almost brushing the walls of the buildings, her head bent, melting into the noonday crowd. Furious that no less repulsive representatives could be found. That people might identify her with *them*.

But unaccountably, as she proceeded, Hilda's apprehension rose. She gave only the most perfunctory greetings to Mr. Scaparetti, of whom she was an old and consistent customer.

"Here it is!" Mr. Scaparetti beamed as he produced Hilda's bag. "See how I gave it the finest workmanship – better even than the original." He raised his forefinger to pursed lips and gave an audible kiss. "Now you will get many years – yes, many more years – of pleasure and pride."

Hilda glanced down, hardly noticing the reweaving of the leather reattached to the clasp.

She reached for her wallet to pay. But the billfold was empty. When she flung the bills on the sheet, she neglected to leave any money inside. She rummaged around in her purse hoping to come across a stray bill, a 20, even a ten. But she found nothing but her handkerchief and a lipstick.

Mr. Scaparetti's face darkened momentarily at her mumbled excuses, but he recovered quickly.

"No need for explanation, dear madam," he said. "Such a good old customer as you, your credit is good with me." He reverently wrapped the renewed handbag in a soft flannel pouch, placed it in a shopping bag, and with a flourish presented it to Hilda.

Hilda barely took notice. She thought back to the words of the brash young money collector. Could he be called a beggar? What big news did he have access to? What announcement was imminent? Did he and his people have special sources of information not available to all?

She couldn't wait to find out. Today, she couldn't bear to travel on the bus with its slow progress, stopping to pick up and disgorge passengers every two blocks.

Hilda's arm shot up to hail a cab. She would borrow the fare from the doorman when she arrived, something she had never dreamed she might do.

Leaning forward, she told the driver her address in a voice as urgent as if the two of them were in the midst of wartime chaos right here and now.

The driver maneuvered westward through the side street.

"Take the park – it'll be fastest this time of day," Hilda couldn't help blurting out.

"No problem, lady. Just leave my job to me."

He glanced back at her. "Relax, lady, relax," he said. "Nobody's going to fall off the edge of the Earth. It's going to keep turning like it always does."

Hilda leaned back, grateful somebody, even a stranger, was taking care of her. Her cheeks were hot. She marveled at her compulsion to fling away so much money – goodness knows how much – to precisely the type of Jews who most repelled her. Well, she thought, they were just the medium to reach a good cause. But she suspected that didn't explain it all, and she felt a curious disequilibrium, scornful of both the money collectors and of herself.

Phil popped into mind. She wished that it was later in the afternoon after school had ended and that she would find him at home. She wanted to spill out the incident to him.

She needed to impress on Phil that if only somebody, somewhere, had taken action for his namesake, Philip, he would have an uncle today, and a grandfather. That if they had stuck together, taken stock of the danger, then the worst might not have happened. But then, she realized, she would not be sitting here in a taxi waiting for the light to change on Central Park South. She might not be married to Hermann. And Phil? Where would he be? Would he even exist? Hilda's thoughts were confused. There was no way to rearrange the past.

Still, she thought there was a lesson here somewhere, something important to convey to Phil.

Then Hilda reconsidered. The repellent, scrawny boys, their coarse epithets barked into the microphone, their comical attire – she knew any description she gave her son must leave out the identity of these stereotypical scroungers.

No, she would paint the scene neutrally: describe that right on sophisticated Fifth Avenue in the middle of the day, hundreds were stopping to dig into their pockets and enthusiastically give money for the cause of Israel's survival. She would emphasize the impromptu sympathy – surprising and heartwarming – that threats to the Jewish land were arousing in the elegant heart of America.

Her anxiety grew to get home and turn on the news. Was the peace still holding? Or were Egyptian or Syrian planes strafing Israeli cities? Would King Hussein follow the sage advice of the Americans and keep Jordan neutral so that if war did break out, Israel would not have to fight enemies on many simultaneous fronts? Would Abba Eban have anything to announce today? And what about the president, the new development that the Jew on Fifth Avenue hinted about? Could he really know something more than the news stations? Would the president use his leverage to strong-arm a compromise to avoid war? She prayed he would.

As she opened the door, keys still in the lock, Hilda heard steps coming toward the hall vestibule.

Joy washed over Hilda. Phil was home.

"School over so early?" she asked.

"Hey Momsie, did you forget? Regular days are already over."

Of course. Phil's class was on the light, staggered schedule leading up to graduation.

Phil loped past her into the living room, flopping down on the couch and draping his legs over the side.

"Greatest thing just happened," he grinned. "We won!"

Hilda waited with a catch in her throat, fingers gripping the front door knob.

Won? Could the news be that good? Had Nasser yielded to international pressure to start direct negotiations?

"Won!" she exclaimed. "How? When? How did we win?" This stunning news so unimaginably good shone amid the dark predictions of the last few days. Maybe the Arab countries had backed down altogether and the threat was lifted?

"Did you hear a bulletin on the radio?" Hilda cried. "Tell me."

"Radio? Radio? Of course not on the radio!" retorted Philip, his tone puzzled.

"You remember the bike trip over the Sierra Nevada's I signed up for this summer? Remember how I didn't have any friend to go with? That Jake's parents grounded him for failing trig?

"Well, Jake's father finally agreed. Since Jake brought up his grade to a C minus, his dad is letting him go.

"So Jake and I have won! We will be rooming together. Now I won't be alone among a bunch of losers, like sissy preppies from Andover. Finally, finally – the summer's starting to really take off!"

The words tumbled from her American son's lips. They sounded like gibberish. She stood still, dry-mouthed. She couldn't place exactly which boy Jake was. She vaguely recalled that she and Hermann had been introduced to his overweight father in a pink shirt riding on a cart at a golf resort.

"Actually, great you got home this early," continued Phil. "If we rush, we might still have time this afternoon to go down to Abercrombie's and order my biking outfits. Macy's might carry some, but they recommended Abercrombie & Fitch as the official outfitter, and they sure will have it all."

Hilda didn't respond.

"Come on, Momsie! I know you love the stuff at Abercrombie's, too. We can look around together. And there aren't many weeks left before my trip leaves. Western Expeditions sent a list of all the gear we have to take." Phil waved a printed paper at Hilda and began to read out loud, "Four short-sleeved shirts, two long-sleeved flannel shirts, rain jacket, mess kit..."

Hilda stood still. "Not today, Phil," was all she could manage. "No, no, not today." With quick steps, she reached the living room and flicked on the television.

But once there, she turned again to face him.

"Oh, darling Phil," Hilda burst out. "I am so happy to have you!"

Phil, startled, stared at his mother. Then he unfolded himself from the couch and bounded over to her. Like he hadn't done since he was a small boy, Phil threw his arms around Hilda. Now she was the small one.

"Thanks, Momsie," he said. "Thanks for everything!"

The announcer's words cut in, solemn and commanding. "Normal programming interrupted, we bring you this special CBS report direct from United Nations Headquarters in New York City!"

Hilda had made it just in time.

She perched herself on the edge of the heirloom lion's paw mahogany chair opposite the television console. She leaned forward.

The General Assembly Hall was packed with delegates. Close-ups showed somber expressions on the faces seated row upon curving row.

Ambassador Eban, carrying his dense bulk with assurance and dignity, advanced regally up to the speaking podium, graceful as a ship of state. Hilda let out her breath, reassured even before Eban opened his mouth or uttered any words.

Such a majestic spokesman would never let the Israelites be driven into the sea.

There was the expectant hush, a hush that extended farther than the United Nations. It reached Hilda's apartment and around the world.

Hilda sat transfixed, immobile except for her hands. The right palm caressed the back of her left hand. Then the left palm flitted over her right hand. The nervous habit repeated again, and again. Hilda's hands flew over each other like two nervous birds.

As she waited, a novel question burst into Hilda's mind, a question uncharacteristic of her reserve and refinement. "After all we have been through," she thought to herself, "don't we have the right to happiness?"

Unconsciously, and for the first time, Hilda used the word "we."

GLOSSARY

Ach Liebchen - Oh sweetheart (German)

Aktion - Nazi term for forced assembly of Jews, usually for deportation, discipline, or murder (German)

Alte - old man (German)

Arbeitet - to work (German)

Chelmno - Nazi extermination camp in Poland

Einsatzgruppen - Nazi mobile killing squads (German)

Fraulein - young woman (German)

HIAS - Hebrew Immigrant Aid Society

Jude - Jew (German)

Konzentration - concentration (German)

Kristallnacht - "Night of the Broken Glass." Night of 1938 Nazi violence in Germany against Jews (German)

Laissez Passer - travel permit according the right to passage

Luftwaffe - aviation arm of Nazi Germany's armed forces

Mein Mann - my husband (German)

Oswiecim - Town in Poland. Site of Auschwitz-Birkenau concentration camp

Pan - Mr. (Polish)

Pania - Mrs. (Polish)

Polizei - police (German)

SA - Initials of Sturmabteilung: Storm Troopers, a Nazi paramilitary organization. (German)

Sabra - native Israeli (Hebrew slang)

Shiksa - Gentile woman (Yiddish)

Tapuz - orange (Hebrew)

Wannsee Conference - 1942 conference at which Nazis adopted the Final Solution calling for the annihilation of European Jewry

Wehrmacht - armed forces of Nazi Germany

Zisele - my sweet (Yiddish)

Zloty - Polish currency

ACKNOWLEDGMENTS

Gratitude to my cousins Gloria and Kenneth Price for their unflagging support and encouragement and to my friend and colleague Inna Shapiro for her superior profession eye and generosity in taking this journey with me. They have made all the difference.

Appreciation for the expert technical assistance of Isaac Arzi and to photographer Ido Lore.

Thankful acknowledgment to the following publications in which these stories first appeared:

- German Lessons in *Israel Short Stories*, Ang-Lit. Press (2011)
- Three Hundred Zlotys in *arc30* (2023)

ABOUT THE AUTHOR

Helen Schary Motro is a writer and attorney whose award-winning writing spans the gamut of opinion journalism in the world's leading press, including the *New York Times*, *Christian Science Monitor*, *Boston Globe*, *Haaretz*, and *Newsweek*.

Motro is recipient of the Common Ground Award for Journalism in the Middle East. She taught law at Tel Aviv University and was a columnist for The Jerusalem Post.

Author of the non-fiction *Maneuvering Between the Headlines*, her short stories, poetry, and essays appear in anthologies and magazines.

As the child of survivors, Motro has written extensively on the Holocaust and the experience of the Second Generation.

AMSTERDAM PUBLISHERS HOLOCAUST LIBRARY

The series **Holocaust Survivor Memoirs World War II** consists of the following autobiographies of survivors:

Outcry. Holocaust Memoirs, by Manny Steinberg

Hank Brodt Holocaust Memoirs. A Candle and a Promise, by Deborah Donnelly

The Dead Years. Holocaust Memoirs, by Joseph Schupack

Rescued from the Ashes. The Diary of Leokadia Schmidt, Survivor of the Warsaw Ghetto, by Leokadia Schmidt

My Lvov. Holocaust Memoir of a twelve-year-old Girl, by Janina Hescheles

Remembering Ravensbrück. From Holocaust to Healing, by Natalie Hess

Wolf. A Story of Hate, by Zeev Scheinwald with Ella Scheinwald

Save my Children. An Astonishing Tale of Survival and its Unlikely Hero, by Leon Kleiner with Edwin Stepp

Holocaust Memoirs of a Bergen-Belsen Survivor & Classmate of Anne Frank, by Nanette Blitz Konig

Defiant German - Defiant Jew. A Holocaust Memoir from inside the Third Reich, by Walter Leopold with Les Leopold

In a Land of Forest and Darkness. The Holocaust Story of two Jewish Partisans, by Sara Lustigman Omelinski

Holocaust Memories. Annihilation and Survival in Slovakia, by Paul Davidovits

From Auschwitz with Love. The Inspiring Memoir of Two Sisters' Survival, Devotion and Triumph Told by Manci Grunberger Beran & Ruth Grunberger Mermelstein, by Daniel Seymour

Remetz. Resistance Fighter and Survivor of the Warsaw Ghetto, by Jan Yohay Remetz

My March Through Hell. A Young Girl's Terrifying Journey to Survival, by Halina Kleiner with Edwin Stepp

Roman's Journey, by Roman Halter

Beyond Borders. Escaping the Holocaust and Fighting the Nazis. 1938-1948, by Rudi Haymann

The Engineers. A memoir of survival through World War II in Poland and Hungary, by Henry Reiss

A Spark of Hope. An Autobiography, by Luba Wrobel Goldberg

The series **Holocaust Survivor True Stories** consists of the following biographies:

Among the Reeds. The true story of how a family survived the Holocaust, by Tammy Bottner

A Holocaust Memoir of Love & Resilience. Mama's Survival from Lithuania to America, by Ettie Zilber

Living among the Dead. My Grandmother's Holocaust Survival Story of Love and Strength, by Adena Bernstein Astrowsky

Heart Songs. A Holocaust Memoir, by Barbara Gilford

Shoes of the Shoah. The Tomorrow of Yesterday, by Dorothy Pierce

Hidden in Berlin. A Holocaust Memoir, by Evelyn Joseph Grossman

Separated Together. The Incredible True WWII Story of Soulmates Stranded an Ocean Apart, by Kenneth P. Price, Ph.D.

The Man Across the River. The incredible story of one man's will to survive the Holocaust, by Zvi Wiesenfeld

If Anyone Calls, Tell Them I Died. A Memoir, by Emanuel (Manu) Rosen

The House on Thrömerstrasse. A Story of Rebirth and Renewal in the Wake of the Holocaust, by Ron Vincent

Dancing with my Father. His hidden past. Her quest for truth. How Nazi Vienna shaped a family's identity, by Jo Sorochinsky

The Story Keeper. Weaving the Threads of Time and Memory - A Memoir, by Fred Feldman

Krisia's Silence. The Girl who was not on Schindler's List, by Ronny Hein

Defying Death on the Danube. A Holocaust Survival Story, by Debbie J. Callahan with Henry Stern

A Doorway to Heroism. A decorated German-Jewish Soldier who became an American Hero, by Rabbi W. Jack Romberg

The Shoemaker's Son. The Life of a Holocaust Resister, by Laura Beth Bakst

The Redhead of Auschwitz. A True Story, by Nechama Birnbaum

Land of Many Bridges. My Father's Story, by Bela Ruth Samuel Tenenholtz

Creating Beauty from the Abyss. The Amazing Story of Sam Herciger, Auschwitz Survivor and Artist, by Lesley Ann Richardson

On Sunny Days We Sang. A Holocaust Story of Survival and Resilience, by Jeannette Grunhaus de Gelman

Painful Joy. A Holocaust Family Memoir, by Max J. Friedman

I Give You My Heart. A True Story of Courage and Survival, by Wendy Holden

In the Time of Madmen, by Mark A. Prelas

Monsters and Miracles. Horror, Heroes and the Holocaust, by Ira Wesley Kitmacher

Flower of Vlora. Growing up Jewish in Communist Albania, by Anna Kohen

Aftermath: Coming of Age on Three Continents. A Memoir, by Annette Libeskind Berkovits

Not a real Enemy. The True Story of a Hungarian Jewish Man's Fight for Freedom, by Robert Wolf

Zaidy's War. Four Armies, Three Continents, Two Brothers. One Man's Impossible Story of Endurance, by Martin Bodek

The Glassmaker's Son. Looking for the World my Father left behind in Nazi Germany, by Peter Kupfer

The Apprentice of Buchenwald. The True Story of the Teenage Boy Who Sabotaged Hitler's War Machine, by Oren Schneider

Good for a Single Journey, by Helen Joyce

Burying the Ghosts. She escaped Nazi Germany only to have her life torn apart by the woman she saved from the camps: her mother, by Sonia Case

American Wolf. From Nazi Refugee to American Spy. A True Story, by Audrey Birnbaum

Bipolar Refugee. A Saga of Survival and Resilience, by Peter Wiesner

In the Wake of Madness. My Family's Escape from the Nazis, by Bettie Lennett Denny

Before the Beginning and After the End, by Hymie Anisman

I Will Give Them an Everlasting Name. Jacksonville's Stories of the Holocaust, by Samuel Cox

Hiding in Holland. A Resistance Memoir, by Shulamit Reinharz

The series **Jewish Children in the Holocaust** consists of the following
autobiographies of Jewish children
hidden during WWII in the Netherlands:

Searching for Home. The Impact of WWII on a Hidden Child,
by Joseph Gosler

Sounds from Silence. Reflections of a Child Holocaust Survivor,
Psychiatrist and Teacher, by Robert Krell

Sabine's Odyssey. A Hidden Child and her Dutch Rescuers,
by Agnes Schipper

The Journey of a Hidden Child, by Harry Pila and Robin Black

The series **New Jewish Fiction** consists of the following novels, written by Jewish authors. All novels are set in the time during or after the Holocaust.

The Corset Maker. A Novel, by Annette Libeskind Berkovits

Escaping the Whale. The Holocaust is over. But is it ever over for the next generation? by Ruth Rotkowitz

When the Music Stopped. Willy Rosen's Holocaust, by Casey Hayes

Hands of Gold. One Man's Quest to Find the Silver Lining in Misfortune, by Roni Robbins

The Girl Who Counted Numbers. A Novel, by Roslyn Bernstein

There was a garden in Nuremberg. A Novel, by Navina Michal Clemerson

The Butterfly and the Axe, by Omer Bartov

To Live Another Day. A Novel, by Elizabeth Rosenberg

A Worthy Life. Based on a True Story, by Dahlia Moore

The Right to Happiness. After all they went through. Stories, by Helen Schary Motro

The series **Holocaust Heritage** consists of the following memoirs by 2G:

The Cello Still Sings. A Generational Story of the Holocaust and of the Transformative Power of Music, by Janet Horvath

The Fire and the Bonfire. A Journey into Memory, by Ardyn Halter

The Silk Factory: Finding Threads of My Family's True Holocaust Story, by Michael Hickins

Winter Light. The Memoir of a Child of Holocaust Survivors, by Grace Feuerverger

Stumbling Stones, by Joanna Rosenthall

The Unspeakable, by Nicola Hanefeld

Hidden in Plain Sight. A Journey into Memory and Place, by Julie Brill

The series **Holocaust Books for Young Adults** consists of the following novels, based on true stories:

The Boy behind the Door. How Salomon Kool Escaped the Nazis. Inspired by a True Story, by David Tabatsky

Running for Shelter. A True Story, by Suzette Sheft

The Precious Few. An Inspirational Saga of Courage based on True Stories, by David Twain with Art Twain

The Sun will Shine on You again one Day, by Cynthia Monsour

The series **WWII Historical Fiction** consists of the following novels, some of which are based on true stories:

Mendelevski's Box. A Heartwarming and Heartbreaking Jewish Survivor's Story, by Roger Swindells

A Quiet Genocide. The Untold Holocaust of Disabled Children in WWII Germany, by Glenn Bryant

The Knife-Edge Path, by Patrick T. Leahy

Brave Face. The Inspiring WWII Memoir of a Dutch/German Child, by I. Caroline Crocker and Meta A. Evenbly

When We Had Wings. The Gripping Story of an Orphan in Janusz Korczak's Orphanage. A Historical Novel, by Tami Shem-Tov

Jacob's Courage. Romance and Survival amidst the Horrors of War, by Charles S. Weinblatt

A Semblance of Justice. Based on true Holocaust experiences, by Wolf Holles

Dark Shadows Hover, by Jordan Steven Sher

Amsterdam Publishers Newsletter

Subscribe to our Newsletter by selecting the menu at the top (right) of amsterdampublishers.com or scan the QR-code below.

Receive a variety of content such as:

- A welcome message by the founder
- Free Holocaust memoirs
- Book recommendations
- News about upcoming releases
- Chance to become an AP Reviewer.

www.ingramcontent.com/pod-product-compliance
Lightning Source LLC
LaVergne TN
LVHW041919070526
838199LV00051BA/2670